MARY'S THE NAME

ROSS SAYERS

cranachan

First published in 2017 by Cranachan Publishing Limited

ISBN: 978-1-911279-11-2

eISBN: 978-1-911279-12-9

Cover photograph © Vasily Deyneka / shutterstock.com

Cover Design and Typesetting by Cranachan

www.cranachanpublishing.co.uk

@cranachanbooks

For Mum, who loves a book with a secret.

CHAPTER ONE

When me and Granpa watched James Bond films, he told me not to be scared because people didn't have guns like that in Scotland. That must've been why the robbers used hammers.

'Empty the tills,' one of them shouted. 'Everybody stay back. Nobody needs to be a hero.'

The robber had the hammer above his head, like he would use it on Granpa if he didn't do what he said. It was like something off the telly, but I couldn't change the channel. I was crouched down under a table, next to the staff room. The robbers couldn't spot me. They were both wearing those masks you wore for the cold—*balaclavas*— that was the proper word.

'I need a winning coupon to put through,' Granpa said, 'To get the till to open.'

The robber had one. He handed it over.

'Barca at home, twelve to one on!' the robber shouted. 'But a win's a win, eh?'

He was using a silly, deep voice so we wouldn't know what his real one was like. Granpa took the betting slip and scanned it. His computer buzzed.

'The safe next,' the robber went on. 'We'll have the insert, as well.'

Granpa leaned down to twirl the clicky wheel to open the safe.

'The safe's nae problem,' Granpa said. 'But the insert takes thirty minutes' notice to open.'

I could see the robber's big teeth showing through the hole in his mask.

'Don't start,' the robber said. 'I know that bloke there's been waiting on his winnings for about half an hour.'

As the robber pointed to a man standing near the counter, the safe beeped five times.

'That'll be the insert ready for opening, aye?' said the robber.

'Aye, very good,' Granpa said. 'Ye've it aw planned oot, I suppose.'

The other robber was going around the security cameras, spraying them with black spray paint. He had a hammer too. When he was done, he stood guard near the door. There was Desk Robber and Guard Robber. Guard Robber didn't come near to the desk, so I didn't get to see his eyes or mouth, but I was ninety-nine percent sure he was the ugliest person ever. Apart from maybe Desk Robber. It was okay to call bad people ugly. They didn't have feelings the way good people did.

It was a Saturday and the shop was busy. The robbers didn't tell anyone to get on the ground though. The men stood with their arms crossed and made mean faces, but no one tried to stop it. One man kept writing his bet on a slip with a little pen. My heart went so fast it was sore.

Granpa was putting the money into their big rucksack as fast as he could. Granpa's boss, Mr Ferguson, was in the staff room. He was staring out the crack in the door, whispering into his mobile phone. I hoped he was phoning

999. If he wasn't, it was just the worst time to fancy a chat with someone.

I started to pee myself and couldn't stop. All down my tights and on to the floor. It was terrible, but it still felt nice, the warm feeling down my legs. It made a puddle and creeped over the carpet towards the staff room. Maybe the robbers could smell it but they didn't say anything. It would've been good if I could've chased them away with the smell of my pee.

Desk Robber looked up and noticed a camera above the desk that Guard Robber hadn't sprayed with paint. He smashed it with his hammer and the glass tinkled down to the floor. I got such a fright I banged my head on the top of the table. I bit into the slimy inside part of my lip so I wouldn't scream. Granpa wasn't scared, or maybe he was just pretending that he wasn't.

'Easy, fella,' he said. 'I'm doing it. Ye'll no get any trouble fae me.'

Granpa was being nice to them but they weren't saying thank you because they were no good, *rotten to the core* robbers.

'Hurry up, man,' said Guard Robber.

Desk Robber leaned over the counter and snatched the money from Granpa's hands and shoved it in the bag. It was probably a lot of money, but the rucksack didn't look full. They could've brought a carrier bag with them, but then maybe they didn't even have five pence and that's why they needed the bookies' money so much.

'Right, let's move it, Johnny,' said Guard Robber.

'Fuck sake,' Desk Robber said. 'Dinnae say my name... *Duncan.*'

'That's no fair, you meant that.'

3

'Boys,' Granpa said. 'On yer way, aye?'

I wished Granpa had stayed quiet like me.

'Shut it, you auld prick,' Desk Robber said, and swung his hammer over the counter. Granpa tried to get out the way, but it smacked into his shoulder. He fell off his wheelie chair. It made a big clatter when it hit the floor, but Granpa didn't even shout *ow* or *oh ya beastie*. The two robbers ran off out the door. No one tried to be a hero and stop them.

I made sure I didn't bang my head when I got out from under the table, then ran over to Granpa. My shoes were wet and squelchy. I wanted to be away from the pee smell, but it followed me.

'Are you okay, Granpa?'

'Never mind me, hen. Are ye awright?'

'I peed myself. I'm sorry.'

'Guess what? Me as well.'

He winked at me. The robbers were gone, so Granpa thought it was okay to joke around. But I didn't feel like joking around. It was the scariest bit of real-life I'd ever seen. Every part of me had been scared. My tummy was still doing a funny rumbling without any sounds.

The other men in the shop came round to our side of the desk, to check that Granpa was okay and help him up. Mr Ferguson came out of the staff room and walked right through my pee puddle. He didn't notice. I went back over and put down lots of football coupons to cover up the wet patch. They went soggy. My hands were shaking, so I put them behind my back.

'The police are on their way,' Mr Ferguson told everyone. 'They've asked for anyone who witnessed the robbery to stay for questioning.'

'You're no keeping me here,' one man said. 'I've got a

lucky fifteen waitin to go on. I'll go doon the road.'

He walked out and lots of other men went with him. The ones who stayed were busy watching Jeff and the football scores on the telly. Jeff tried *Countdown* for a while but he didn't like it. It wasn't football-y enough for him.

Soon the ambulance men came and the policemen too. The policemen weren't in the mood for joking but the ambulance men were really nice to me.

'Is this the young lady here?' said a tall paramedic with a red beard. 'I heard an eight-year-old girl scared off those robbers. Was that you?'

'No.'

I don't know why, but I started crying then. I had held it in when the robbers left, but I couldn't help it when the ambulance men were talking to me. They thought I had been a brave girl, but really I had been the opposite and hid under a table. The red beard paramedic made a face like *oops I made her greet*.

'Well, I was told you were very brave and I was to make sure you rode with your grandad in the back of the ambulance. Does that sound good?'

'Okay,' I said, 'But it's Granpa, not grandad.'

'Right you are. Look, we've got a special pair of trousers for you. They're green, like ours.'

'And like my eyes.'

'And like your eyes.'

I got to go with Granpa to the hospital and it made me stop feeling shaky because I knew we were safe in the ambulance. Ambulances didn't chase robbers like police cars. Granpa said there were people called *ambulance chasers* but I'd never seen them. Not even Usain Bolt was fast enough to catch an ambulance.

The trousers they gave me were all crunchy whenever I walked or sat down. *Crunch crunch crunch.* I kicked my legs back and forward just to hear the noise.

The ambulance had a clean smell, like how the colour white would smell.

'Mary,' Granpa said. 'Ye might need to say sorry to Mr Ferguson.'

'Why?'

'He's blaming ye for the funny smell coming fae his shoes.'

Granpa got the job in the bookies about a year before the robbery.

'Things'll be a bit different fae next week, Mary.'

'Why, Granpa? What's wrong?'

'Nothing's wrong. I've had to get a job again. I'm starting at the bookies near the Craigs. So I'll be working while ye're at school. Since I'm new, I have to work a Saturday as well. They'll no let me off with it. But the manager's telt me that as long as you keep oot the way, ye can come with me. It's only four hours and we can get a chippy after. Is that awright?'

Granpa had a job from then on. It was the first one I'd seen him doing. I knew he'd worked in a factory donkey's years ago. Donkey years were even longer than dog years. I thought he didn't have to work anymore because he'd worked so much when he was young.

I had to go to the bookies every Saturday. That was one of my days off school, so I wasn't happy at first. I normally would've gone to Braehead Park with Leona or for a ride on my bike. But when I stopped being friends with Leona, I looked forward to the bookies more.

Plus, Granpa told me work was very strict and you had

to go in or you'd get *the sack* which was the worst thing you could get. Really that meant you got fired, but they put your things in a sack and chucked you and your sack out on the street in front of everyone.

Bookies was short for bookmakers, but they didn't make books. They took people's bets on horses and football and lots of other things. There weren't any other people my age in the bookies. Young people weren't allowed. Granpa's boss, Mr Ferguson, would see me come in and say, "Hello Mary" and not tell me to get out. He had given me *special permission.*

Four hours was a long time and it could get boring, but there were things you could do to make the time go faster. I used the little pens to write down bets I thought would be good. It was sort of like guessing what would happen in the future. One time I wrote down: *Granpa will buy me a lolly on the way home.* I was supposed to put down numbers next to the bet but I wasn't completely sure about those. I knew 100/1 meant it had no chance of winning and so I worked out 2/1 must've meant it had a much better chance. *Granpa will buy me a lolly on the way home 2/1.* I gave it to him when there was no one in the queue.

'What's this?' he said. 'A lolly? Och and ye've even done odds as well. How much are ye putting on?'

I didn't understand.

'Ye've got to stake some money yerself. If ye put a pound on at 2/1, ye'll get back three pounds. That's two pound winnings and yer original stake.'

'I just want a lolly.'

He scrunched up his nose and his glasses got pushed up into his eyes.

'We'll see if yer bet comes up on the way hame, will we?'

That bet did come up. I got a strawberry milk ice lolly from the shop on the way home. Granpa said I *bashed the bookies* that day.

I hadn't always lived with Granpa, but that was before I had memories. My story was the saddest one I knew, so I didn't tell it to anyone, even though I thought about it a lot.

My mum had been called Alice and my dad had been called Robert. They met in a place called Stenhousemuir and that wasn't far from Stirling where I lived with Granpa, but I had never been there. Granpa said Stenhousemuir wasn't *worth the bus fare*. My mum and dad fell in love and got married like in a film. If people got married at the start of a film it meant they would break up later. But a wedding at the end of a film meant they lived happily ever after and you didn't need to see what happened later.

My parents had a baby and that was me. I completed the family: Mum, Dad and me. Alice, Robert and Mary. Three was our magic number.

Granpa said I was named after my mum's mum. There weren't many Mary's about so it was a good, special name and I liked it. It was from the Bible. I tried to read the Bible once, but I gave up almost right away. Even Granpa said some of it *went right over his heid*.

Granpa's name was Arthur because his mum and dad liked the man who had made up the Sherlock Holmes stories. It was an English name, but you could call your children anything you wanted. Even English names for Scottish people, or Scottish names for English people. Arthur was my dad's dad and I called him Granpa.

Granpa gave his second name to my dad and my dad

gave it to me. Sutherland. Mum's second name had been Fowler, but when she got married, she got the choice to swap her name for our better one. She made the right choice and was a Sutherland from then on.

Most of the things I had, like my second name, I got from other people. Granpa said I got my green eyes from my dad. The freckles on my nose were from my mum, but they only came out when it was sunny. My long brown hair was the same as my mum's too. Sometimes I wanted to cut my hair short, so it didn't get in my face when I did handstands. I kept it long to be like her.

Granpa had short hair. It was white but he swore *on his life* it had been blond before I was born. He wore fuzzy cardigans and liked to hang his glasses in the little pocket on his chest. My cardigans weren't as warm. They were good for any weather though, and they went with skirts or trousers. Granpa let me wear whatever I wanted.

A bad accident happened in my mum and dad's car and they died. Mum died in the car and Dad died in the hospital after they took him out of the car. It wasn't their fault. There was a big queue on the motorway for a long time after the accident. Granpa was looking after me that day because my mum and dad were going out for tea. A baby was a lot of work and they needed a break.

'Yer gran on your mum's side had just moved to Canada,' Granpa told me. 'I spoke to her and we agreed it was best to keep ye in Scotland. I wisnae for letting ye go to her, anyway. Old bat. I wanted ye aw for myself.'

He told me the story when I was six. That was when I had my light-up shoes. When Granpa told me the story, I was mostly paying attention to him, but I was also bashing my shoes together to get them to light up. Then I noticed that he had started crying and I'd never seen him do that before.

'I love ye, Mary. It's you and me against the world.'

'Will we win, Granpa?'

'They dinnae stand a chance.'

I didn't know who *they* were, but I agreed. That was the first time he said he loved me. I knew he always felt it, but it was the first time he'd said the words. After that, I thought he'd tell me he loved me all the time. But he didn't. It was just that one time. That was enough. I remembered it.

I thought I might've liked to be like the people at my school, with a normal family. But living with Granpa was great and that was normal for me. Just me and him. You could have a family with just the two of you. That was allowed. Two was a magic number as well.

If Mum and Dad were around, I could've shown them how good I was on the keyboard and they'd have loved me too. And Granny as well. I never met her, but Granpa kept pictures of her in the house. We could've had a big picnic all together and smiled at the camera for a family portrait.

Granpa said there were some forms to fill in because I was really young and had to move house. It wasn't a normal thing for a baby to stay with a granpa. He must've filled them all out perfectly because I stayed with him from then on.

There had been a funeral for my mum and dad. Granpa said a lot of friends came, but some couldn't because they were in faraway places like Canada and Tillicoultry. I don't remember the funeral. I bet loads of people came. I would've definitely put my money on that bet at the bookies.

♪

CHAPTER TWO

When we got back from the hospital, Granpa had his right arm in a sling. He looked like an Egyptian mummy, who was almost completely unwrapped, apart from the last bit. He kept sliding his arm out of the sling to do things.

'Granpa, dinnae do that.'

'Wheesht, you. How else am I meant to make yer tea?'

When he took the sling off, he could still do all the things he did before, only he said *ow* and *jeezo* a lot more. He couldn't lift the big pot with his left arm, so the sling had to come off when it was stovies for tea. That was allowed. But any other time I shouted at him to put it back on.

'Ye're no Florence Nightingale,' he said.

'I dinnae know who that is,' I said. 'But I bet people kept their sling on when she told them.'

The doctor told Granpa that he wasn't allowed to drive, but that didn't bother him. Granpa didn't have a car. We got the bus or walked everywhere. It was much better for the planet that way. If Granpa had bought a car, I would've been sad for the planet, but also happy that we didn't have to walk all the way home after we went swimming at The Peak. There had been a place in town called The Rainbow Slides, but it closed down before Granpa was able to take me. The slides were on the outside of the building and I wished they hadn't knocked it down to make a car park. It sounded a lot more fun than The Peak.

The next day, two policemen came to our house. It was a Sunday so we were having a lie in but they came and *bang bang banged* on the door to wake us up. Granpa came into my room and opened my curtains. He didn't even give me the usual *five-second warning*. My room went from night to day in one second. It was still dark under my duvet so I pulled it over my head. It was always night-time in the world under my covers.

'Get up, Mary,' Granpa said. 'Ye dinnae want the policemen thinking ye're a lazy bairn, do ye?'

'I dinnae care what they think.'

'Ye should. Being a lazy bairn is illegal these days. Lazy bairns go to the jail and never come back. Even when they get released, they're too lazy to leave their cells. They lie there forever, no moving and whispering, *'somebody help meee, I dinnae want to stay in my bed noo, I've changed my miiind.'*

'I dinnae believe you.'

'Have I ever lied to you before, Mary?' Granpa winked. 'I'm off to open the door. I'll buy ye as much time as I can.'

I knew Granpa was kidding me on, but I jumped out of bed. I left my curtains open. I guessed the house had to be bright in case the policemen wanted to investigate and *dust for prints*.

Granpa had talked to the police at the bookies before he went off in the ambulance, but they had more questions to ask. The security cameras at the bookies had been *no use at all*.

The policemen were both quite fat. They couldn't

have run after any robbers. One had a grey moustache. I didn't know moustache hair could go grey. I wondered if moustache hair could fall out like head hair did. You wouldn't even know if a man's moustache had gone bald; you'd just think he didn't want a moustache. Girls hardly ever went bald. That was another reason that I was glad I wasn't a boy.

Granpa sat in the living room and talked to the policemen. He didn't like the neighbours seeing him in his dressing gown, but he was wearing it with the policemen. He had *nothing to hide* from them. I had to go into the kitchen, even though the policemen said it was okay for me to stay. Granpa didn't want me to hear what they were talking about, but it was obvious they were talking about the robbery.

I had been at the robbery, so maybe I had important information that only someone who was under-a-table-behind-the-desk could've seen? I didn't have any information like that, but the policemen still should've checked with me.

I shouted from the kitchen, 'He disnae have his sling on.'

The policemen laughed but didn't make him put it on.

After they left, there was an outdoor smell in the living room. They didn't dust for any prints, which made sense because the robbers had never even been in our house. I was good with the duster anyway. There was no dust to find prints in.

'Did they catch the robbers, Granpa?'

He shook his head.

'No yet. But they will, dinnae worry. A witness said their getaway car was a red van with a picture on the side. The picture was a cow drinking a glass of milk. Must be a milk delivery van. Cannae imagine there are too many of them kickin' aboot.'

'That was silly of them.'

'Criminals aren't smart people, Mary. If they were smart, they wouldnae be criminals, noo would they?'

Granpa made jokes a lot, but when it was something serious he always made sense.

By the Tuesday, Granpa had to go back to work. I didn't think that was fair.

'Mr Ferguson's made it clear that I'll no have a job to go back to if I take time off. I'm no happy about it, but sometimes in life ye've got to say, "Yes, sir", even when every part of ye wants to... well, say something else.'

'You were going to swear there.'

'But I didnae. Disnae count!'

That was one of our games. If I caught Granpa swearing, he had to give me fifty pence. He swore a lot less after we started playing. He said I was costing him a *flipping fortune.*

'But what if the robbers come back?'

'They're daft, but I dinnae think they're that daft.'

Me and Granpa were both unhappy about him going back to work, but we couldn't do anything about it. And the robbers were still *on the loose,* but Granpa wasn't worried.

Granpa's birthday was the 13th of March and that made him sixty-six because that was sixty-six years later than 1949. Granpa made me work it out. I had to write it down in the back of my colouring book but I didn't tell him that. I would never get Rachel Riley's job on *Countdown.* Granpa fancied her, but she was clever so that was okay.

I picked out his birthday card when we went up the town.

I could only find ones which said *Grandpa*, but Granpa didn't spell his name with a 'd'. Instead, I chose one that had two otters holding hands while they floated in the water. It was the cutest thing I'd ever seen.

Granpa gave me the money to buy it, so the surprise wouldn't be spoiled. The lady who served me said, 'Who's this for, darling?'

'My granpa.'

'D'you want me to put some confetti inside? It'll not cost you extra.'

I nodded and said thank you. It was a shame that I couldn't make it a special spy card like Granpa did for my birthdays. He always made a secret compartment at the back of my birthday cards. That was where he put a pound coin, or maybe even a fiver, if I was lucky. I had no idea how he did it.

Normally, it was only me and him for Granpa's birthday. We'd sit and have carrot cake, which was his favourite, or maybe go to the cinema to see a PG or 12A. Sometimes, I wanted to see a 15 film but Granpa said there was an invisible barrier to stop anyone under the right age getting in and you could get barred from the cinema. I wasn't sure if that was real, but I didn't want to chance it.

Granpa wouldn't watch 'U's or cartoons though, even if they were amazing like *Frozen*. I didn't see *Frozen* till it came out on DVD.

On his sixty-sixth birthday, eight of Granpa's friends came round to our house. It was a Friday night. I'd never met most of them before, but they seemed to know me and my name. The new faces kept saying that they'd not seen me since I was *this* high. They didn't talk to me for long, and after they'd said something nice they went and sat down.

They liked getting a *soft seat*.

'What lovely brown hair you have,' said a lady.

Her hair was white, but she had some bald bits where you could see the purple lines trying to get out of head. She looked a lot older than Granpa. I couldn't see any of his head veins.

'Thanks,' I said. 'I'm a brunette.'

If you were a girl with brown hair, you were a brunette. Boys couldn't be brunettes. I thought the word must be Scottish because the first bit, you said it like *broon*. I would usually have said brown. Granpa tried his best not to sound too Scottish around me so I wouldn't pick up his *bad habits*. I said some things Scottish-y though. Sometimes a word like *braw* or *pure chilly Baltic* was better than a boring English word.

We were all together in the living room. I sat on the carpet, at the feet of the ladies on the couch. It was almost ten o'clock and Granpa hadn't told me to get to bed yet. The telly was off because it would've been rude to turn it on, even though it meant we missed the news. Watching the news together was something we always did, even when it was scary. Granpa said it was important I knew what was happening in the world. He didn't want to put a *sugarcoat* on anything.

Most people had fizzy wine in tall glasses. One or two had brandy that Granpa poured from a special bottle. There had been dust all down it.

'It's a special occasion after aw,' Granpa said.

The brandy had been in the cabinet for so long, I thought it was an ornament. Ornaments were like action figures for grown-ups that could break really easily, so you could only look and not touch.

Granpa had forgotten all about being angry at his work and his bad arm and the robbers. It was as if it hadn't even happened. He went through to his room and came back with his guitar. His friends cheered. He used the strap so he could play standing up. Granpa's arm must not have been hurting or maybe he was trying to ignore the pain.

'What are you going to play for us, Arthur?' A man asked in a big, deep voice.

'Something bloody loud,' said Granpa. 'So you can hear it.'

'My plan failed, Arthur,' Malcolm from next door said. 'I sent those boys to the bookies so you'd no be able to play that thing ever again!'

Malcolm laughed so much his face went red and he started coughing and put his hankie up to his face.

I wanted Granpa to play Elvis, but I was scared to say in front of the other people. But then, Elvis was old and so were they, so maybe I could've said it. Elvis was good for dancing.

'Right, here's yin,' Granpa said. 'Sing along if ye can. You as well, Malcolm, if ye can put doon yer brandy for a minute.'

Everyone laughed again *ha ha ha*. Granpa was great at making people laugh.

He played and everyone listened and tapped their hands and feet. When Granpa sang he put on a posh voice like a real singer on the radio. He was strumming up and down really fast as he sang one of the best ones he knew.

There's a girl by the loch and she's mighty fine,
There's a girl by the loch and she's mine all mine,
There's a girl by the loch and she's mighty fine,

And she's going to take me to cloud nine.

There's a dame in my heart and she comes my way,
There's a dame in my heart and we met halfway,
There's a dame in my heart and she comes my way,
And I hope that she'll be here to stay.

It was great how Granpa could remember all the words. Most people remembered some, but not all of them. No stopping or saying, *oh wait how does it go again?* People who did that just ruined the song.

When he finished, everyone clapped and said, "Well done, Arthur". Granpa slowed his arm down and played a new song. He flicked just one string at a time and played the tune that way.

Sweetheart, where are you?
I miss you, tonight.
You never even said goodbye.

Are you there in the dark?
Or every time my heart beats alone.

Sweetheart, come home now.
I'm asking you, dear.
I promise you'll shed no more tears.

While he was singing, I heard the ladies on the couch whispering.

'I love this one.'

'Takes me back.'

'He used to play it for her.'

I guessed they were talking about Granny. But Granpa didn't write the song, so I knew it wasn't about her.

When everyone had gone home, me and Granpa sat in the living room and listened to an Elvis CD. It was the best choice because Elvis only sang hits, so we never needed to skip a song. Granpa was drinking brandy from his glass with the big, round bottom. He gave me some to try, but it made my throat feel like fire and I had to drink milk to cool it down.

'Give us a wee blast, hen,' Granpa said.

That was code for putting the radiator up high for a little while. The living room warmed up quick and it made me sleepy.

'Granpa, do you think Granny can come back and see us?'

'Noo, there's a question. Why?'

'The ladies thought the sad song was about you and Granny.'

He smiled and took a drink of his brandy.

'Naw, naw. I dinnae think she'll be back. I think she likes it better where she is noo.'

'But is she not all by herself?'

'Och naw, she's with aw her family and friends. Apart fae us, that is.'

I was glad Granpa knew she couldn't come back. She was dead and it was impossible. If Granpa thought she could come back, I would've been worried that he was going crazy. Like old people who ended up in the special home. Granpa called it *the loony bin,* but it was nothing like *Looney Tunes.*

It made me happy thinking about Granny having a good time, wherever she was. Granpa told me she had gone to sleep in the hospital and not woken up again. *The cancer got her*. Sometimes you couldn't beat it, no matter how hard you tried. I never asked Granpa any more about her in case he got too sad and couldn't cheer up again.

'I'll be seeing her soon enough. One of these days.'

'You cannae go to her yet, Granpa. You've got to be alive to make my tea and help me with my homework till I get to high school.'

'Good point, Miss Sutherland. But what happens when ye get to high school? Will you no need a hand anymair?'

'I'll be clever enough to do my homework myself by then. That's plenty of time for me to get even cleverer than I am now.'

'There's a terrifying thought. Let's get to our beds.'

He stood up and picked a bit of confetti from his cardigan. 'Still finding this bloody stuff everywhere.'

Granpa let me decide if I wanted to go back to the bookies the next day.

'Ye can stay with Malcolm fae next door,' he said. 'He's normally away on his travels, but he's back hame for a while.'

'Em,' I said. 'I suppose so.'

'I did tell him ye were the bravest girl I knew and ye wouldnae let those robbers scare ye fae coming with me.'

'Oh.'

'Ye'll prove me right, won't ye, Mary?'

I was scared but excited that Granpa thought I was brave.

'Aye,' I said. 'Let's go.'

There were loads of football matches on Saturdays. Some men would put bets on football they were going to watch at the stadium. Imagine that. You put a bet on a team and you were there watching them right in front of you. If they weren't trying hard, you could shout at them and tell them to get a move on. If your team won, you could go right back to the shop and get your money. You'd know for sure it was a winner because you'd just seen it with your own eyes and not someone on the telly who could be making it all up.

Some men bet against the team they supported. Granpa said they didn't want their team to lose, it was a *just in case* bet. If their team lost then they would get some money and that would cheer them up a bit.

The two big teams were Rangers and Celtic. They were in Glasgow and if men were going to their games they'd come in early because they had a big drive to get to the stadium. Those teams hated each other. But you'd still see a Rangers fan and a Celtic fan talking to each other about their bets and who they *fancied,* so they didn't hate each other that much. Fancying a team was completely different from fancying a person. I used to tell my friend Leona she fancied Paul Reed from our class but it didn't matter who she fancied because she wasn't my friend anymore. I didn't fancy anyone.

Granpa supported Kilmarnock. Their games weren't on the telly very much, unless they were playing Rangers or Celtic.

'I only support Kilmarnock cause my dad did,' he said. 'If ye must, support Man United or Real Madrid. Ye'll be much happier.'

Kilmarnock's stadium was called Rugby Park. They couldn't even name their stadium properly.

Stirling Albion were the closest football team to us. Granpa said they went *up and down like a yo-yo*.

Not many women came in to the bookies. Maybe *once in a blue moon*. I'd never seen a blue moon. Women didn't love betting like the men did. Granpa said that was why the men liked me being there. I brought a *feminine touch*. I was good luck for their bets.

'Never start betting, Mary,' Granpa said.

'Why not?'

'Ye'll no be able to stop.'

'I would. I'd stop whenever I felt like it.'

'Just like that?'

'Just like that. No more bets for me, mister bookie man.'

'Good girl. Forget the bogey man. It's the bookie man ye need to fear. The bookie man sneaks into yer wallet and steals away all yer money. The bookie man always wins.'

He worked there, so he must've been right. It was sad that the other men didn't know the bookies would always win. It was a secret and I wasn't to tell the men, or they'd never put on any more bets. Another secret was me and Granpa's Secret-Pocket-Money-Spy Game.

That Saturday, after the robbery, was when the game started. I was sitting next to Granpa at the desk. His face was whiter than usual because he'd drank too much brandy the night before. I always made sure to smile at the customers, even when they didn't smile back. Granpa was too ill to smile.

'Mary,' Granpa whispered. 'Ye want to play a spy game with me?'

'Are we going to make dens in the living room like last time?'

'No at home. I mean here, in the bookies.'

'Oh. Aye, definitely.'

'Right, take this and put it in yer pocket.'

He gave me a bunch of twenty pound notes all folded and neat. I put them in my jacket pocket.

'We're not stealing, are we, Granpa?'

'Dinnae be silly, Mary. These are my wages. I thought I'd make it a game for ye. Noo, yer mission is to sneak all my wages oot in yer pockets. And ye'll get a wee treat if ye accomplish yer mission. How does that sound?'

He winked at me.

'Deal,' I said.

It made being in the bookies a lot more exciting. We were spy partners just like in James Bond. Apart from that Bond didn't have partners because they usually betrayed him. I was James Bond and Granpa was M or Q. One of the old ones.

'Remember, this is our secret. Mr Ferguson kens aboot our game, but ye're no to say anything to him. Ye understand? No a word?'

'Promise.'

I went under the desk, to see if the cleaning lady had missed any bits of glass from the robbery. She had done a good job because I couldn't find any and the carpet smelled of lemons instead of pee. I looked up at the security camera. It was staring back at me, but its eye had been smashed by Desk Robber's hammer. He had made it blind.

When his shift was done, Mr Ferguson made Granpa show him what was in his pockets and looked in his carrier bag. He must've told Mr Ferguson to do that. Like when you think the good guys are about to get found out because they've got the secret package and they get searched by the baddies. But wait! They gave the secret package to Mary and she escaped with it. Granpa had thought of everything.

I was to keep the money safe all the way home, in case there were other spies watching us. When we got home, Granpa said, 'Mission accomplished.'

He was rubbing his hands together, all happy and not hungover anymore. Granpa likēd the game just as much as me. I passed him his wages. He looked through all the money and gave me a fiver. A whole fiver.

'That's yer pocket money.'

I was so happy I hugged him. I didn't hug Granpa a lot because he had to bend down and his knees usually made a horrible cracking noise, but he deserved a hug that time. My reward was my pocket money, so that was why I called it the Secret-Pocket-Money-Spy-Game. It was a hard name to say, but since it was a secret I only ever said it in my head.

CHAPTER THREE

My school was Braehead Primary and I was in Primary 4. It wasn't as good as Primary 3. Or even Primary 2. Every year had got better—until Primary 4. That year was when I realised that teachers didn't really help you. They wanted you to do well with your reading books and sums, but when you were sad, it wasn't their job to make you feel better again. They just said, *"Things will get better, Mary."* or *"Oh, I'm sure you'll make other friends".*

Mrs Lithgow was my teacher. She had bright red hair that she dyed to make it that colour. Nobody mentioned it, even though grown-ups weren't meant to have hair that colour. She had sweaty bits under her arms, especially when she wore the light grey top, but nobody mentioned that either.

When she got mad, she got really mad and I was scared even if it wasn't me that was in trouble. Her shouting was so loud that other teachers could hear it across the social area between classes. Miss Young from next door would come into our classroom because she knew someone was in trouble and she wanted to shout at them too. They would look at each other and say things like,

'Is that him causing trouble again?'

'It is, Miss Young.'

'And after he behaved so well all of last week.'

'I know. I'd hate to have to get his parents in.'

'Maybe he can come and sit in my room till he's calmed down.'

One time, I sneaked under the windows of the staff room and heard one of them saying they wanted to *'wring that boy's neck'*. I would've tried to stop them, but I was only wee. The next second, they were laughing and calling each other by their first names, like Margaret and Denise. When they went into the staff room, they changed from grumpy teachers back into normal grown-ups.

One thing I did like at school was music. On Thursday afternoons, the music teacher Mrs Stafford came and she had hundreds of instruments. All types of strange ones that you had to bang or shake or scrape and those were called *percussion*. I wondered if she took them home at night. Her house must've been noisy.

The best was the keyboard. I got lessons on Thursday lunchtimes from Mrs Stafford. I loved staying inside and having the empty classroom to myself while everyone else was outside. I'd just started doing left hand chords. Not full ones obviously, just the root note. That was hard enough. If I begged her, Mrs Stafford would write the names of the notes on the white keys in marker pen. She was worried it wouldn't rub off, but it always did.

'You'll never learn this way,' she said.

'Just a few more lessons.'

'And a few more after that?'

'I'll have them memorised by then.'

We only had a toy keyboard at home so I never got as much practice done as Mrs Stafford wanted. I asked for lessons every day, but Mrs Stafford could only come once a week because she went to all the other schools in Stirling too.

'Do you not think I need them more, Mrs Stafford? I dinnae care about missing lunchtime.'

'Their lessons are just as important as yours,' she said. 'Plus, I'm already doing your grandfather a favour.'

I was good for my age, but not as good compared to people who could play without sheet music or looking at the keys. There was a man on the telly called Jools Holland. He only came on late at night. If it was an extra special night, Granpa let me stay up to watch the news and the programme with Jools. He played piano better than I'd seen anyone else do it. His hands were like wriggling spiders when he played.

I was nowhere near as good as Jools, but I was still better than everyone else in my class. Paul Reed always tried to push me away so he could show off and play the *Jurassic Park* theme tune, but no one was impressed.

'Do you even know what those keys are called, Paul?' I said.

'I dinnae care. Dinnae tell me.'

'They're D, C sharp, D again, A and G.'

'God's sake, Mary. No wonder you've got no pals.'

Everyone liked it better when I played *Super Trouper* because I could play more than just five stupid notes over and over.

Granpa and me played the Secret-Pocket-Money-Spy-Game for weeks and weeks and all through the Easter holiday. I went with him to every shift when I was off school.

Granpa brought something special to work one day. A present, all covered in wrapping paper. He must've bought it while I was at school.

'Who's that for?' I said.

'Mr Ferguson,' Granpa said. 'An Easter present. Ye can give it to him if ye like. Here's what to say.'

I carried the box to Mr Ferguson's office. His door was held open by a little wooden slice on the floor. I put the present on his desk.

'Happy Easter,' I said.

'You shouldn't have,' Mr Ferguson said. 'I've not got you anything.'

'It's to say thank you for letting me come to work with Granpa, even though I'm not supposed to.'

'What the regional manager doesn't know can't hurt him,' he said, smiling.

'And sorry for your shoes smelling like pee.'

He ripped off the paper. It was a pair of shoes. Not suede ones like he had before, but shiny black ones with really thick bottoms. Sort of like a policeman's shoes. I liked the way the shoebox opened, like a treasure chest showing the gold inside.

'Thank you, Mary,' he said. 'This is very kind of Arthur. I'll be more careful where I stand in future. Thank your granpa for me, will you?'

I didn't get an Easter present from Granpa. I got an Easter egg, but that didn't count. Mr Ferguson getting a present didn't make any sense. He had made Granpa go back to work with a sore shoulder. They hadn't been friendly to each other after the robbery.

'Have you forgiven Mr Ferguson, Granpa?'

'Cause of the shoes?' he said, 'Naw. Just want to keep in his good books. Dinnae get too friendly with him, Mary. He's no right in the heid.'

Mr Ferguson seemed okay to me. Sometimes he got quite angry when people didn't wash up their dirty plates and cups, but I would've been annoyed too. The cups with old coffee in them smelled the worst.

I spent most of the time doing my colouring books in the staff room. I could have as much hot chocolate as I wanted from the machine in there. Lydia showed me how. She worked Monday to Friday so I only saw her during school holidays. Her eyes were like a panda's because of all the make-up she wore.

There weren't any pandas in my colouring books. I took my time with every page, making sure everything was the right colour and staying in the lines and not leaning too hard on the pencils. I knew Granpa liked it when I made things last.

The Secret-Pocket-Money-Spy-Game was getting a bit boring. It was the same thing every time and it didn't feel like being James Bond at all. James Bond got different gadgets to try out in the lab and then they'd come in handy later in the film, even when it seemed like they were no use at all. There were no gadgets for me, only the money. But Granpa was always so happy when we got home and the mission was accomplished, so I kept playing and said nothing.

Sometimes, when a man had a winning bet, Granpa gave him his winnings then put his slip under his computer keyboard. Then, later on, he would slide it back out and scan it again.

'Y'see, Mary,' he said. 'When a punter wins on a horse, the man who owns the horse gets winnings as well.'

He took more money out the till and put it in a drawer. He didn't tell me how the man who owned the horse would get the money from the drawer, but I guessed that was probably Mr Ferguson's job.

During the Easter holidays, we played our game every day. Sometimes twice a day.

'Granpa, why are you getting so many wages?'

'I've been here a year noo. Ye get a big pay rise when ye work somewhere for a year. Are ye no enjoying the game anymair?'

'Oh no, it's fantastic. Like being a real spy.'

'Good. Here's another lot to put in yer secret stash.'

The Easter holidays, that was when the bundles of his wages got much heavier. They were harder to hide in my jacket pocket and I could barely get my hand around them. I wasn't ready to be a proper spy.

The last day of school was Wednesday June 24th. We got off at two o'clock, instead of three, but Granpa worked till half past two, so I had to wait in school till he could come and get me. I told Granpa I could've walked home, but he said it wasn't safe.

'It's no that I dinnae trust ye. It's that I dinnae trust everyone else.'

I sat next to the fish tank in the welcoming area and read the books they had for visitors. The books for really wee ones were easiest: one about a big dog, another about a little hamster. They could always talk. It didn't matter what it was, a cushion or a light-bulb, everything could talk in a children's book.

There was a book of poems too. Grown-up poems that didn't rhyme. I chose one called *Mr and Mrs Scotland Are Dead* because it sounded exciting. After I'd read it, I couldn't even work out what had killed Mr and Mrs Scotland. Was it a murder or an accident? There weren't any answers at the back of the book.

Even the teachers weren't staying till three. They were hugging each other and saying, *"have a good summer"*. The welcoming area was right next to the main door, so I got to wave to all of them as they left.

'Oh, you're still about, Mary,' Mrs Lithgow said. 'Hope you have a nice summer. Come back and visit us. Mrs Stafford wanted me to wish you all the best too.'

'I hope you have a good holiday, Mrs Lithgow. I'll only be in the upper wing, it's not that far.'

She gave me a smile, but looked a bit confused. She had a carrier bag full of the presents our class had given her. I thought being a teacher would be worth it just for the presents at summer and Christmas. Mrs Lithgow could hardly see over her desk for all the bottles of wine.

'I'm glad I have the summer to get through all of these,' she said.

At playtime, I heard Freddie Cooke from Primary Six say his mum had given him wine to give to his teacher, but he'd drank it on the walk to school.

'Where's the empty bottle then?' another boy had asked.

'I threw it in the burn,' Freddie said.

'Which burn?'

'Yer maw's burn.'

'That disnae even make sense.'

But everyone had still laughed. It didn't matter if the boy's mum had a burn or not.

Granpa didn't give me a present to give Mrs Lithgow and she told me she *understood*. The bottles clinked together when she went through the double doors to the car park.

I liked being in school after home time. There was no chance of getting into any trouble or being told to get back to class. And no one was around to make fun of me for being a *Mary-no-mates*. Through the window, I could see Leona walking with Hannah Hunter. I didn't care what they were doing during the summer.

Granpa came at 2.54pm. He was wearing his work clothes. Red polo shirt and black trousers. It wasn't that different from my school clothes, only my polo shirt was white. My jumper was maroon and I had it wrapped around my waist. That was how cool people wore it.

'Sorry aboot the wait,' he said. 'Were the teachers awright with ye sitting here?'

'Aye, Granpa. They're all happy that it's summer.'

'Summer? Someone should tell the weather.'

Our house was only a ten-minute walk from the school. Out the car park, past the parish church, past the paper shop, all the way to the end of the street. Our street was called Springfield Road, just like in *The Simpsons*. Lisa Simpson was eight, the same as me. She had been eight forever though. I wanted to be nine as soon as I could.

Granpa made me cheese sandwiches and left the crusts on. It was a waste to throw the crusts in the bin. I nibbled all round them quick, so I was only left with the soft middle bit.

'I've got something to tell ye, Mary,' Granpa said. 'We're going on holiday this summer.'

'Really? You're not joking?'

'Would I joke aboot something like this?'

'Probably.'

'Well, I'm no.'

'Where are we going then?'

'It's a surprise, so I cannae tell ye yet. But we'll be away aw summer. Ye dinnae mind being away aw summer, do ye?'

'Naw! Not even a bit. But what about your job, Granpa? Won't you get *the sack* if you go away for the whole summer?'

'That's aw sorted, Mary. Mr Ferguson felt bad aboot making me go back to work straight after I hurt my shoulder. They've hired someone to work my shifts for the summer. Ye'll need to pack yer stuff. Ye may as well take everything.'

'Are we getting on a plane? Because Walter Tompkins said he had to use his mum's passport when he went to Spain.'

'Ye dinnae need a passport for where we're going, Mary. Think closer to hame. Will we make it like a game? Another spy adventure?'

'Aye. How?'

'How aboot, you be the spy and I'm yer, well, yer person that has to get ye somewhere safe? Cause the baddies are after ye. How aboot that?'

'There's not really baddies after us, is there?'

'Course no. But if there were, we'd need to go really fast, wouldn't we? We'd need to grab our stuff and get a move on.'

'Should we go fast then?'

'We should go like Usain Bolt. What if we leave... tomorrow morning?'

I made my hands into fists I was so excited.

'Is that enough time tō pack?' I asked.

'Ye'll need something to put yer stuff into first, won't ye?'

We went next door to see Malcolm. He travelled a lot because of his work. He had spare suitcases in his loft and he climbed up to get us one. The loft had a hidden ladder which slid out from the ceiling and gave me a fright. Granpa held the ladder and I looked up, but all I could see was Malcolm's bum wobbling as he reached for something.

'Right,' Malcolm said. 'This looks just the ticket.'

He handed down a wee red suitcase to Granpa. It had two wheels on the bottom so you didn't have to carry it.

'What d'ye think, hen?' Granpa asked me.

'It's perfect,' I said. 'Thanks, Malcolm.'

'Ya beauty,' Malcolm said, his head still up the loft. 'I knew I still had my *Bat out of Hell* LP.'

Earlier that day, Mrs Lithgow had asked us all where we were going for our summer holidays.

'I'm going with my dad to Florida,' Paul Reed said.

'Majorca,' said Leona Turnbull. 'With my mum and dad and my best friend Hannah and her family.'

I felt sorry for Hannah. Leona would probably find a new best friend in Majorca and she'd be chucked away like rubbish.

'I'm just staying in Stirling with my granpa,' I said.

'At least you'll be with your best friend,' Paul said.

Everyone laughed. They wouldn't have laughed if they'd known about my holiday. My holiday was going to last the whole summer.

Packing was exciting but sore on my arms. Clothes and shoes were the obvious things. I took books and toys that I thought I might need too. The Harry Potter books took up too much room, so I only took the first three. They were the easiest to read and the least scary. My space shuttle from *Moonraker* flew straight in my bag. My Elvis mask too. It was just a piece of cardboard with a picture of Elvis on and a bit of string to hold it on your head, but when I wore it I felt just like *The King*. I couldn't make my voice go as low as his though. You never saw spies packing all their things, especially not toys. But that was what I needed for my mission.

I ran through to the living room to give Granpa the good news.

'That's me packed,' I told him.

'Ye were quick. Sure ye've got everything? Toothbrush? Wellies? Big jacket?'

I ran back to my room because I'd forgotten those things. Apart from that, though, I was packed.

'Right, that's me really done this time.'

'Toothbrush?'

'Aye.'

'But how will ye brush yer teeth tonight?'

I ran back to my room to take my toothbrush out of the case.

Granpa didn't rush with his packing.

'Are you taking those pictures of Granny?'

'I am.'

'Will you need them?'

'I'd like to have them with me. The summer's a long time and it'll be nice to be able to see her.'

I didn't have any photos of people. Not even of Mum and Dad. I preferred to remember them in my head. That way I could put sideburns on my dad even though he never had them in real-life.

'Should we go and see yer mum and dad one last time before we leave?'

'Definitely.'

'Better put on your wellies and big jacket then. Ye didnae pack them did ye?'

'You told me to!'

'I think I would remember saying something daft like that.'

We left our bags at the front door, ready for the next day. It was a thirty-minute walk to the cemetery. Past the primary school, up the big Broomridge hill, past the high school and through the football pitch below the main road.

'Wait till I tell everyone in my class about our holiday when we go back,' I said on the walk there. 'They'll not believe me.'

'Ye dinnae really like any of that lot, do ye, Mary?' said Granpa. 'Who cares what they think.'

'I dinnae care. But I want them to know.'

Granny's grave was at the cemetery too. Granpa bought some carnations on the way so he could put them at Granny's grave. He always asked the man at the counter if they had any flowers that were *on their way out*. Those were the cheapest and they *did the trick*. I loved the look of flowers, but they never smelled as good as I thought they would.

'Would ye like some for yer mum? Granpa asked me.

I nodded.

'Pink ones, please. How come we never buy any for Dad?'

'Your dad hated flowers. Terrible hay-fever.'

I liked finding out things about mum and dad I didn't know.

Everyone knew to be quiet when they walked around the cemetery, even though there weren't any signs saying so. I could hear cars beeping from the main road, but that was allowed because they might not know there was a cemetery nearby.

'You head along to yer mum and dad,' Granpa said.

'But I don't normally go without you.'

'I fancied having a chat with yer granny, just the two of

us. If ye dinnae mind?'

I didn't mind.

I walked over the muddy grass. Walking over mud in my wellies was one of my favourite things. The mud could try, but it would never get through to my socks. My wellies were dark green and I could pretend I was a farmer checking on my land and my animals. There had been wellies with flowers on them at the shop, but I wanted proper ones. Real farmers didn't have flowers on their wellies.

I made sure to walk right down the middle of the grass between the headstones because it wasn't nice to walk right on top of dead people. I thought that was silly at first because it wasn't like they could wake up, but Granpa said it was about *respect* which was really important. If you walked right on top of where people were lying it was like saying, *"ha ha you're dead and I don't care"*.

The flowers at Mum and Dad's grave from the last visit had gone droopy and brown. I took them out and threw them over the fence and into the bushes. I put the new pink ones through the holes of the little round pot. They were the brightest thing my eyes could see. Bright enough that people walking by would stop and have a look at the pretty flowers and read my Mum and Dad's name. They'd know that someone still loves Alice and Robert Sutherland.

It was okay to step on top of graves, but only if you knew the person. You were never, ever to dance. Mum and Dad's names were on the same grave so I could talk to them both at the same time.

'Hiya, Mum. Hiya, Dad. Me and Granpa are going on holiday tomorrow. I dinnae know where we're going but Granpa says it's going to be fantastic. I won't be able to come and talk to you for a while. I'll bring you back a present. I cannae wait to see Leona's face when she finds out I went on holiday. We're still not pals, but that's fine because I dinnae want to be her friend anyway.'

A woman came round the corner but I kept talking because Granpa said it was *nothing to be embarrassed about.*

'And that's school finished till next year. When I go back I'll be a P5. Our class is going to be in the upper wing with the P6s and P7s. I'm a wee bit scared, but I'll get to use the new iPads so that's nice.'

Obviously Mum and Dad couldn't talk back, so our chats never lasted long. I said bye and that I'd see them soon and went back to see if Granpa was still talking to Granny.

Dead people were under the ground everywhere. But not many alive people above the ground came to visit them. They were all too busy. I knew I would still come when I was older, even when I had other things planned. It was the right thing to do.

Granpa was on his knees in front of Granny's stone.

In loving memory of
Isabel Lorraine Sutherland
1951 – 2002
She leaves the world a richer place.

One time, I'd asked Granpa about the last bit. He never talked fancy like that.

'Some fella at the headstone place talked me into it.'

Granpa always said a good thing about living in Scotland was you didn't need to come and water the flowers because the weather was so bad and the rain would do it for you.

'Almost didnae see ye there, Mary.'

'How's Granny?'

'No bad. She was talking aboot ye.'

'What did she say?'

'She said, "*when is that girl going to get her silver swimming certificate?*"'

'I'm trying so hard, Granpa, but I can't keep straight doing the backstroke. I'm trying, Granny.'

'She kens ye are, hen.'

CHAPTER FOUR

I tried to get Granpa to tell me where we were going, but he pretended to lock his lips, then threw away the key. He said real spies didn't *divulge their secrets* so I would have to wait and see. Lying in bed that night, I thought of Mum and Dad again. If only they could've come with us. It was silly, but when my room was dark, I thought they could've been there, somewhere, watching me.

'Are youse coming too?' I said.

'We'd love to,' said Mum.

'Can't wait,' said Dad.

But obviously they didn't. That was just me imagining what they would've said. Mum's voice was lovely, like a news person on the BBC. Dad's was deep. Like Sean Connery.

Granpa woke me up at six in the morning. I'd never been awake that early. My eyes were sticky and full of crunchy sleep nuggets. I rolled them down my cheeks and flicked them across my room. It was already sunny outside and that helped to keep me from falling back asleep.

We ate lots of toast to fill us up for the journey and to use the last of the bread.

'You've got to tell me now,' I said.

I was scraping the last of the strawberry jam out of the

bottom of the jar. The knife made a clacky sound against the glass which made my ears hurt.

'I've an old pal called Iain Watson,' Granpa said. 'We used to work together. I hadnae spoken to him in years, till he rang me up a few months ago. He read my name on the *Stirling Observer* website after the robbery and found my number in the phone book. He lives in a place called Skye. D'ye ken where that is?'

'Above our heads, where the clouds are?' I said.

It was a silly joke and I wanted to say it before Granpa did. He laughed and rubbed the top of my head.

'Ye're getting too clever, hen,' he said. 'It's an island up north fae here. Iain says it's braw. That's where he lives, in a place called Portree. He's gonnae let us stay with him for the summer. How does that sound?'

Por-tree. No one else in class had said they were going there.

'Brilliant. What's there to do in Portree?'

'I'm no sure. Ye'll need to ask Iain when we get there. Anyway, ye're good at making yer own fun, aren't ye?'

Making your own fun meant using your imagination because there wasn't a park or a cinema. But that was okay because I was actually really good at making my own fun. I didn't even need anyone to hang around with. It had been ages since I'd hung about with Leona and I was doing fine.

Skye was an island but it still counted as Scotland. That made it less exciting because I already lived in Scotland all the time. I would've preferred to go to a country where people had strange voices and *time difference*. Alan Robertson from my class went to Australia and saw kangaroos. He told our class that one kangaroo almost made his dad crash their car when it jumped out in front of them. You didn't get wild animals like that in Stirling, but maybe there would be some on Skye.

'Get that apple juice doon ye,' Granpa said. 'The taxi's due soon. We're getting the Aberdeen train, but we get off at Perth.'

Granpa wrote down the trains we had to get on a slip of paper.

7. 34 to Perth
8.51 to Inverness
12. 55 to Kyle of Lochalsh
? - Portree bus

Granpa didn't know exactly what time the bus went to Portree, but he said there were bound be lots of buses going to Portree and not to worry. He gave me the bit of paper to keep safe. It was a lot of pressure.

The house looked almost empty when we left. All the big stuff stayed obviously, the telly and couches, but Granpa took almost all of his other *personal* things. He had a black rucksack over his shoulder and was pulling along a suitcase too. Its wheels rattled non-stop on the ground.

'How's your shoulder, Granpa?'

'It's feeling grand today.'

Some days his shoulder hurt so much he could only use his left arm to do things.

I was in charge of my red case. I liked pressing the button and making the handle disappear. I had a bag for life from *Morrisons* too. It was full of the sandwiches we made. Cheese, ham, jam, chocolate spread. We even used the outsiders of the loaf.

Granpa was skinny, but he still had enough muscles

to carry his rucksack and not be out of breath. I had seen an old picture of him when he had a moustache and was standing outside a pub. His body hadn't changed much from those black and white days.

The taxi came and the driver helped us put our bags in the boot. You had to sit in the back seats in taxis. You weren't the driver's friend, so you weren't allowed to sit next to him.

'Say cheerio to the house, Mary,' Granpa said.

'Dinnae be stupid, Granpa.'

'Well, I'm going to say it. Bye house.'

'Fine. Bye house.'

'What a daftie ye are, Mary. Talking to a house.'

The taxi driver talked a lot and didn't let me or Granpa say much. We just nodded and Granpa said *'Ye're quite right'* whenever the driver stopped to take a sip of Red Bull.

We went through the town centre. I'd never seen it so quiet. We were one of the only cars on the big Craigs roundabout. We could've driven round and round as many times as we wanted, like a penny swirling down the wishing well at the supermarket. But the driver had a job to do so we came off the roundabout before we even did one lap.

Being inside the train station felt like being outside even though we were inside. Granpa got our tickets from the man in the office. He was behind a glass screen with little holes to let your voice go through.

'Granpa, you should get that for the bookies—a glass screen. Then you'd be safe from anyone.'

'What aboot robbers fae the circus who eat glass?'

I was ninety-nine percent sure those didn't exist.

Granpa had it all planned out, so we didn't have to wait long for the train. A posh lady over the speakers told us the train was on its way.

The next train at Platform 2 is the 7.34 *to* Aberdeen.

There was a little gap before she said 7.34 and Aberdeen, like she was checking her jotter to make sure she said the right thing.

We sat at a table with four seats so there was plenty of room for our bags. The seats were blue with little green and grey squiggles on them. I could've coloured in the seats much nicer.

It was about thirty minutes to Perth. I watched Bridge of Allan zoom by the window and Granpa read the *Metro*. I turned the pages when he gave me a nod. While he was reading, I put the bit of paper with the train times in his jacket pocket without him noticing. It was just too much pressure. It was safer with Granpa.

We got to Perth and stepped off the train. The fancy word for getting off a train was *alighting*. I had only ever heard the lady on the speaker say it. If someone said to you, '*I alighted the train*', you'd tell them to stop talking so posh.

The Perth station was much bigger than the Stirling one. Lots of stairs going in all directions and I knew that without Granpa I would've got lost.

'Next stop Inverness,' said Granpa. 'Bit of a wait though. Will we stretch our legs?'

We walked out from the station and into the street. It was almost time for the grown-ups to start their work so there were lots more cars going about. We walked by a big park and there were fancy, expensive looking houses over the road just like King's Park at home.

'Granpa, those bags are heavy. We shouldnae walk too far.'

'I'm fine, Mary. There's life in this old dog yet.'

He was meaning himself, an old dog. I was taking him out for a walk. We had been walking for a little while when I saw a bookies on the next street over.

'Look, Granpa, it's the same as the one at home.'

'Cannae get away fae the place, can I?'

'Oh, and look what's outside.'

I was excited when I saw the van. The red van with the picture on the side. The picture of a cow drinking a glass of milk. It was up on the pavement in front of the bookie's doors. The police had been looking for the van for months and I had found it without even trying. Then I remembered it wasn't a good van and I got worried. It was the police who were meant to find it, not me and Granpa.

'Christ,' said Granpa, putting his hand through his hair. 'Here's a dilemma.'

'Should we phone 999?'

It was like he didn't hear me.

'Mary, I'm gonnae ask ye a favour. Come here.'

He took me down the street next to us. We went past the *West Mill Street Library* and turned into an empty lane with no cars. He took off the bags and put them against a wall. There was a leaky tap and he stood right in the puddle it was making.

'Stay here, awright? Right here and dinnae move. I need to make sure the people are safe. Ye didnae pack that mask of yours, did ye?'

'The Elvis one? It's in my bag. Why?'

'Be a good girl and get it oot for me.'

I opened my case to get the mask out. I had no clue what an Elvis mask had to do with anything. While I was looking in my bag, Granpa was looking in his too. He reached into his rucksack and brought out something wrapped in a black bag. It wasn't very big and I couldn't tell what was inside. I hadn't seen him pack it. He took the mask off me and gave me a wink.

'Granpa, dinnae leave me.'

'I'll only be a minute.'

He gave me a serious *don't you move* look and walked round the corner and left me with the bags. I started breathing really fast just like when the robbery happened. Granpa had never left me out in the street myself before. And it was Perth. I didn't know about Perth. I only knew Stirling. If he didn't come back I would never get to Portree and never get home and have to live in Perth forever. I crossed my legs so there was no way I could pee myself again.

I wasn't sure what to do, so I stayed still like Granpa told me. Some people passed and I thought I should tell them something, but I couldn't think what to say. I sat down on the bags and tried not to cry even though I wanted to. From where I was, there wasn't anything wrong. No robbers, it was like a normal day. I couldn't hear anyone shouting or getting hurt. I took out a sandwich wrapped in foil and smelled it. I guessed chocolate spread. I took out another one and smelled it. Definitely cheese.

An old man was walking his little white Scottie dog. He got a fright when he came round the corner and saw me.

'Morning, dear. You okay there?'

I nodded and hoped he would go away.

'You out on your lonesome?'

I shook my head and really hoped he would go away.

'Looks like you're off on your holidays.'

'I'm going to Skye,' I said.

'Beautiful place. Have you been before?'

Just then, Granpa came back. He was breathing hard through his nose. He still had the black bag but it looked much fuller and heavier. He wasn't wearing his jacket anymore.

'Mary, let's go.'

He grabbed his rucksack and started walking so fast I had to run to keep up.

'Ah, she's with you, pal?' the dog-walking man said. 'I was keeping an eye on her.'

Granpa didn't say anything back. It took all my strength to pull my case along and hold the sandwich bag and run all at once. I knew Granpa would never leave me behind, but he wasn't even turning around to make sure I was keeping up. He knew how fast I could run though, so he probably guessed I'd be right behind him.

We went back up the street towards the bookies and turned left towards the station. I didn't see police cars anywhere. We were almost at the station before Granpa slowed down to put the black bag in his rucksack.

'Granpa, what happened? Was it the same robbers? Did they get away?'

'Mary, ye dinnae need to worry aboot those men again. The police got them.'

'I didnae hear the sirens or see any cars.'

'Plain clothes police. Dinnae be stupid.'

He was using his angry voice. I started crying.

'Stop that, Mary. Folk are looking at us.'

'I dinnae care. I want to go home.'

'We're on holiday. Ye're no gonnae let those bloody robbers ruin our holiday, are ye?'

He wiped away the tears from my cheeks and blew a raspberry on my neck. I started laughing.

'There's the smile that broke the King's heart.'

'That's cheating. I'm not happy with you.'

'Aw naw, Mary's upset with me. Would it help if I had chocolate?'

He pulled out a Dairy Milk from his rucksack. I took it.

'Only because I'm hungry,' I said. 'Where'd your jacket go?'

'Oh, em, I gave it to a wife ootside the shop. She was feeling a bit chilly, having to stand aboot while the police were inside.'

'And where's my mask?'

'I put it in my bag. I'll give it back later.'

On the train to Inverness, Granpa read the *Metro* again, but I didn't turn the pages for him. He didn't turn the pages either. The chocolate bar was warm and soft. I licked the melted chocolate off the wrapper when I was finished.

'I wanted to see the robbers get caught,' I said. 'I wanted to see them get put in handcuffs.'

'Ye wouldnae have liked it, Mary. It's no like on the telly. There's loads of shouting and swearing. And they dinnae give ye fifty pence every time they do it.'

CHAPTER FIVE

Granpa took out a red waterproof jacket from his suitcase and put it on. I wondered if he had really given his other jacket to a lady outside the bookies. On telly, when a man gave a lady his jacket, it was only for a wee while, then he got it back when she wasn't cold anymore. I was cold all the time and no one ever gave me their jacket.

'Did one of the robbers take your jacket, Granpa?'

'Christ, ye're obsessed with my bloody jacket. I gave it to someone, I told ye.'

'But jackets are expensive.'

'It was an old jacket.'

'And why did you take Elvis?'

'The mask? I took the mask... in case the robbers spotted me ootside and kent it was me who phoned the polis. That's my phone oot of credit as well.'

'Oh. I'm really glad the police got them, Granpa.'

'Me as well.'

'I still dinnae think you should've gone so close. The whole holiday could've been ruined.'

'I'd gladly never be involved in another robbery. Promise.'

He smiled at me. The jacket was gone and so was the bit of paper I'd put in the pocket. I didn't tell Granpa about that. I didn't want him to get angry again. I smiled back.

The Inverness station wasn't as complicated as the Perth one. The train we were waiting on took us to a place called Kyle of Lochalsh. There were two boys called Kyle in my class at school. One of them had the nickname 'Kyle the paedophile', which rhymed but didn't make any sense to me.

We ate our sandwiches on the train station benches. It wasn't even twelve o'clock yet. It was the earliest lunch I'd had, ever. I got all the chocolate spread ones to myself because Granpa thought they were *a waste of good bread*.

There was a lady with a dog on the bench behind us. A man who worked at the station came over and started petting the dog.

'Lovely, she is,' said the station man. 'I've got four Boxers at home, myself. All rescues.'

'What's a rescue?' I whispered to Granpa.

'It's a dog ye get on the cheap,' he said. 'Their owners call them *'rescues'* like they saved them fae a burning building or something.'

I leaned over the bench.

'Excuse me,' I said to the station man. 'Did you save your dogs' lives?'

His face was confused, like I had asked him to do a sum like 9 x 8.

'Well, in a way, aye. They would've been put down if it wasn't for me.'

'What does *"put down"* mean?'

'Oh, well, em.'

Granpa turned round to join in.

'What are you and yer friend talking aboot, Mary?'

'The man's telling me about putting dogs down,' I said.

Granpa did an over the top shocked face and I knew he was doing it on purpose. The station man's cheeks went red.

'Let's move, Mary,' Granpa said. 'Shocking.'

Granpa picked up all the bags and moved them a few benches down. The station man gave the dog one last pat on the head then walked away.

'What time's our train, Mary?'

'Five to one.'

'Are ye no even going to check the list?'

'I've got it memorised,' I said, tapping my head.

There hadn't been much to memorise. *12.55 to Kyle of Lochalsh*. The Portree bus didn't have a time next to it. Granpa would never know I had lost the bit of paper.

The train to Kyle was the best journey of the lot. Lots of bright flowers passed by the window and the glass kept the smell from getting up my nose. There were amazing views of big blue lakes. But I didn't say lake in front of Granpa. It was to be *loch*, even though they were really the same thing. If you were Scottish, you had to say *loch* for some reason, or it meant you were English.

I fell asleep for a minute then woke up with a hot feeling on my face. The sun was coming through the window and making a bright rectangle on me.

'Ye'll no sleep the night,' Granpa said.

'I will so. I can always sleep.'

'What, even if there was a big hurricane ootside, rattling yer bed like this?'

He leaned over and shook me about and it was quite tickly and I couldn't stop myself laughing.

'I would definitely sleep. We dinnae get hurricanes in Scotland anyway.'

'Ye do in Portree. Big yins. Ye'll need to screw yer bed doon in case ye go flying oot the windae.'

I really hoped he was joking about the hurricanes. That

would ruin the summer. No sun at all, only hurricanes trying to throw you out the window all the time. I'd have rather stayed home and been bored in Stirling.

Granpa only joked about silly things, hurricanes or when he said birds used to be dinosaurs. He never kidded on about serious things. That was how I knew the robbers were locked up for good.

Kyle of Lochalsh was right next to a loch. We sat on a wall and looked out over the water while we waited for the bus to arrive. There were big jaggy rocks right beside the water and I walked on to them. Not too far, though. I didn't want to break an arm or a leg before we got to Portree.

The sun shone on the water and made a white line down the middle. I couldn't stare at it for too long. It was so bright and shiny and if I stared at it for too long it made me need to sneeze. The water was sparkly like a magician was doing a spell on it and something amazing was about to jump out.

'Does anything live in this water, Granpa?'

'Nessie comes here on her holidays.'

Granpa had cheered up in Kyle. It was like the further away we got from the robbers, the happier he was. I was the same. We had left them behind, miles away. I was back in Granpa's good books and he was back in mine.

The bus came and we got seats in the very back row. Granpa didn't want to, but he didn't realise that was where cool people sat. At school, when the bus came to take us on a trip, I always tried to sit up the back. People were usually saving the empty seats for someone else though. Leona used to save me a seat but my seat turned into Hannah's seat. Sitting down the front with the teachers was okay too.

I watched the driver through the window. He was putting

all our bags in the belly of the bus. I was so sleepy I didn't even care about the old bus smell or that the driver didn't put a film on the telly at the front. I had to concentrate hard to lift my eyelids up. It was like a game. I fought hard, but in the end I let my eyelids win.

The road to Portree was twisty and turny. When the bus swung one way, my head rolled to the other side. Sometimes, I'd wake up on Granpa's arm, but other times on the hard window. I kept my eyes closed to make falling asleep easier. I heard some things Granpa was saying to the people in front of us. It sort of sounded like he was talking on a phone.

'Naw, I'm just a customer. I got the number from the poster in the loo. It said, "*Have you witnessed dishonesty?*" ...In the shoes, aye. It looked a bit suspect to me so I thought I'd let ye ken... I'd like to remain anonymous... Much appreciated. It was a local call, I promise.'

My brain was too tired to try and work out what he'd been talking about. I decided it was probably a dream. Granpa's phone was out of credit.

I opened my eyes. I closed my eyes. We were outside. Granpa had carried me off the bus because I had been in *the land of nod.* I didn't want Granpa to know I was awake though. He would've put me down and I was too tired for that. Cuddling into his shoulder was comfy enough for sleep.

The next time, I only opened one eye. The car smelled of smoke and Granpa and the man driving were speaking so fast and laughing so hard I couldn't understand anything they were saying. With my eyes closed, it was like listening to the radio. One of those programmes where they're too mean to play music.

'Ye're going to have to walk, hen,' Granpa said. 'I ken ye're awake.'

'Two more minutes,' I said.

'Come oan. Ye've no even said hello to Iain yet.'

I stepped out of the car and into the driveway. Granpa's friend Iain was taking our bags out of the boot. He had mine in his hand.

'Is this yours, Mary?' he said.

I nodded and walked towards him.

'Mary,' Granpa said. 'This is Iain Watson. And Iain, this is Mary.'

Iain took my hand and shook it and winked at me.

'It's a pleasure,' he said. 'Arthur's told me all about you.'

'He didnae say anything about you,' I said. 'How do you spell your name?'

He took Granpa's bag out of the boot.

'The right way.'

Iain had glasses like Granpa and seemed about the same age. He was taller though, and Granpa didn't seem so tall anymore. The top of Iain's head was bald, but he had a little ring of white hair going from the top of one ear to the other.

We were on a street and quite high up, at the top of a hill. I kept out the way while they put the bags in the house and I crunched the orange stones in Iain's driveway under my feet. Iain had a type of car that was more like a jeep. I had been in it and not even realised I had been for my first ride in a jeep. Leona had probably never been in a jeep.

Past the house across the road, I could see the water. It was a loch that went all the way into the distance. It wasn't a loch at all, it was the sea. If you swam in one direction enough you'd end up in another country, if you kept on going and didn't need to get out and have your tea. A champion swimmer could've maybe ended up in Australia with the kangaroos. I wondered how far you could swim out to sea if you had a silver certificate.

I walked into Iain's house. The first room was the living room, which joined on to the kitchen. There was no door between them, only a wee counter, so you could cook while you watched the telly. The living room had a nice green carpet and everything was cream coloured in the kitchen. I followed Granpa and Iain's voices through the kitchen and down a hall. They were in a bedroom and Granpa was unpacking and Iain said things like, 'What did you bring that for, you daftie?'

Further down the hall was a room with the big light on. My red case was sitting just inside. I was so happy to have my own room, even though it looked like a grown-up's. The furniture was heavy-looking and wooden, like in a catalogue. I would fill the wardrobe and drawers with my stuff, then it would feel more like home. I needed a wee lie down first though. The covers on the bed were silky and felt good wrapped around me.

'What have we got here?' Granpa asked.

I didn't move and tried not to let myself smile. I knew he was standing at the door.

'Thinks she can just collapse on the bed and no have to do any unpacking? Ye're some girl, Mary.'

He could definitely tell I was smiling. I felt him move closer and tuck in the covers under me, nice and tight.

'It's been a long day, hen. You come through when ye've had a wee rest.'

He kissed me on the forehead, put out the big light, and closed the door over.

When I woke up, the clock next to the bed said 9.33pm. I got up and walked quietly, which was easy because the bedroom had a thick brown carpet and my toes sunk right into it. I opened the door and peeked out. I could hear Granpa and Iain talking in the kitchen.

I tiptoed down the corridor. The door wasn't closed over completely. They were sitting at the kitchen table. Iain was laughing and pouring Granpa a drink. It was light brown stuff which I knew was whisky. It had the dancing bird on the bottle. I liked the sound of the glasses clinking together.

'In the shoes?' Iain was saying. 'In the fucking shoes?'

He had a strange laugh which sounded more like a cough.

'You tell me,' Granpa said. 'How often d'ye check under yer insoles?'

Iain nodded.

'You sorted everything out with the house?' he said. 'And the girl's school?'

'It's aw done,' Granpa said.

'And the job?'

'Notice served, no problem.'

'And you're telling me you just scanned the slips again, and they paid out twice?'

'Aye, somebody should probably tell them there's a flaw in their system, eh?'

They had a good laugh at that, but I didn't know what they were on about. I was a bit worried. On telly, people who listened in on other people talking almost always got caught. I was stuck. If I went back to the bedroom and made a noise in the hall, they would hear it and know I was a nosey parker. I breathed through my nose to be as quiet as I could.

'You'll like it here, Arthur. The only problem might be finding things for the wee one to do.'

'Hopefully she'll make a pal or two,' Granpa said. 'She never brought anyone hame in Stirling though. She had a pal last year. Leona something. But I've no seen her in ages. Wee lassies these days, they can be right nasty.'

'They were nasty in our day as well, if you cast your mind back.'

Iain pointed at Granpa with his glass. Granpa pushed his glasses up with his middle finger.

'True. But it'll be good for her to have other lassies around. Older women as well. Growing up with just her granpa for company cannae be good for her.'

'Don't be daft. Hell, if it wasn't for you she'd be in bloody foster care. Or in Canada with the bitch-in-law.'

'I ken ye're right, but it's no been easy on my own. Isabel would've loved Mary.'

'Oi, what did we say?'

'No dead wife talk.'

'Right. Talk me through yer story one more time, Arthur.'

'I kent the first yin would be waiting by the door. Caught him in the stomach, he went doon winded. The second one swung for me, but his stance was aw wrong. It took a fair few whacks to keep him doon, mind ye.'

That was when I stepped on a creaky bit of the floor and Iain looked up, staring right at me. I pushed the door open and did a yawn, so they'd think I was just out of bed. My heart was going *like the clappers* and I could feel it thudding in my ears. I wondered if you could sick up your heart from being so scared.

'It's alive,' Iain said.

'Good evening, young lady,' Granpa said. 'Sleep well?'

I shrugged and rubbed my eyes.

'I hope you like your bedroom?' Iain asked me. 'We can make it a bit more girly soon.'

'It's fine, thanks,' I said quietly, 'What were you talking about?'

'Was someone listening in?' Granpa said, but he wasn't mad. 'Just reminiscing aboot our old boxing days. Is that no right, Iain?'

'Of course, Arthur,' Iain said. 'There weren't many better in the ring than your granpa, Mary.'

'D'you have any milk, Iain?' I asked.

'I think I can accommodate that request, Mary. If all your needs are that simple, I think we'll get on grand.'

He brought out a glass bottle, not like the plastic ones we had to recycle at home. It didn't have a green or blue top so I didn't know how skimmed it was. It tasted brilliant anyway.

'Did you like the view we have over the water?'

'It's braw,' I said. 'Is there a beach down there?'

'Not like you're thinking of, Mary. It's mostly stones and gunk and seaweed. You wouldn't want to sunbathe on a Portree beach, put it that way.'

I thought maybe there would be good sand further down the beach if I followed it for miles and miles. I could go further than anyone ever had and find a secret beach no one knew about but me. People would pay me and be my friend if I took them to see my secret beach.

'Can I go swimming in the sea?'

They both laughed at me.

'I wouldn't recommend it,' Iain said. 'You'll freeze your

bum off, for a start. Then again, I think there's a group of oldies in the village that go swimming in the winter. Polar Bears, they call themselves.'

'And could I join?'

'I'll look into it.'

'Oh no, wait. I'm only here for the summer. I cannae join if they only swim in winter.'

'Good point. Maybe you can make your own group, Mary. The Penguins or something.'

He winked at Granpa and that was them laughing again. They were laughing at everything the other said, even when it wasn't that funny. I wondered if they were drunk. Normally Granpa only drank at Christmas and his birthday. If only alcohol didn't taste so disgusting then maybe I could've had some with them.

'I'm going back to sleep if that's okay, Granpa.'

'Before ye go, look at what Iain's got.'

He was pointing at something in the living room. It had a sheet over it and I hadn't noticed it before. Iain turned on the big light and I peeked under the cover. It was a fancy electric keyboard. Even bigger and better than Mrs Stafford's!

'Did you buy it just for me?' I said.

'Not quite,' Iain said. 'I used to fancy myself as a bit of an Elton John, back in the day. Never was very good at it, to be honest. It's been collecting dust in my back room.'

'Can I play it, please, Iain?'

'I would love you to, Mary. Maybe not tonight though. After we get back tomorrow?'

'Iain's going to give us the tour in the morning,' said Granpa.

I pressed the C key. It was heavy and thudded back into place when I let go.

I hugged Granpa and Iain nodded at me before I went back down the hall. I would've listened at the door again, but Iain followed me out and shut the door right over. I was almost in my room when I heard Granpa shout, 'Mind and brush yer teeth, Mary.'

I had almost got away with it too.

I was so glad they had only been talking about boxing. I didn't want Granpa to be in any trouble for beating someone up. But in boxing, the whole point was to whack the other person. It was allowed.

I'd never known Granpa had been a great boxer when he was young. He only told me things about my mum and dad, but I'd never had anyone to tell me things about Granpa. I hoped Iain had more old stories about Granpa and would tell me all the bits and pieces I didn't know about him. I wanted to know *the truth, the whole truth, and nothing but the truth* about Granpa.

CHAPTER SIX

It was scrambled eggs for breakfast.

'Are you ready to see all that Portree has to offer, Mary?' Iain said.

'I think so. What is there?'

'D'you like breath-taking views and awe-inspiring scenery? Because if you don't, then we're a bit stuck. There are boat tours that take you out on the water. To see seals and things, but I'm not convinced they're any good. They could point at a stone in the distance and say, "That's a seal's head. Fifty quid, cough up."'

'I'd like to see the seals.'

'I'm sure your Granpa will take you.'

It sounded as if Portree was more of a grown-up place for folk who liked hills and pictures of the sea. Malcolm from next door used to show me and Granpa his holiday pictures and they were fine but not professional and his thumb was in half of them.

Mrs Lithgow showed us photos of her trip to Africa in class once. The photos were of her with black people so you could always spot her straight away. She couldn't dye her hair in Africa so it was blonde instead of red. Most of the photos were a bit sad because of all the hungry people in the empty houses, but looking at them got us out of doing real work so no one complained.

'Can I go and see things on my own?'

'You'll need to ask your Granpa.'

'I'm no sure,' Granpa said. 'I dinnae usually let her out on her own. And fae what she said last night, she's planning on taking a dip in the bloody icy water.'

'I'm a good swimmer,' I said. 'I've got a bronze certificate.'

'When I was your age,' Iain said. 'If I'd got a bronze certificate, my dad would've said, "*Bronze? Why not silver or gold?*" But I'm not like my dad, Mary. Well done.'

I smiled, but really I was annoyed because I'd forgotten to bring my bronze certificate with me. It would be at home when we went back and I could take a picture of it and send it to Iain so he knew I was a good swimmer.

Then I would keep going and get silver and gold, even though they were much harder than bronze. Iain's dad couldn't say anything to me if I ever met him. I bet Iain's dad didn't even have any certificates at all. But Iain's dad was probably dead, there was no need to worry about having to impress him.

It was only a ten-minute walk into the village. I hoped we could go in Iain's jeep, but that was just for going on long drives or *off-roading*. You wouldn't think granpa's would want to walk places since they normally had sore knees and backs, but Granpa and Iain were both still quite fit and walked faster than me even.

'Keep up, shorty,' said Granpa.

On the walk, there was a little waterfall which looked magical, like out of a fairy tale book or a *Disney* film. I knew Granpa wouldn't let me go near it on my own because there weren't any fences around it to keep you out and you could fall in if you weren't careful.

You could almost always see the sea in Portree. It was there in the background whenever you looked about. Lots of boats floating on it, not going anywhere, just bobbing in the one place. I guessed there weren't garages for boats like you had for cars. If you had a boat, you had to leave it floating in the water and hope no one would steal it. It would be hard to steal a boat though. You'd have to swim out to it and get soaking wet. What if there wasn't any petrol in the boat? You'd just be floating there feeling like a numpty, dripping like a *drowned rat*. The main thing you'd worry about was the sea. A big wave could come out of nowhere and turn it upside down. I bet there were hardly any boats ever stolen in Portree. It didn't look like a place robbers would live.

'Do you have a boat, Iain?' I asked.

'I've got loads of boats,' he said. 'Only I've forgotten where I parked them all. So, in other words, I've got none. Do you only hang about with boat owners?'

'Naw, but you should save up and get one, then you can take us anywhere we want.'

'I like your plan. But why would we want to go anywhere?'

He pointed to the view and it was the best one I'd ever seen. I went up to the railing that looked over the harbour. All the colours of the houses in a row were absolutely amazing, like a stone rainbow. A white one, a pink one, a blue one, a green one. Then one that was a mixture of blue, green and yellow. We didn't have any houses so bright in Stirling.

It was the prettiest street I'd ever seen. I decided right then and there that I wanted to live in one of those houses. The pink one. I wanted the pink one. When I was a grown-up, I'd buy it and I'd be the lady who lived in the pink house. I'd be friends with all the other people on the street. The man from the blue house, the family from the green one. People would come and take pictures with me and I'd give them juice and biscuits. Everyone would want to be my friend because I was the pink house lady and everyone in the village would know how friendly I was.

I didn't tell Granpa in case he said, "*Ye're no allowed to buy those houses*" or something. He always had a reason why I couldn't do things. He could ruin the dream, but not if I didn't tell him. Not if I kept it to myself. This dream would be mine and even if anyone asked me if I had a dream, I wouldn't tell them.

We went past a Co-op and down a street which had a post office and gift shops. I thought of what sort of present I should get for Mum and Dad's grave. It would need to be something waterproof.

I looked down a lane where a man was hanging flags from above a doorway. It was the Scotland flag, the yellow one with a red lion, whatever that was called. A lady went past and said, 'Oh, you're tempting fate with so many flags. The gale force winds will be on their way!'

They both laughed. The man said, 'I'm going to need to put up a Union Jack and the EU flag to keep everybody happy.'

At the end of the street, there was a big open space with lots of cars coming and going.

'This is Somerled Square,' Iain said. 'All the buses come in and out of here.'

'Ye were here last night, Mary,' Granpa added, 'When Iain picked us up. Everyone heard ye snoring on the bus.'

'I dinnae snore.'

'Ye do. It sounded like someone tuning bagpipes.'

I could see a big yellow building with a sign outside -

Portree Independent Hostel.

'What's a hostel, Granpa?'

'It's like a hotel for smelly people,' he said, frowning, 'Ye'd be in a room with aboot ten other people. Bunkbeds, probably.'

That sounded great. Like a big sleepover. Only I didn't have nine other friends to stay with me.

Iain was pretending to be a proper tour guide and was giving us facts about Portree.

'Mary, did you know that Skye is the second biggest tourist destination in Scotland? Only behind Edinburgh.'

'I didnae know that.'

'Would you like to live here when you grow up?'

I thought about the pink house.

'Maybe,' I said, trying to think of a reason which wasn't the pink house. 'I need to live somewhere with a good university.'

'Very good. Your granpa teach you to say that?'

'Aye, we've got a plan,' I said.

'What are ye gonnae study when ye leave high school, Mary?' Granpa said.

'Music. So I can be a concert pianist.'

'And what aren't ye gonnae do?'

'Run away and join ISIS.'

'Good girl.'

Iain laughed. ISIS was a bad group of people and they were always wanting women to join because there were too many men and not enough women to keep them company. It was on the ten o'clock news a lot, the women in the airports going to ISIS. They were always dressed normal, like you wouldn't know they were *terrorists*.

We went down a set of steep steps to get to the harbour. The houses were even prettier close-up. All the coloured houses in a row. There were lots of people looking and taking pictures. That would be a bad thing about living in the pink house - the people outside taking pictures all the time. The clicking of their cameras could keep you awake.

The first building was called *The Lower Deck*. It was a sit-down restaurant. Then next door was a fish and chip shop. The chippy had a sign saying you could book boat trips from there. That was funny. You could go in and say, "*One sausage supper and one boat trip please*". You couldn't say that in the chippy in Stirling. Well, you could try, but they'd think you were really daft.

The smell coming out the door was great. Vinegar and fat. It wasn't open yet but I could hear the bubbles in the fryer going. When we went to the chippy in Stirling, Granpa always made a joke about how the fish had been in a big fight and they had all been battered. It wasn't a proper visit to the chippy if Granpa didn't make his silly joke.

The pink house was called *The Pink Guest House*. It was white around its windows. It looked like a French Fancie cake. It would be delicious and creamy if you bit into it.

I thought about what I would change when I owned it. I didn't think I would keep it as a guest house. Probably too many visitors to look after all the time. I'd only want one or two folk popping in for juice and cakes, that would be easier. I'd definitely still have it painted pink though. I could put a new coat of paint on every year and people would come and help me. I would give out paintbrushes and say, "*lend a hand*". Everyone would know me. *The pink house lady from Portree*. That's what they would call me.

There was a long pier in the distance. I thought it would

be fun to run down and jump off the end of it. Like in a film where people are on holiday and you know they're happy because they don't care about getting wet. But the water wouldn't be warm like in a film.

Lots of men in wellies were walking here and there, looking like they had work to do. We got to the end of the road, so we went back on ourselves.

There was a slope which went right down to the beach in front of the harbour street. Like Iain said, it wasn't really a beach. Mainly stones and muck.

'Am I allowed to go down there?' I asked.

Granpa looked at Iain.

'Go ahead,' Iain said. 'Tide's out plenty. Just watch your feet for glass. And be careful of the seagulls. They're a menace.'

Granpa and Iain waited up on the street and I went down the slope and stood right next to the water. The salty smell went up through my nose and landed on my tongue. I didn't have my wellies on, so I didn't let the water touch my shoes, but I could've if I'd wanted to. It was right there in front of me. All the bobbing boats were there too.

The seagulls were great to watch. They walked into the water just like people. Lifting up their legs really high before putting them down, so the water must've been cold. They looked white and clean, but then they'd stretch out their wings and underneath was horrible and dirty.

If someone threw a chip, they were right after it. Three or four of them, into the water, fighting for it. Then the slower seagulls floated in and circled around, pretending they didn't even want the chip anyway. But you could tell that they were all desperate for a chip.

There were little ropes going from the beach into the

water. They were tied to the boats to stop them floating away. Tied to the wall, but not the handrail, definitely not. The sign said *TYING TO HANDRAIL PROHIBITED*. I couldn't tell which rope was for which boat because they disappeared under the water, hiding below the surface. If a rope was right at the top of the water and a seagull tried to float over it, it couldn't. Its face would be like *"what's going on? I've stopped"* and it needed to do a funny wee shuffle to get over the rope and keep floating.

Granpa and Iain were leaning on the rail and talking. I was waving but Granpa didn't see. I waved harder, but he still didn't see me.

'Granpa!' I shouted. 'Look!'

Finally, he saw me and gave me a wave. I showed him how close my foot could go to the water and then I rushed back at the last minute so the water couldn't get me. It actually did get me a little bit, but Granpa couldn't tell. Just the tip of my big toe was wet.

A dog came down the slope. It was a greyhound. And it was grey. A grey greyhound. I recognised it from when the dogs raced on the telly in the bookies. Only, the dogs in the bookies were lightning fast. This one wasn't in a hurry at all. It walked down slowly and started rubbing its head on my jeans.

'NIPPY!' someone shouted from up on the street. 'Get back here.'

A boy came down the slope. I guessed he was probably a P6 or 7. He had dark brown hair and a *My Chemical Romance* T-shirt. His jeans were loose and looked comfy.

'Sorry,' he said. 'Nippy, get back.'

Nippy walked back to the boy with its head down. She looked like she needed go for forty winks.

'It's okay,' I said. 'I like her.'

'I'm not supposed to let people pet her.'

'But that's what dogs are for.'

'No, this one's going to be a racing dog.'

Nippy yawned, blinked slowly a few times, then laid down.

'I don't think she will be. She's too slow.'

'She's saving her energy.'

'Maybe if you pet her, she'd go a bit faster.'

'My dad says not to.'

'That sounds stupid.'

'Are you calling my dad stupid?'

I could feel my face going red. I put my head down and pulled my sleeves over my hands.

'Well, it is quite stupid,' I said. 'Having a dog and not giving it a clap.'

'Shut up. You're not even from here.'

'You're right. I'm Mary.'

'I'm Lewis. You shouldn't talk about people you don't know, Mary. I'll get Nippy to attack you if you call my dad stupid again.'

Nippy was scratching her head with her paw and getting sandy dirt all over herself.

'Your dad's stupid.'

I laughed, so he'd know I was kidding on. Lewis didn't say anything else. But he looked annoyed and walked back up the slope. Nippy didn't follow him. He had to come back down the slope, put her leash on and drag her away.

I could've made friends with Lewis, but instead I'd made fun of his dad. Even *I* knew that wasn't how to make friends. But it was fine. I didn't want to be friends with an idiot like him anyway.

I went back up the slope to Granpa and Iain.
'Who was that lad with the dog?' Granpa said.
'No one,' I said.
'No one. That's a funny name. Is he yer boyfriend?'
'I dinnae like him.'
'Sounds like a boyfriend to me.'

♪♪

CHAPTER SEVEN

We went to the *Isles Inn*. It was a pub with hotel rooms upstairs. Granpa said that's what made it an inn. There was a pool table up the back. I liked the sound of the balls clicking and clacking together. It was pool, but I liked the word *snooker* better. The balls snooked off each other. *Snook snook snook.*

Iain went up and put a 50p on the edge of the pool table. 'We're next,' he said, to the men who were playing.

That was the rule. If you wanted to play next, you put 50p on the table. I thought about hiding the 50p for a laugh, but oh no, they took it quite seriously.

Granpa and Iain had a pint of beer each. It looked nice and foamy, but I knew how horrible it tasted and I was happy with my cola. The cola came out of this little juice gun. The lady behind the bar fired it into a glass. Lemonade was coming out of it one second, then she pressed a different button and it was cola. I would definitely buy one of those juice guns when I had money of my own. It would go perfect in the pink house kitchen.

Granpa and Iain were good at pool. They were doing all the things I'd seen proper players on the telly do. Crouching down to look at the balls from my height, putting the blue stuff on top of their cues, pushing and pulling the cue back and forwards loads of times before they actually did the shot. They knew all the fancy pool words too. *Screwback* was a funny one. Then they were talking about the balls *kissing* each other which made me laugh.

'Och, you've snookered me, Arthur,' Iain said. 'You didn't even mean that.'

'Is it not pooled?' I said. 'He's pooled you?'

'Ye just say snooker, anyway,' Granpa said. 'Wheesht while we're playing.'

Iain won and they shook hands and said, *"well played"* and *"good game"*. Like in tennis, only they weren't doing it over a net.

The lady behind the bar called out, *"Watson, table of three"* and that was the sign for us to get our lunch.

'Nothing wrong with her,' Iain said. He nodded to the lady behind the bar and winked at Granpa. He smiled and shook his head like Iain was being silly. The lady was really pretty and Iain was right, there was nothing wrong with her.

I was eating my fish fingers when I noticed a girl waving at me from across the dining area. I waved back. She had a bright yellow top on to match her bright blonde hair. Her hair was curly, but good curly. She was having fish fingers too, so we had something in common. She was pointing at her plate and smiling. I smiled back and lifted up mine.

'What are ye doing?' said Granpa. 'Get yer plate doon.'

'But that girl over there-'

'I dinnae care aboot that girl over there, Mary. Sit and eat nice.'

'That's Kevin MacLeod's girl,' Iain said. 'Grace.'

Iain knew the names of loads of people in Portree.

'Like saying grace at the table?' I said.

'Just like that. Do you and your Granpa say grace?'

'Naw. That's just on telly in America. It's not fair to thank God for food when really it's Granpa who bought it for me.'

'So what's she's saying is,' Granpa said. 'I'm God.'

I put my plate down, but kept looking over at Grace when I could. She was with a lady who I guessed was her mum. Her mum had blonde hair too. I had already made an enemy of that boy Lewis, so I needed to make a friend as soon as I could. Grace looked older than me, but not a lot. I guessed she was nine or ten and probably going into Primary 6.

I thought that if Portree was like Stirling, then the older girls wouldn't want to hang around with girls in lower years like me. I would need to make sure Grace knew I was good to hang around with and not like a little baby. I was extra careful with my knife and fork and didn't make any screechy sounds on the plate. I even ate some peas.

After lunch, Granpa and Iain went back to playing pool. Granpa looked really happy. I was quite bored watching them after a while. They always played *one more game* because whoever lost didn't want to be the last loser which meant there was always a rematch.

'Will there ever be a final winner?' I asked. 'Like a champion?'

'It's unlikely,' Iain said. 'We're too competitive. Whichever one of us dies first, the other will be champion.'

It would never end. I thought it would be much better to come up with a way of choosing a winner and that would be that. They could move on to a new sport like tennis and find out who was the best at that. But they'd never be better than Andy Murray. You didn't get many Scottish people who were best in the world at something but Andy was special. Granpa had taken me through to Dunblane when he got married to Kim. It was rainy that day and her dress wasn't as nice as Princess Kate's, but it was great to see Andy in real-life.

Grace and her mum got up from their table. Her mum went out the door, but Grace came over and sat in the chair next to me.

'Hiya,' she said.

'Hiya. I'm Mary.'

'I'm Grace.'

'Do you live in Portree?'

'Aye. I know that man,' and she pointed at Iain. 'But I've not seen you or that man before.'

'That's my granpa. We're here for the summer on holiday.'

'That's good. Where are you from?'

'Stirling.'

'Is that near Glasgow?'

'Sort of.'

'I'm ten, what age are you?'

I guessed right. There was a year and a quarter between us and I'd need to work extra hard.

'Eight and three quarters.'

'I can show you the best places to go if you want.'

'Aye, please.'

'Mostly we just go to the Lump.'

'The Lump, what's that?'

'It's just a hill. But it's good. I'll show you.'

'Great. Give me two seconds.'

I went up to Granpa and put my hands together so he'd see I was praying.

'Granpa, can I go with Grace for a little while? Please? She's ten.'

There was a much bigger chance of Granpa letting me

go with Grace, once he knew how much older she was. She could take care of the both of us. I didn't notice Grace coming up behind me.

'Hiya,' said Grace. 'My mum says it's okay.'

'Does she now?' said Granpa. 'What d'ye think, Iain?'

'She'll be fine with Grace,' Iain said. 'Now hurry up, it's your shot.'

'Back here, no later than three,' Granpa said.

Grace and me ran out of the pub. I was faster than her and I had to slow down to let her lead the way.

Portree was only a wee village, but a lot of cars came from all directions so crossing the road could take a while. But then the driver might give a little wave and you were fine to cross in front of them.

The Lump was the hill behind the harbour. If you saw a picture of the harbour houses from faraway, up the back you'd see a hill with trees on it. That was the Lump. On the way up the hill, there was a *Royal Bank of Scotland*, then an old building which had a sign saying *Gathering Hall*, then a church, then at the top of the road was the *Portree Hospital*.

'Why's it called the Lump?' I asked.

'It just is,' Grace said. 'My brother says it's because it's a little dump, and when you put those two words together it makes lump. But it's not a dump at all. That's him just being stupid.'

It looked like we were going to the hospital, but then Grace turned left just before it and took me up a gravel path. There were signs telling you all the things you were to do and not to do.

DANGER!

Keep to footpath & steps
Beware of falling rocks
Do not climb or sit on fence
Do not climb trees
Do not climb rock face

'Are there really falling rocks?' I said.

'I've never seen any,' Grace said.

Grace hadn't seen any, but I was going to be on the lookout anyway because I really didn't want to be hit by a big rock. But then the hospital was right next door. I'd probably survive.

Grace took us off the main path and to the left, up some steps which were quite tricky to climb. There were wooden bits at the front of the steps so you could see where the steps started and ended. Whoever made the steps didn't have enough money to use cement.

'Aw no, I can hear Thomas,' Grace said. 'That's my brother.'

At the top of the steps, was a tower. It was like part of a castle except with no castle under it, just the tower. A cylinder of old brick with moss growing all over. There was a boy at the top of the tower leaning over the side.

'Grace the disgrace!' he shouted down. 'Who's that with you?'

'Come down and I'll tell you,' Grace said.

'You just want up here, don't you?'

'Are you here yourself?'

'James was here, but he had to go home. Is Mum at the house?'

'Yes, she says you left your plate on the living room table again.'

'No chance, that was Dad's plate. He always blames it on me.'

His head disappeared from the top of the tower and as he made his way down, it sounded a bit like thunder, with his feet clobbering the stairs. Then, quick as a flash, he was at the door of the tower. There wasn't actually a door, it was only a doorway.

'What's your name?' he said.

'Mary. I'm here on holiday.'

'I'm Tom. Grace is stinking isn't she, Mary?'

'Shut up, Thomas,' Grace said. 'No one calls him Tom, Mary. It's to be Thomas. Mum and Dad don't like people calling him Tom.'

'Shut up, Grace, I can be called what I want. Everyone at school calls me Tom.'

'Like who?'

'James and Lewis and Billy and Stuart-'

'Stuart's at the high school. You're not friends with anyone at the high school.'

'How much d'you want to bet? Just because you don't have any friends.'

'I've got a friend standing right next to me, idiot.'

'Oh, well done,' he said. 'One friend. Do you want to be friends with me instead of her, Mary?'

'Can't we all be friends, Tom?' I said.

I made sure to say *Tom*, so he wouldn't be annoyed at me like he was at Grace.

'I suppose we can all hang about,' Grace said. 'But we're brother and sister so we can't be friends.'

That made sense. Grace and Tom couldn't be friends because they were already brother and sister. They couldn't be more than one thing.

'Come on, let Mary go up the top,' Grace said.

Tom put his hands across the doorway to stop me, but

then took them away because he was only joking. He had brown hair and Grace had blonde hair. Maybe Grace had got her hair from their mum and their dad must've had brown hair like Tom. Alex Sinclair in the year below me at school had ginger hair even though both his parents had brown hair. Everyone said he was adopted.

'What age are you, Mary?' Tom said.

'My Granpa says it's not right to ask a lady her age,' I said.

'But you're a girl, not a lady.'

I hadn't thought of that before.

'I'm eight and three quarters.'

'I'm eight too. If you stay longer in Portree, you could be in my class next year.'

'I'm only here for the summer. I have my own school at home.'

He looked a bit disappointed at that. I was glad he wanted me to stay around though.

I went through the doorway and it wasn't as nice as I thought it would be. There were puddles and glass bottles had been left on the ground, or smashed, and the jaggy pieces were lying around. One label said, Lambrini, and I had never heard of that drink. There was a fousty smell and I didn't understand why Grace liked it so much. She came in behind me.

'It's better up the top,' she said.

I ran up the stairs. Not super-fast though, because the stairs were still wet and slippy. Everywhere on the walls, people had put their names on the bricks. Like scraping their initials or love hearts into them. *NOEL + LERNER '15.* If 15 meant 2015, that must've happened not long before I got to Portree. *LIFE AINT NUTTIN BUT A THUG.* That sounded American because it was like what a rapper would say and didn't make any sense.

'How do they get their names on like that?' I said to Grace.

'You need something sharp. Thomas has a screwdriver he uses.'

The top of the tower was fantastic. I could see for ages in the distance. Over the tops of the harbour houses and boats in the distance you couldn't see from down below. I could see the water till it touched the sky. And all the houses, every single one in Portree, I could see them. I was higher than anyone else for miles. I forgot all about Grace being there behind me. I ignored Tom who was making faces at us from down below. All I could see was Portree and the rest of Skye further away.

I was the Queen of Skye, standing at the top of her tower. I owned everything, especially the pink house. I was sort of like Mary, Queen of Scots. Except I didn't get my head chopped off while my dog was under my dress. I didn't even have a dog.

I came back to the real world when I heard the voices. A big group of people coming up the same path Grace and me had taken to the tower. There was a lady at the front leading them about, pointing at things and talking about them. She pointed to the tower and all the people waved at us. Me and Grace waved back.

'What's happening?' I said to Grace.

'That's Michelle. She does walking tours. She takes the tourists round Portree and tells them the history of the village.'

'That sounds good.'

'You have to pay for it. I'll show you about for free.'

That was a much better deal.

'The tower's proper name is the Apothecary Tower,' Grace told me. 'They used to keep medicine in here.'

The tour lady led her group through the trees and round the corner, till I couldn't hear her anymore. All I could hear was the sea swishing and the wind rushing. I couldn't even hear Tom because he'd disappeared.

'I'm going to find him,' Grace said. 'Sometimes, he tries to jump on to the Gathering hall roof. Mum says I'm to make sure he doesn't. I'll be back in a minute.'

She went back down the tower's steps and walked the path into the same trees the walking tour disappeared into. I wanted to tell her to stay. I wanted to tell her I wasn't allowed out by myself. But I couldn't. She was ten and she never would've been friends with me again.

A man came running up the hill. He was dressed in normal clothes, so I knew he wasn't a jogger. He stopped to catch his breath below the tower.

'Hiya,' I said.

He got such a fright. He put his hand on his heart.

'Och, Jesus,' he said. 'What a scare you gave me. Awright there.'

'Are you chasing someone?'

'Kind of,' he said, taking big long breaths. 'I was doing a walking tour and I lost the rest of the group.'

'They went that way,' I said, pointing into the trees. 'Not that long ago.'

He gave me the thumbs up, but he was still crouched over because of all the running. It wasn't that big a hill, but he was holding his sides like he had a massive stitch. He had long curly brown hair; the sweat had made it stick flat to his head. I thought he would've been quite good looking with a *short back and sides* like Granpa. He was carrying a clipboard, but I couldn't see if it had a pencil attached with a bit of string.

'I'm Mary. What's your name?'

'Em, Craig.'

He was so tired he'd forgotten his name for a second.

'Do you live here?' I said.

'Naw, I'm visiting a friend. But I need to find him first.'

He laughed to himself at that, but I didn't get the joke.

'But since I came all this way,' he said. 'I thought I'd be a tourist for an hour.'

'Do you know any fun things to do? I'm looking for tourist stuff too.'

'Naw, sorry. I'll mainly be working on a special project while I'm here, Mary. It's only for grown-ups though. I won't bore you with it.'

He stood up straight.

'Right, just around this corner you said? I'll catch you around, Mary.'

He zoomed round the corner.

'Bye, Craig!' I shouted.

Grace came back a little while later. I had stayed put at the top of the tower and that's where she found me.

'I couldn't find Thomas anywhere,' she said. 'He must've gone home. Hope you weren't too bored.'

'It's fine,' I said. 'I pretended I was queen of the castle.'

'I do that too,' she said.

We both laughed. In the real world, you didn't get two queens of the same place, but we could do whatever we wanted in our tower.

CHAPTER EIGHT

Grace walked me back to the pub.

'Iain's house is on the other side of the harbour,' I said.

'I know where you mean,' Grace said. 'That's Coolin Hills.'

'There's a green jeep parked in the drive.'

'Okay, I'll maybe come round someday. See you later, Mary.'

Grace ran off so she could get back and clean her room before her tea. Her parents were fine with her being out herself as long as she liked. She was so lucky.

Granpa and Iain weren't playing pool anymore. It looked like they were sleeping in the comfy chairs, but when I came in they sort of jumped up and were ready to leave.

'Good timing,' Granpa said. 'Did ye have a nice time? Is that Grace yer pal noo?'

'Aye, I think so. She's really nice and she's ten. Her brother Tom is my age. He was there too.'

Granpa yawned.

'So two friends, is it?'

'Kind of. They're brother and sister, so we can't all be friends at the same time, obviously.'

'Obviously. Right, back to Iain's for tea. We've got something special for tonight, hen.' He picked up a carrier bag and shook it. 'Lobster!'

'Me and your granpa did a bit of shopping while you were away,' Iain said.

'Will I like it?'

'I hope so. It was expensive.'

I touched the lobsters through the carrier bag. They were hard and the bag was wet.

'Are they crunchy?'

'Only if you eat them alive.'

That was the most disgusting thing I'd ever heard.

The lobster was okay. Granpa and Iain went on about it like it was the best thing they'd ever had. It didn't taste like much to me. I would've preferred chips and cheese.

Granpa and Iain had more whisky after their tea.

'Are you going to drink every night of the holiday, Granpa?'

'If ye dinnae want me to, Mary, I'll stop. Only, my shoulder's been really sore lately. A wee dram helps it hurt less.'

'Oh, that's okay then.'

As long as there was a reason for the drinking, it was fine. Iain didn't have a good reason, but I wasn't in charge of him.

We all sat round the kitchen table and played pontoon, but not for money, only to score points.

'Does Portree have any bookies?' I asked.

'Not a single one,' said Iain. 'Are you missing it, Mary?'

I shook my head. I was happy there were no bookies in Portree. All the bad things that had happened to us had been because of bookies. The robbery, Granpa getting hurt, the thing that had happened in Perth. It was good news because if there were no bookies, then those robbers definitely wouldn't turn up in Portree. Granpa said they were already locked up, so there was nothing for me to worry about.

'What did you and Grace get up to today?' Granpa asked.

'We went to this tower. Grace says its proper name is The Apoth... The Apath... The Medicine Tower. I went to the top and I was the Queen. We were both the Queen actually.'

'Very good. And her brother was there as well, ye said?'

'Aye. He's okay, a bit weird.'

'Wouldnae expect anything different from a wee boy.'

Granpa was the card dealer, which meant that if it was a draw, he would win. I thought that was unfair, but he said that was the way it worked in casinos. The *house* always won. Because they were a big house and you were as small as a caravan or a wee garden hut. When I got twenty, and Granpa got twenty, Granpa won. I never got to be dealer because I wasn't fast enough with the cards.

Then we played rummy and I won.

'Three fours and a ten, Jack, King, Queen of Spades,' I said.

'You mean Queen, King,' Iain said.

'Queen is the highest face card,' Granpa said. 'In the rules we play. Is that no right, Mary?'

'Aye, because there's not much difference between them. They're all worth ten so why can't the Queen be the highest? We've got a Queen in real-life anyway, not a King. It makes sense. It's fair.'

'That's one way of looking at it, I suppose,' Iain said. 'But playing card companies aren't sexist, Mary.'

'She said no such thing,' Granpa said.

They started arguing then. No, *debating*, that was the

better word. Because they weren't really angry at each other, but they had different opinions and were shouting them at each other like the politicians did on the telly. They were debating what Granpa should be teaching me. But I thought Granpa was teaching me great. I learned everything else I needed to know from the news.

'It was me who decided Queen should be top, not Granpa,' I said after a while.

'Och, ignore me, Mary,' Iain said. 'I've had one too many. I've missed having a good argument with your granpa here. Only a bit of banter.'

One second they were shouting and the next they were pouring more drinks and playing more card games. Even though Iain had had *one too many* he was having another. He scooped up all the cards and was busy sorting them.

'Mary, you'll like this,' he said. 'And watch closely in case I make a mistake.'

'Is this the one ye used to do down the Orchard?' Granpa said.

'New, politically correct version. Not perfect yet, but Mary's a good tester.'

He had all the cards in the deck and shuffled them before he laid them out. I could see every one.

'They're all there. Right, Mary?'

I nodded.

'Would you care to cut the cards?'

I took some cards off the pile and he slapped the others on top. He did more shuffling and sorting.

'Okay, Mary, I'm going to tell you a wee story.'

And as he told the story, he dealt cards face up to match.

'One day, the Queen (Q♥) was walking her five (5♥) corgis when she noticed one (A♣) had gone missing, leaving her only four (4♥). She thought about shouting for the King (K♥) but remembered he had died about six (6♥) decades ago. She only had eight (8♠) pence on her mobile phone, so she couldn't send a text. Instead, she phoned nine, nine, nine (9♦9♣9♠).

'The person answered and said, "What's your emergency?". She said, "This is the Queen (Q♦). I was walking my five corgis (5♠) and one (A♠) has gone missing so I only have four (4♠). I would've shouted for the King (K♦) but he's been dead for six (6♦) decades."

'The man on the phone said, "My name is Jack (J♠). I'm going to need more details from you. What's your full name?"

'She said, "Queen (Q♣) Elizabeth the Second (2♦). I was born in nineteen twenty (2♥) six (6♠). I'm eighty (8♦) nine (9♥), and I've ruled since my coronation in nineteen fifty (5♣) three (3♥). I have four (4♣) children and thirty (10♦10♠10♣) godchildren."

Jack (J♣) said, "That's impressive. What's your address?"

She said, "It's one (A♦) Buckingham Palace, of course! Which was built in seventeen (7♠) oh three (3♠), by the way. Then she said, "Wait, I am the Queen! (Q♠) I should be demanding details from you!"

'The phone operator said, "My name is Jack (J♦) Kingston (K♣). I was born in nineteen eighty (8♣) eight (8♥), making me twenty (2♣) seven (7♦). I've only had this job three (3♣) days and yesterday a man claiming to be the King (K♠) of Jamaica (J♥) phoned asking me to send seven (7♥) million pounds in aid. So, I'm having a hard time trusting you are who you say you are. You say you were walking your five (5♦) corgis and one (A♥) went missing, leaving you four (4♦). But I know for a fact the Queen has six (6♣) corgis, so really you are missing two!" (2♠)

'The Queen said, *"You're joking!"*

'And Jack said, *"Yes, I'm joking* (Joker). *The Queen actually has seven (7♣) corgis so three (3♦) are missing."*

'The Queen said, again, *"You're joking!"*

'And Jack said, *"Yes, I'm joking* (Joker). *I've never believed you were really the Queen, but I give you a ten (10♥) for effort."* And he hung up on her.'

I clapped and clapped. It was just the best story, trick —whatever you call it—I'd ever seen. He'd used every single card, even the joker cards which I didn't see when he showed me them all at the start, so I really didn't see them coming. He kept shuffling during it too, so how had he done it? I had no clue.

'Very good,' said Granpa. 'The ending needs some work, I think.'

'True,' said Iain. 'Never known what to do with that last fucking ten.'

They laughed. Normally when someone swore in front of me, Granpa would tell them *"not in front of the wee one"*, but he didn't say it to Iain. Because it was Iain's house and he could swear all he wanted in his own house. I was still keeping an ear out if Granpa swore though. He'd owe me 50p if he did.

I was bored of cards. Granpa and Iain started playing for money while I went to play the keyboard. Granpa had packed my keyboard books without telling me and they were on the stand.

It was an electric keyboard, and I could make it as quiet or as loud as I wanted. It was my first time playing one where the keys were so heavy. My fingers weren't used to it and I could hardly even press them down. It wasn't like the keyboard at school at all. I practised for about fifteen minutes then I put up the sound so Granpa and Iain could hear me playing *Super Trouper*. That was my best one. They were humming along, so they must've liked it. I put the sound back down when I did *On the Sunny Side of the Street*. That was really tricky and I couldn't even try the left hand of that one.

There was a knock at the door.

'It's past nine,' Iain said. 'What's someone wanting at this time?'

He opened the door. It was Craig, the running man from earlier.

'Evening, pal,' Craig said to Iain. 'Sorry to bother you. I wonder if I can have a minute of your time? I'm a student at the Highlands and Islands University. I'm doing a handwriting analysis for my dissertation. It would really help me out if you could write a few words in my folder here. It'll really only take a minute or so.'

'Could you not do this during the day?'

'I'm trying to get my results as soon as possible. That means putting in the extra hours. I've been at it most of the day and I'm keen to get a few more samples. Would you mind?'

I got up from the keyboard and went to stand at the door.

'Hiya, Craig.'

I could tell by the look on his face that he wasn't expecting to see me.

'Hello, Mary,' he said. 'Fancy meeting you again.'

'Craig was up the Lump at the same time as me.'

'Well,' Iain said. 'Any friend of Mary's is a friend of mine, I suppose. In you come.'

Craig wiped his feet and came with us into the kitchen.

He shook hands with Granpa and we all sat around the table.

'Ye fancy a drink, Craig?' Granpa said.

'I better not. Thanks, though. Like I said, I just need you gents to write a few words for my handwriting dissertation. Both of you, if you don't mind?'

'Aye, go on then. Although, no to be rude, what's the point of it?'

'A lot of people have asked me that. I'm going to be comparing the examples I collect against a control sample. It's all quite boring unless you're in my field, to be honest.'

Craig gave Granpa and Iain a piece of paper and a pen each.

'D'ye no want Mary to have a go as well?' Granpa said.

'Grown-ups only. Sorry,' said Craig. 'Okay, the first word I want you to write is *Scotland*.'

They both wrote down Scotland. Iain's 'S' was huge, like a big twisty snake. I picked up one of Iain's pens from the counter and wrote down Scotland on a bit of paper too. Craig said it was to be grown-ups only, but maybe my writing would be so good he'd use it in his project anyway.

'The next word is *Wallace*.'

The rest of the words he made us write out were: *Edinburgh, Aberdeen, Glasgow, Skye, Portree*.

'And lastly,' Craig said. 'If you write the numbers one to ten for me, the figures, not the words.'

When we were done, Craig flicked to a certain page in his clipboard. He kept looking back and forth between what Granpa and Iain had written and what was on the clipboard. He didn't look at mine. I tried but I couldn't see what was so special about the page in the clipboard. Granpa, Iain and me were just looking at each other. I wondered if they had done a good job, or if their writing was rubbish, like a P1's first jotter.

Craig did a sigh like he was disappointed.

'Thank you,' he said. 'You've been very helpful. But I've several more houses to get to tonight, I'm afraid.'

'Do ye no need our details?'

'No, I've got all I needed. Thank you, gents.'

'Did you find your friend yet, Craig?' I said.

'What's that?' he said. 'Oh, right. Not yet, Mary. Soon, though, I hope.'

Craig gave me a wave as he was going out the door.

My fingers were too tired from the heavy keys to play anymore that night. I sat with Granpa and Iain till I felt tired. They were talking about Craig.

'Bizarre,' Iain said. 'They've clearly run out of topics for dissertations at universities these days. Handwriting? What was that all about?'

'Who kens?' Granpa said. 'I doubt mine will be much use to him, anyway. My shoulder was hurting so much I had to use my left hand. What I scrawled looked nothing like my handwriting.'

♩

CHAPTER NINE

Grace came to Iain's house the next morning. I had been hoping she would.

'Hiya, Mary. Are you coming out?'

'Aye! But I'll need to check with my granpa first.'

Granpa said it was fine, as long as I stayed with Grace. I reminded him that she was ten.

'And ye've got that phone on ye?' Granpa asked.

I nodded. Iain had given me an old mobile phone of his. It was quite heavy and didn't even have a camera, but it had some money on it so I could text and phone. Granpa still wasn't completely happy with me going out without him. Iain had convinced him Portree was safe. It was so safe lots of people didn't lock their doors. Like in *the good, old days*.

'Phone me if ye need picked up or anything. And back no later than one for yer lunch.'

He stood at the front door and watched us as we went down the hill.

'Mary,' he shouted, 'Should I look into getting us on one of those boat tours?'

'Definitely,' I called back. 'Tomorrow?'

'Tomorrow it is.'

Grace took us to the Lump again. She crossed roads without

even checking both ways. I wanted to tell her that wasn't safe, but that would've made me seem a right geek. But then you saw people with things like *geek* and *nerd* on their T-shirts and they were wearing them on purpose. Maybe it was cool to be a geek. Only if you called yourself it, though. It wasn't nice to hear it from other people.

Grace took me past the tower and on a dirt path. It went round the top of the Lump and came out at this great big open space. It was a circle of grass with a little wall around it. Like a grass bowl.

'What's this for?' I said.

'This is where they have the Highland Games,' Grace said. 'It's amazing the things they throw. Logs the size of tree trunks. I couldn't do that.'

'Me neither. I couldnae even lift it a tiny bit probably.'

'Have you seen them then?'

'Aye, but only on the telly.'

'You should come when the Games are on. It's August, I think. My dad says you can get five thousand people here sometimes.'

I couldn't imagine that. Five thousand people around that grassy circle. No one else was around that day, only me and Grace with loads of room to spin around without even touching your fingers on anything. Like when I got to the gym hall before anyone else and could jump around and hear my plimsolls squeaking and echoing.

'Let's play Performance,' Grace said.

Performance was a new game to me and Grace had to explain the rules. There was this big flat slab on one part of the hill. It was sort of like a platform or a stage. Grace told me that the game was that you'd do a performance and then the other person would say what score you got out of ten, like on *Strictly Come Dancing*. If you sang a song and you did it really well you might get an eight or nine or if you were brilliant, maybe even a ten. Grace said she never gave out scores lower than a five because it caused arguments.

I did an Elvis song - *Burning Love*. But Grace had never heard of it.

'How d'you not know it? It's one of the best songs ever,' I said.

'I've heard of Elvis, but not *that* song.'

'Well, you need to listen to them all. He was the King. That was his name. The King. People called him it because he was so good.'

'Did he have a Queen?'

'I don't think so. I suppose if he had a wife then she would be the Queen. I'm not sure if he had a wife or not.'

'Queens are always old, though, aren't they? I'd rather be a Princess; like Kate.'

Grace wanted to be a Princess, but I still wanted to be a Queen. We played at that. Me being Queen and telling her what to do, and her being the Princess and doing things I wanted. Then Tom came and the game changed completely.

'Go away, Thomas,' Grace said.

'Mum said I was *allowed* to play too,' Tom said. 'She said you're not *allowed* to say I can't.'

'Why don't you go and play with Lewis? He came round this morning looking for you.'

Lewis. The boy with Nippy, the slow greyhound.

'I don't like him anymore,' Tom said. 'He told Mum I was listening to CDs with *Parental Advisory* stickers and she went into my room and took them all away.'

'Tom,' I said. 'Does your friend Lewis have a dog? A greyhound?'

'Aye, but his dad never lets anyone near it. How did you know?'

'I met him yesterday. I don't like him either.'

'Correct decision.'

'Do you want to play Royal Family with us?' I asked.

Grace rolled her eyes and did a big sigh, which wasn't really Princess behaviour.

'Can I be the King?' Tom asked.

'You always have to be the one in charge,' Grace said. 'I'm not being bossed around by you, Thomas.'

'Dinnae worry,' I said. 'I'm still Queen and I'm above the King.'

'But the King's always the boss,' said Tom. 'The Queen isn't above the King.'

'Well, in our game I'm the Queen and I'm the leader no matter what.'

Tom decided he was going to be Iron Man instead. So, we played Royal Family with the Queen, the Princess and Iron Man. It was hard for it to make sense when Iron Man kept flying around everywhere. I wasn't interested in trying to save this Pepper lady Iron Man was so obsessed with.

When we got out of breath, we lay down in the middle of the Bowl. If you were in a plane and looking down at us from the sky, we would've just been three wee ants in the middle of the big circle of grass.

'Mary,' Tom said. 'See that tree over there?'

He was pointing at a big tall straight one, with no leaves or even any branches on top. It looked more like a big stick planted in the ground.

'That's a funny looking tree,' I said.

'There's a man buried under there.'

'Don't listen to him,' Grace said. 'He's making up stories again.'

'How much d'you want to bet?' he said. 'Dad told me, and Mum was there and she nodded, so you know it must be true.

'What man?' I said.

'A hanged man,' Tom said. 'They used to hang people in Portree. In the square. And the last man they hanged, they put him up here on the Lump and planted a tree on top of his grave.'

'Why would they put him up here?' Grace said. 'What's the point?'

'Maybe there was nowhere else to put him,' he said.

'Was he a bad man?' I said.

'A murderer.'

'They dinnae kill people like that anymore, do they? I asked.

'No, they're not allowed,' Grace said. 'Because you can never know for absolute sure that someone's guilty. Killing them isn't fair. Someone else could confess the next day and then you'd have killed the wrong person.'

'Sometimes it could be fair,' I said. 'Like if something happened to you. If people did really bad crimes and you saw them happening and you knew for sure it was them that did it. And you could point them out in the court and say, "*That's them judge*". Maybe it would be better for everyone if they were gone and couldnae hurt anyone anymore.'

'What if they've got a family?' Grace said.

'I bet they dinnae. I bet they've been baddies all their life.'

'But they might.'

Tom got up and was trying to catch a butterfly. He was

swiping at it and had no chance.

'Are we still talking about killing people?' he said. 'I would do it. Cut their heads right off.'

'You'd be too scared,' said Grace.

He jumped over and karate chopped Grace on the neck and he made a noise like *waataah*. Grace jumped up and was kicking at his shins. Shins were the best place to kick because they hurt the most.

'You did that way too hard, Thomas,' said Grace. 'You always ruin everything, you prick.'

I hadn't heard Grace swear till then. I hadn't known she would be good at it. She knew the right swear word to use, right off the top of her head.

'I'm telling Mum you swore,' Tom said, then he ran off, down the hill, till we couldn't see him anymore.

'Do you really think he's a... prick?' I said.

I never usually swore, but I wanted Grace to think that swearing wasn't a big deal to me. She might think that I did it all the time, non-stop, in Stirling. Swearing was mostly for cool people like rappers and singers in rock bands.

'Most of the time,' she said. 'Mum calls him worse sometimes.'

'Like what?'

'Em... git.'

'I think prick's worse than git.'

'What about *little* git. She normally says little git.'

'I still think the 'p'-word is worse. I mean prick.'

'But it's the way she says it. And you need to be able to see her face too. It's like her eyebrows are being pulled up by coat hanger hooks.'

Grace walked me all the way back to Iain's without me even asking her to.

'What's in the garage?' she said.

The garage had a big red door. It was always closed. I decided to play a joke on Grace, like how Granpa would do to me.

'It's a plane in there,' I said. 'Iain can fly planes and he has his own one.'

I was smiling because it was such a good joke. I couldn't help wanting to laugh.

'You couldn't get a plane in there, Mary,' Grace said. 'They're having you on. I'll come for you another day.'

She ran down the road and I waited until I couldn't hear her shoes slapping against the pavement. My joke hadn't worked. I thought it was a good one, but Grace was older and maybe it was easier for her to tell the difference between jokes and the truth. And maybe it was harder than it looked. Granpa must've been joking for years and years —that's why he was so good at it.

♪

CHAPTER TEN

I was excited all through the night about going on the boat ride. It was the same feeling as before we left for the holiday or Christmas Eve or the night before the Grand National. Granpa had all the information we needed from a sign in the village. We were going at two o'clock. Iain didn't want to come because he thought he'd get soaked and that it *wasn't for him*. He'd been on a boat before, but I hadn't. I wanted to do lots of things I hadn't done before on holiday and then I could tell everyone in class when we went back home. They would be really interested and listen to me. Maybe even Leona would too.

We got all wrapped up in our waterproof jackets and put our wellies on. It was sunny outside but Granpa said the water from below the boat would be sloshing right over the edges.

Me and Granpa went down to the harbour street with the coloured houses. It was called Quay Street. I looked at the pink house again. It was hard not to stare at it because it was so perfect. I thought maybe I should live in another house across the harbour, then that way I could see the pink house all the time out of the window. Because if I lived in the pink house, I wouldn't have a view of the pink house. It was a hard decision.

We got to the chip shop at ten to two. That was where you waited for the boat tour. There were other people there like us, in their waterproof jackets. They must've known one of Granpa's favourite sayings too: *better to be safe than sorry*.

'It's gaye dreich,' one old lady said.

'Ye're right there,' Granpa said.

Granpa understood what she meant but I didn't. She wasn't saying *gay* like *gay people*, or *gay* like happy. There was a third way of using it just for Scottish people.

The poster said, *Stardust Sea Eagles Boat Tour*. The most important thing was the sea eagles. Eagles that lived in the sea. Or maybe they lived near the sea. I was sure that birds couldn't breathe underwater. I hoped an eagle would land on the side of the boat and I could pet it on the head.

There was a man walking up the street, coming from where all the boats were tied up. He was tall and had a short beard. *Stubble,* that was the word. He was wearing black waterproofs, from head to toe. Most waterproof clothes made you look puffy and ugly, but I could tell this man wore waterproofs more than he wore normal clothes. He looked *right* in them. He made them look cool.

'Sea eagles tour, yeah?' he said to all of us.

His accent was Australian, the same as the people on *Neighbours*. Granpa told me *Neighbours* used to be on the BBC and didn't have any adverts but I wasn't sure if he was kidding on.

'All right guys, I'm the skipper. If you wanna make your way down to the bottom there. My boat's the one with *Stardust* written on it. I'll be out in five.'

He went into the chip shop and we all walked down slowly. There were nine of us. Me, Granpa, three women who all had on sunglasses, and two old couples. The old couples didn't know each other.

There was a little slope, the same as the one at the other end of the harbour. We went down it, but not all the way. There wasn't a beach, just water. The *Stardust* boat was there waiting for us. It was blue all-round the bottom and white on top. It was bobbing left and right and sometimes it bumped up against the slope and made a thunking sound. I was worried it might get damaged with all the bumping and get a hole. It could *spring a leak* and we'd all have to swim back to the harbour. I had my bronze certificate in swimming but that was only for swimming in pools like the one at The Peak. Real water with fish and waves was different.

The old couples were chatting about the places they had visited and it was like a competition to see who had been the most places.

'We came fae Fort William.'

'We've been there. We were at Islay.'

'It's braw there, we've been. Before that it was Ullapool.'

'We practically live there!'

The skipper man came back and he had a little bag and was eating a Mars bar.

'A hungry skipper is an angry skipper,' he said.

We were all laughing. He rushed his lunch down him because he had been out on a boat all morning and had to work during lunchtime too. Maybe he had fish and chips every day. I wondered if you could get sick of having a chippy tea every day. Probably not.

He jumped over on to the boat and was sorting things. Then he came back and helped everyone get on board. We were to hold his hand and put our foot on the edge and he'd pull us over. When I got to the front of the line he said, 'Aha! My First Mate has arrived. Allow me, darl.'

And he lifted me up like it was easy peasy and plonked me down inside the boat. Granpa was smiling.

'She'll be asking me to do that noo,' Granpa said, while he was stepping on.

We sat down on the little benches which went around the inside of the boat. The cushions were all wet. I didn't want to get a wet bum but no one else seemed to care. I sat down and tried to ignore the wet feeling underneath me.

'Welcome on board, folks,' the man said. 'We've got decent weather for it today so let's give it a bash. My name is Andy, and I'll be your skipper this afternoon. Where are we all from then?'

Everyone went round the boat saying where they were from. When it got to us I was ready to say Stirling, but I didn't get the chance.

'Livingston,' Granpa said.

And then it was on to the next person.

'Why'd you say Livingston?' I whispered to him.

'We're spies, remember?' he said. 'We've got to have a good cover story.'

I hadn't realised we were still doing the spy game. And I had already told Grace I was from Stirling.

Andy held up something bright orange.

'Take a good look at this life float,' he said. 'It's the only one on board, so you'll all need to fight for it in the event of an emergency.'

I wasn't worried too much about the life float. *Women and children first*, that was boat rule number one, and I was both.

'If something happens to me, I get injured or feel like

a swim and jump overboard, there's a white phone above my steering wheel there. On it is a big red button. Press it and the rescue team can get our location and come find us. Hopefully.'

Safety wasn't a joke, but Andy was making it fun to listen to. Andy gave us all the important information but we were having a good time too. We had paid eighteen pounds each, which was a lot. He was making sure we got our *money's worth.*

We set off and I got a bit of a fright because the engine was really loud it was hard to hear anything else. *Brrrrrrrrrr.* Non-stop. I was at the back of the boat and I could look over and see all the water getting churned up, like the bubbles in a fancy bath. Me, Granpa and the other passengers sat in the open air and Andy stood in the cabin at the front, steering the boat. I thought it would be good to be in the cabin, out of the wind, but I didn't want to miss seeing anything.

One thing I noticed, was that the men liked to stand up. Even when the boat was all wobbly and it was really hard to stand up, they still did it. Granpa and the two other old men, standing all the time. One of the men almost fell over, but he didn't take a seat, he kept on standing and smiling, pretending that he hadn't nearly fallen over.

Maybe the men were showing off that they could stand up best while the boat was going and it was a competition. Andy stood up too, but he was allowed and he was really good at it. He knew which way the boat was going to tip because he'd move his foot a little and he'd be straight again. The men all stood with their legs apart to help them, but Andy's were the furthest apart. He definitely won that part of the game.

'Granpa, sit down,' I said.

'Och wheesht, I can see better this way.'

The three women with the sunglasses were from Italy. They had said so when Andy asked them. Unless they were spies too. But their voices sounded foreign and surely they couldn't fake that. They all had on scarves that nearly covered their faces and they didn't look at anything through the binoculars. All they did was huddle in to each other and look cold.

Andy took us to the side of a cliff. It was giant. Lots of trees and things were growing out at strange angles and I wondered how anything could live up there. There were meant to be some eagles living up there, but they weren't coming out, which was a shame. Andy turned the engine back on and we kept going forward.

Sometimes, the water would really whack the boat and we'd all get chucked about. The water would come into the boat and splash on my face and I could taste salt water in my mouth. It was absolutely horrible. I spat it out into the water. Granpa said you were allowed to spit into the sea. It didn't count as proper spitting.

'It's been forty years since the first pair of white-tailed eagles were introduced to the U.K.,' said Andy. 'You know how many pairs there are now?'

There was a long gap because no one seemed to know. I looked at Granpa but he shrugged.

'Three?' an old lady said.

'More than three,' Andy said.

'Ten?' her husband guessed.

'It's one hundred, guys. Which is still not a lot in forty years.'

I think Andy was a little annoyed. I bet he wanted us to guess high, so he could shock us, but the old couple ruined it.

Finally, we found sea eagles on this little island next to the main part of the land. A male and a female. They sat there, watching us, watching them.

'Let's see if we can get them to come to us,' Andy said.

He took out a slimy fish and injected it with a big needle thing.

'What we do is, pump the fish with steroids,' he said. 'Then when the eagles eat 'em, they get massive and we can spot 'em easier. Good for tourism.'

That made sense, but Granpa was smiling.

'Is that a joke, Granpa?'

'I'm honestly no sure,' he said.

'It makes sense,' I said. 'That they'd want the eagles to be really big so we can see them.'

'But what if they got so big they could snatch unsuspecting wee girls fae boat tours?'

'Naw, dinnae be daft, they'd snatch grown-ups. There's more to eat on a grown-up.'

'That's a lovely thought.'

'It's true.'

Andy threw the fish over the side of the boat and it plopped under the water. One of the eagles was coming towards us. Not very fast though, just taking its time because it must've known the fish was especially for it.

'This is the female, by the way, folks,' Andy said. 'She doesn't mind coming close to the boat. The male is very shy, y'see.'

But then a cheeky seagull swooped down and grabbed the fish and was off with it.

'Now watch the male chase it,' Andy said.

He was right. The boy eagle that had been relaxing went chasing after the seagull because it had stolen the fish that was meant for his wife. But they got too far away and turned into dots. If they had a fight over the fish, I missed it.

'Let's try another,' said Andy.

He did the same, putting the needle into the fish and throwing it over the side. The girl eagle got it that time. She flew right down and was away with it in two seconds flat. The old couples tried to take pictures, but they were all disappointed because it had been too fast for them. I couldn't take any pictures because my phone didn't have a camera.

Eagles were the opposite of people really, with the boys being shy and the girls being loud and running about. In class at school, it was always the boys being noisy and making trouble. But the girl eagle wasn't a nuisance like boys were. She was confident and came to get fish because she had to eat. The boy couldn't be bothered and it was left up to the girl.

I thought maybe I could be like the girl eagle when I grew up. I could impress people with my looks, but that wasn't the most important thing. I could also be confident and better than the boys. I didn't want a boyfriend though; it would just be me and I could have the fish all to myself.

After that, Andy took us round the back of the little island, hoping we would see a few more eagles.

'Keep an eye out for seals, too,' he said.

'There!' Granpa shouted.

I looked but I was too late. Then I saw my own seal, only its head poking out of the water before it went back down again. They were even faster than the eagles and you were lucky to spot one. It was like the game where you had to bash the moles back down. They came out at random. I thought maybe they were coming up for air, but Andy said they could hold their breaths for ages. They were nosey, up to see what the noises were and if anything exciting was happening above the water. But we must've not been very exciting to the seals because they didn't stay long.

The dolphins didn't turn up that day which was quite annoying. I had heard they were the friendliest animals ever, apart from maybe dogs. If I was a dolphin, I'd have definitely come to see the boat and let people pet my wet head.

'Andy?' I said.

'Yes, beautiful?' he replied, with a smile.

'You know dolphins… are the female ones better? Like how the female eagle is better?'

'I didn't say the female was better, did I? I think the male is dominant in dolphins. Sorry to disappoint you.'

But Andy couldn't disappoint me. He was too nice and smiley.

'Back to the harbour now, folks. Hold on.'

It was much colder on the way back for some reason. And there was a lot more water jumping into the boat and spraying my face. I put my head between my knees and that way I couldn't get wet.

I heard one of the old ladies shouting at her husband.

'Sit down, Brian.'

And then she screamed. I looked up and the old man wasn't on the boat anymore and everyone was looking over the side and yelling. The boat stopped. Andy pushed to the front of everyone and he had a rubber ring and threw it over. I wanted to go and look, but Granpa had his arms right round me and his hands locked in that special way at my front so I couldn't move a muscle.

'No need to worry,' Granpa said. 'The skipper kens what to do.'

And he did. Of course he did. Andy had the old man back on the boat a few seconds later. He pulled him right up over the side. The man had the ring around his waist and looked like a weird ballerina. He was the most soaked I had ever seen someone. And he'd lost his specs. There was a lot of shouting and the man's wife still looked scared, even though he was back on the boat.

Andy was taking off the man's clothes. I looked at Granpa.

'He'll catch hypothermia if he stays in the wet clothes,' Granpa explained. 'It's best to get them off quick.'

That was smart. Everyone was putting clothes and towels round the old man's shoulders. Then Andy had this big shiny jacket out of nowhere. Like the hugest bit of tin foil in the world. He wrapped it round the old man like a soggy sandwich you'd put in the fridge to dry out.

'Really hold on tight this time, folks,' Andy said, and he went into the room at the front.

The boat was going even faster than it had before. It was as if Andy had pressed the special *turbo* button for emergencies. Granpa still had a hold of me; I wasn't going anywhere.

Everyone had calmed down a bit by the time we got to the harbour. The man was smiling so he was feeling fine and not that cold. Andy got really serious after the man fell in, shouting and not smiling and making sure everyone got out the way so he could help. But he had cheered up too, back to his normal way, happy and winking at people. It was good he could be serious too because he could save lives that way. If he had kept joking around when the man had fallen in, that would've just been no good and the man might've died. Andy was fantastic at his job. He was our *skipper*.

Andy had his arm around the tin foil man.

'You're my first to go overboard, you know that?' said Andy.

'S-sorry to tarnish your record,' the old man said.

'Just bloody sit down in future, all right?'

The man smiled and nodded. It was always best to listen to Andy.

There was an ambulance waiting for the man at the harbour. It was a two-minute walk to the hospital, but they were being extra careful. The man got in the back of the ambulance, and his wife did too, but first she gave Andy a big hug and kissed his cheek. Andy smiled and I heard him say, 'Stop being silly.'

We were all watching, apart from the Italian ladies, they had disappeared after we got back. I didn't think they had enjoyed the trip very much.

When the ambulance was away, Granpa shook Andy's hand.

'That trip had a wee bit of everything,' said Granpa.

'You can say that again, mate,' Andy said. 'I think I'll need to postpone the four o'clock trip and go for a pint—or ten.'

Imagine that. Not being able to decide whether to have just the one pint of beer or ten of them. I went up and hugged Andy and he had to crouch down to hug me back. His jacket was wet and scratchy on my face, but I liked it.

'That was amazing, thank you,' I said.

'You're very welcome, darl. What was your name again?'

'Mary.'

'Thanks, Mary. I'm glad my First Mate was there to watch over the boat while I dealt with the man overboard. I don't know what I'd have done without you.'

He rubbed my head and I felt his freezing hands on the skin under my hair. I had forgotten all about being the First

Mate. Andy thought I was looking after the boat while he was saving the man. But I wasn't, because I'd forgotten all about it. I didn't tell Andy. I liked him thinking I could do that, even though I hadn't a clue what he thought I'd done. I couldn't wait to tell Grace that I was First Mate, and that the skipper thanked me, and that a man fell in the water. It was the kind of story that would get a *perfect ten* at Performance.

♪♪

CHAPTER ELEVEN

'Why did he make you First Mate, and not an adult?' asked Grace.

'He just did,' I shrugged.

Grace and me were at the Lump again the day after the boat trip. She had taken me to a different bit altogether. Instead of going left to the tower, or straight forward to the Bowl, we went down the path on the right-hand side of the hill. Grace led me down these wooden steps which went right down on to the stony beach. We were on the other side of the hill and you couldn't see the harbour at all. The view was of the other side of the island with more houses and a petrol station. We must've passed the petrol station on the way into Portree, but I had been asleep for that bit of the journey. It made sense; where else were all the cars getting their petrol from?

There was a shed and it was locked. Around it was a load of things. Ropes and big logs and old bits of boats and nets. You could pick through the piles and find mostly rubbish but maybe treasure too. I thought it would be a laugh to put a big net around yourself and pretend you were a fish that got caught by a fisherman.

'Is the man who fell in the water alive?' Grace said.

'I only saw him going in the ambulance. He must be.

He was smiling.'

'Do you know his name?'

'Brian, I think.'

'We can go to the hospital and say, "*We're here to see Brian*", and they'll let us see him and we can make sure he's still alive.'

'Stop being daft.'

'I'm not being daft. The hospital's right there.' Grace pointed to where all the cars were parked. 'It's important that you check on him. Imagine what your granpa'll say if he hears you don't care if Brian is dead or alive.'

'Do you know Brian?'

'No, but he sounds like a nice man. I don't want him to die. Do you, Mary?'

'Of course not. Do you think Granpa expects me to go and check on him?'

'Maybe.'

'But what if we get caught?'

'We're not doing anything wrong, Mary. You can only get caught if you're doing something wrong.'

'Aye, but what if the doctors at the hospital say, "*You shouldn't be in here. Guards! Come and take these girls away. They're only wee girls.*" What then?'

'You're being a scaredy cat, Mary. They don't have guards. It's not like on the telly.'

'But what if it is?'

Grace wasn't listening anymore. She grabbed my hand and was pulling me so my arm stretched and it was sore. But I let her drag me and I decided that I'd blame her if anything went wrong because she was older. She was ten. She was supposed to know what she was doing.

She took me back up the stairs and down the gravelly

path. The path came out right at the hospital, so it had only been two minutes from Grace saying we should go, to us actually being there. I barely had time to think about it.

'Have you done this before?' I said.

'No, I told you, I've never met Brian.'

'I meant visiting someone in hospital.'

'My mum gave blood once and I went in with her. It'll be fine. Stop being such a chicken, Mary.'

I hated being called a chicken. It was what bullies said to make you do stupid things. It was even worse when someone went *buck buck buck* and did the chicken walk in front of you. Grace wasn't a bully, and she didn't do the bucking or the walk, so I forgave her.

'I was already going to go in,' I said. 'Before you called me a chicken. You calling me a chicken didnae change my mind.'

Grace ignored me and walked right in, not worried at all, right up to the reception.

'Oh hello, Grace,' said the lady at the desk.

I wasn't surprised that she knew who Grace was - people in Portree were mostly all friends and knew everyone else.

'Hiya, Kelly,' Grace said. 'We're here to visit someone.'

'Really? Who?'

'Brian.'

'Brian who?'

'Brian... who fell in the sea yesterday.'

'That's a funny last name, *Whofellintheseayesterday*. I don't think we have a Brian *Whofellintheseayesterday*.'

That was exactly the same joke that Granpa made after he'd seen me with Lewis. Grown-ups all had the same rubbish jokes. They needed to come up with some new ones.

'You know what I mean,' said Grace, and did an annoyed sigh.

'I'm sorry, Grace,' the lady said. 'I can't let you and your friend in by yourselves. You can come back with your mum if you want? How is she, anyway?'

'She's okay. Right, we'll come back later then, bye.'

We walked away and back to the bottom of the gravelly path.

'That was still good that you tried,' I said. 'It was quite exciting, eh?'

'We'll get in, Mary, don't worry. We just need to wait for her to be on the phone or something and then we can sneak past the desk. She won't be able to see over it.'

'But she said we're not allowed.'

'She has to tell us that, in case her boss is about, Mary. She doesn't care if we go in or not. And she's my mum's friend.'

'Oh. Great.'

If I didn't argue, Grace would think I was a good laugh and cool. And she would maybe forget I was two years younger.

We slowly walked back down to the entrance and stood leaning out of sight.

'Listen,' Grace said. 'That's her on the phone.'

Grace dropped down to her knees and started crawling. It was automatic doors so they opened, but the Desk Lady Kelly didn't notice because she had turned the other way on her swivel chair. We had swivel chairs in school, but only for the teachers. You couldn't trust the boys with swivel chairs.

I followed Grace. We were on our hands and knees like army men. But women instead of men. And hard flooring instead of soft mud.

We were inside the hospital and it was as easy as Grace said it would be. The hospital was only a small one and there weren't any people about in the corridors to catch us. In *Casualty*, people were running about the hospital non-stop. We wouldn't have been able to sneak into the *Casualty* hospital, no way.

Grace seemed to know where she was going and once we got down the corridor a bit, we could stand up again.

'Right,' said Grace. 'That sign says *Short Term Care*, he'll be there, probably.'

We followed the sign through a pair of white swinging doors. It was sort of like a living room. Big comfy chairs and a telly and newspapers on a table and a little kitchen. We went through another set of doors and it was a normal hospital corridor again. I could hear a voice I recognised from one of the rooms. It was quite loud.

'Still can't believe it. My first to go in the water. But I don't care about that, as long as you're feeling all right, mate.'

It was an Australian accent.

'That's Andy's voice,' I said.

'The boat man?' Grace said.

'He must be visiting Brian,' I answered. 'Let's go and see.'

We went and stood in the doorway. Brian was in the bed in his pyjamas. His wife was sitting on a chair with a magazine on her lap. Andy was standing, wearing his waterproofs. I thought he must've worn them every day, non-stop.

Brian was the only one in bed, the other five beds in the room were all empty. They were all still busy talking. I knocked on the door and they all looked round.

'Yes?' said Brian's wife.

'That's the wee lass from yesterday,' said Brian.

'Mary?' said Andy.

My insides went all warm when Andy said my name. I was too scared to go in, but Grace walked in and I had no choice but to follow her.

'I'm Grace,' she said. 'We've come to make sure you're all right after your accident yesterday.'

'How nice,' said Brian's wife. 'I'm Miriam, it's nice to meet you Grace. And to see you again. Mary, was it?'

'Hiya,' I said. 'Are you feeling better, Brian?'

'I am indeed,' Brian said. 'I'm getting out tomorrow morning. Are you here on your own, girls?'

'Grace is ten,' I said. 'She's old enough to look after us.'

'I can see that,' Miriam said. 'And your parents know where you are?'

'Aye,' Grace said. 'They thought it was a good idea.'

'My parents don't know,' I said. 'But that's fine because they're dead.'

It went quiet after that.

'Well, it's very nice of you to visit,' Miriam said. 'Would you like a biscuit, girls?'

Me and Grace took a biscuit. Andy was eating a Bourbon. I had one too. I normally would've taken off the top biscuit and licked all the brown cream out, but instead I ate it like a grown-up. If Andy looked, he would know he was right to choose me as his First Mate.

'I guess this serves me right,' said Andy. 'For boasting about how I've never had a man overboard.'

'If anyone asks,' said Brian. 'I jumped in.'

They were laughing. I was sad for Andy. He couldn't tell people how safe it was on the boat anymore because Brian had fallen in the water. People in Portree would tell each other and there was no way of keeping it a secret. Maybe no one would want to go on his boat and he'd have to get another job. It was a one in a million chance, but I thought that, once I had the pink house, Andy could help me serve the juice and biscuits. And do all the heavy, manly things I couldn't. I would even let him use the juice gun if he asked nicely.

We didn't stay long. Grace grabbed my hand and squeezed it.

'We need to go now,' she said.

She started running, so I went off after her. I looked back and gave Andy a wave. He winked at me. It was a different sort of feeling from when Granpa winked at me and I blushed.

Grace had forgotten the way we'd come through the hospital and took us into a different room by accident. It was just a little room with only one bed. The man in the bed turned to us. He was in his jammies too. His face was all bruised and it hurt to look at him for too long.

'Sorry,' Grace said. 'We didn't mean to come in.'

'That's all right, girls,' the man said. 'I can't get to sleep anyway.'

He had an Irish accent. It wasn't as nice as Pierce Brosnan's, but what was?

'Are you okay?' I said.

'It looks worse than it is,' he said.

'What happened?'

'You can't ask that, Mary,' Grace said.

'No, it's all right,' he said, 'Although I don't want to scare you.'

'We won't be scared, will we, Mary?'

'Definitely not.'

'Well,' he said, 'A man came into my house last night.

And he claimed I had stolen some money of his. He didn't like it when I told him I didn't have it. He accused me of writing some note he had. The police think he might've had a screw loose.'

'Are the police going to catch him?' Grace asked.

'They'll try. But he didn't leave many clues, I'm afraid. And he was wearing a balaclava so I couldn't get a good look at him.'

'I hope they do.'

'Me too,' I said. 'People who wear balaclavas are just the worst people you can get. They should stop selling them.'

A nurse came up behind us.

'Are these friends of yours, Gerry?' she asked.

'Oh, hello, Heather,' Gerry said. 'These girls were just...'

Grace took off running past her. I was a few seconds behind but I caught up. I checked over my shoulder, but I could only see the nurse's blonde hair so she had her back to us. She didn't care about chasing us.

We went down the corridor and back through the living room type area. There was another nurse in there and she shouted at us but we were moving too fast to hear what she said. We burst through the door, down another corridor, right past the main desk and out the doors. Freedom!

'Hey, girls!' the receptionist shouted after us.

I kept following Grace and didn't look back. We kept running all the way to the tower. Mission accomplished.

♫

CHAPTER TWELVE

We were both so out of breath that we couldn't talk for a minute. Panting and laughing and holding our sides because we had stitches.

'What if she comes up here?' I asked.

'She can't, Mary. She's working. You can't just walk out of your work.'

That made sense. Granpa never walked out of the bookies during his shift. Or if he did, it was to tell the Asian men, who were smoking outside, not to chuck their cigarettes on the floor after they'd smoked them. They were to put them in the bin because Granpa was sick of sweeping up *fag ends*.

'We could've stayed longer with Brian,' I said. 'They were letting us stay.'

'But it wasn't exciting once we found them. Why'd you want to hang around with old people?'

'Andy's not that old.'

'Do you fancy him?'

'I dinnae fancy anyone.'

I felt my cheeks get hot and red.

'You can still fancy him, even if he's older than you,' said Grace. 'That's okay. I don't like his beard, so I don't fancy him. I fancy Daniel Radcliffe. But I need to meet him so I can ask him out. He's got a nice smooth face.'

'I dinnae fancy Andy. I don't fancy anyone. Harry Potter has a beard sometimes.'

'Does not.'

'He does. Big black hairs on his chin and his cheeks.'

Grace wouldn't believe me, but I had seen it on telly. The Harry Potter man being in other films, where he wasn't Harry Potter. He grew a beard for those ones, so people would be able to tell that he wasn't Harry Potter anymore. Harry Potter wouldn't have suited a beard, that's why J.K. Rowling didn't give him one.

We were at the top of the tower. There weren't any seats up there, so you had to lean on the edges of the stone. I had to go on my tiptoes but Grace didn't.

'Can you see Andy's boat?' Grace asked.

It was hard to tell from up there. A lot of them looked the same.

'I cannae tell. It says *Stardust* on it.'

'You'll not be able to read anything from up here,' Grace said.

'Unless you had super-vision. Or a pair of binoculars. We should get a pair of binoculars and then we can have a look at the people on the boats. And if they fall in we can go and tell people.'

We could've gone and told Andy.

'That sounds too much like a job, Mary. Like what lifeguards do. I don't want a job!' Grace threw her hands up to the sky. 'I'm never getting a job.'

'Why not?' I asked. 'Jobs can be good things. Like being a spy, or being a plane pilot, or working in the bakers. Think of all the cakes.'

'Do you know how long you have to do a job for, Mary? All your life.'

'Not *all* your life. You dinnae work every single day.'

Grace closed her eyes and nodded her head.

'My dad's been a teacher for ages and he's still going to have to teach for about fifty more years. Maybe until he's dead.'

'Oh, he willnae die. Teaching's not dangerous, not like being in the army.'

'I didn't mean he'll die at work. I meant he might die of old age.'

'When does that happen?'

'Seventy, I think. My granny was seventy when she died.'

Granpa was sixty-six. That would mean he only had four years left.

'But loads of people are older than seventy,' I said. 'If you get to a hundred, the Queen sends you a birthday card. My Granpa says that's her main job, to write out those cards.'

'If you die after you're seventy,' Grace said. 'When they put your name in the paper, they'll put "*Mary died of old age*", instead of an accident or being murdered.'

'What if you're seventy-one and you get murdered by a robber?'

Grace made a scrunched-up face. I could tell she wasn't sure. She was thinking for quite a while.

'Then they'll just put,' Grace said. 'Mary, 71, died of old age after being shot by a robber.'

Grace could answer any question, like Granpa could. Maybe once you turned ten you got better at working out questions that were hard to answer. I wouldn't get shot by a robber, though. Robbers in Scotland didn't have guns.

'Anyway, Grace,' I said. 'You can ask your work to let you off for the summer if you want. That's what Granpa's doing. He gets all the time off he wants.'

'That doesn't sound right. My dad only gets the summer off because he's a teacher. And my mum only got time off because she had babies. Those are the only ways you can get loads of time off.'

The boats in the water didn't do anything exciting, but they were still good to watch. It was like a postcard come to life and you could dive right into it if you wanted. The noises were hard to explain because there wasn't really anything noisy happening, only little things like the water swishing and a man laughing every now and then. And the seagulls being screechy, but I tried to ignore them.

'I didn't know your parents were dead,' Grace said. 'Till you said in the hospital. Did they die a long time ago?'

'Aye. I dinnae remember them.'

'That's better then.'

'Aye. I suppose so.'

Granpa didn't say anything about the hospital when I got back to Iain's. I was *in the clear*. It was like I was going on my own missions without Granpa. He had taught me all about how to do missions and keep secrets, but I could keep secrets from him too. Grace and me were the new spy partnership and Granpa was old news. We were a girl only spy force, like *Charlie's Angels*. The film was on ITV once and Granpa complained it wasn't as good as the version in his day. But it had Cameron Diaz in it. She was more beautiful than anyone, and he didn't complain about that. Cameron was really a boy's name, but I let her off with it.

Me and Grace didn't have a Charlie telling us what to do because we could come up with our own missions. There were normally three angels but I liked that it was only the two of us. We didn't need anyone else.

Tea was sausage, chips and beans. It was one of my favourite teas.

'What were you and Grace up to the day?' Granpa asked from the kitchen.

'We were at the Lump,' I answered. 'We played Performance and Hide and Seek and Army Women.'

'Army Women?' Iain said. 'What does that entail?'

'Crawling around and shooting people. We'd see someone on the path, or even as far away as down in the harbour, and we'd pretend to shoot them.'

'Like a sniper? You don't get that many snipers in the army, Mary. They're more special ops. I've never heard of any women snipers.'

'Then me and Grace will be the first.'

'I look forward to that day.'

Iain didn't believe girls could be snipers, but girls could be anything they wanted. They could even be football players. It was on the news a lot about how the England Women's team were doing well and how they had beaten Canada 2-1. I hadn't known Canada even had a football team, but the England ladies had beaten them. The news never normally cared about women playing football, but the men weren't playing so the girls got a chance to be on telly. I didn't care about football and I never wanted to play it as a job, but I was glad other ladies could if they wanted.

Granpa sat our plates down in front of us and joined us at the table.

'Tuck in,' Granpa said, scraping his knife and fork together.

'I heard today,' Iain said. 'Gerry from a couple of streets over is in hospital. Apparently, a lad broke into his house the other night and did a right number on him.'

'Christ,' Granpa said. 'And here I was thinking Portree was free fae that sort of thing.'

'They think it was for money, but Gerry's not particularly well-off, as far as I know.'

'What if he tries to come into our house?' I asked.

'Me and your granpa are a match for anyone, Mary. We'd not let anything happen to you.'

There was a knock at the door. I got such a fright, I dropped my knife on my plate and bean juice went all over the handle

'Dinnae worry,' Granpa said. 'Criminals dinnae usually knock first.'

Iain answered the door. A wee breeze blew through the living room and went across my bare legs. I could make out some of the words the person at the door was saying. I heard my name.

'Right, you better come in then,' Iain said.

Granpa got up and went to the door too. I peeked over the top of the counter. It was Grace's mum. I recognised her from the pub when I first met Grace.

'This is Linda MacLeod,' Iain said. 'Grace's mother.'

'Mrs MacLeod,' Granpa said, sticking out his hand. 'It's nice to properly meet ye. Arthur Sutherland.'

'Yes,' she said, shaking it. 'Have you heard about what's gone on?'

'Ye'll have to enlighten me.'

'Mary and Grace broke into the hospital today.'

She put her hands on her hips. I felt like my tea was going to come back up.

'Broke into the hospital?' Granpa said. 'First I'm hearing of it.'

'Kelly, she's a friend of mine who works the desk, she

phoned and said Grace and another girl went in after they were specifically told not to. I assume it was Mary, they've hardly been apart these last few days.'

Granpa curled his finger at me, the sign for me to go over and stand with them. Something in the kitchen pinged and Iain went through to see what it was.

'Is this true, Mary?' Granpa said.

I nodded. I didn't want to talk because I could already feel my throat getting choked up like I might cry. Being in trouble was the worst feeling, ever. I had known we wouldn't get away with it. It was all Grace's fault.

'Grace isn't the kind of girl to do this by herself,' said Mrs MacLeod.

'Let's no rush to blame folk,' Granpa said. He turned to me with his serious face. 'Mary, why'd ye go into the hospital?'

I had to concentrate my hardest to make sure I didn't cry when I started speaking.

'To see Brian,' I said quickly.

I had my head down, staring at the floor. I liked Mrs MacLeod's strappy silver shoes, but I didn't tell her.

'Brian? Who's Brian?' Granpa said, then realised. 'Och, Brian! The one who went overboard. Ach well, there ye go, Mrs MacLeod. A perfectly good reason.'

Granpa thought that would cheer up Mrs MacLeod, but it didn't. She looked like she was *sookin a lemon.*

'They were checking on the welfare of an old man who'd had an accident,' Granpa said. 'I'd say our Mary here is a good influence, if anything.'

Mrs MacLeod's nostrils grew into two big, black holes.

'Are you drunk?' Mrs MacLeod said.

'He's not sober,' shouted Iain from the kitchen.

'I've had a couple of whiskies,' Granpa said. 'No that that's any of yer business.'

'And you were in a state on Friday at the pub,' Mrs MacLeod said.

'Listen, dear, dinnae paint me as some sort of alcoholic who cannae look after his granddaughter.'

'Well, maybe if you didn't let her run riot this wouldn't have happened.'

Granpa waved his hand like she was talking rubbish.

'They're only wee yins,' he said. 'They're supposed to get into mischief every now and then.'

'No wonder Mary's like this,' Mrs MacLeod said. 'Your hands-off method might've worked in the good old days, but it's a different world out there for children now.'

'Och, calm yersel.'

'I can only hope you'll be disciplining Mary for this incident.'

'Incident!' He shouted through to Iain in the kitchen, 'Iain, d'ye hear this? An incident! Ye sound like these bloody teachers.'

'You've clearly got a problem with authority, Mr Sutherland and you've passed it on to Mary.'

'And now you're a psychiatrist, too,' Granpa snorted. 'Ye ken what, it's been lovely meeting ye, Mrs MacLeod, but we're about to have our pudding.'

'Fine,' Mrs MacLeod said. 'But, rest assured, Grace won't be seeing her again.' And she took off out the door.

'Have a nice night,' Granpa called after her. 'And dinnae worry, I'll give Mary ten of the best as punishment. Like the good old days!'

Granpa slammed the door. Iain had been listening to everything and was laughing to himself in the kitchen.

'Charming woman,' he said.

'Mary,' Granpa said, crouching down and sighing. 'Ye cannae go into places like the hospital without telling me.'

'But you just said it was good-'

'I ken, hen, because it's my job to stick up for ye. But ye need to check these things with me first, awright?'

I nodded, but I was annoyed because he knew it was a good thing I'd done by going to see Brian. I didn't deserve a row.

'Am I not allowed to see Grace anymore?'

'I'm sure Grace's maw will calm down in a day or two.'

But I could only think of how fed up I'd be if she didn't. I would be back to not having any friends. If I couldn't see Grace, then I wouldn't be able to see Tom either. Not that I really wanted to see Tom, but I couldn't even if I wanted to. I would have to go to the pub with Granpa and Iain for the whole summer. And even if I learned the rules, I was too wee to hold a pool cue properly.

'How is Brian, then?' Granpa said.

'He's fine,' I said. 'He gets out tomorrow.'

'Ye hear that, Iain? Brian's getting out tomorrow.'

'Fantastic,' said Iain. 'We should celebrate. Would you look at that, the drinks are already poured.' Iain waved his hand over their glasses of whisky. 'Should we invite him over?'

'Who?' Granpa asked.

'Brian.'

'Who's Brian?'

They laughed. They didn't care that much about Brian, they only wanted a reason to have another drink. Grown-ups drank alcohol to celebrate things. You knew it was a good celebration if there was expensive alcohol like champagne. And someone popped it and maybe spilled some on the carpet and no one even cared.

Granpa didn't stay mad at me for long. Iain was making him laugh about Mrs MacLeod and how she had *put him in his place*. I was trying to work out a way to make sure I could see Grace again.

'What if I went and said sorry to Mrs MacLeod?'

'Ye'll do no such thing,' Granpa said.

'But I want to see Grace.'

'Ye'll see her, dinnae worry. Her maw's just angry the night, she'll be fine tomorrow. If worst comes to worst, I'll go round to her house when her dad's in. *"Broke into the hospital"*. She made it sound like *Mission* bloody *Impossible*.'

Granpa wasn't paying proper attention to me because he was playing cards with Iain at the kitchen table again. They played every night. They put BBC Radio 2 on and Iain had a cigar and opened the window to let the smoke float away.

They played all sorts of games. I didn't know any of them. It was either whisky or beer bottles or both beside them. But I never saw them stumbling around or falling down like drunk people did on telly. Maybe because they were always sitting down.

Granpa forgot to tell me to brush my teeth. I did it anyway. My tongue felt furry and there were bean skins stuck between my teeth. It felt quite grown up, doing it, even though no one was making me.

CHAPTER THIRTEEN

Grace came to the door the very next morning.

'Sorry about my mum,' she said.

She had on her nice yellow dress and I wished I had a dress like that. You were supposed to dress in bright colours in the summer, but I didn't have many bright clothes. I had my blue jeans, but they were too heavy and hot for running about in.

'She said I'm not allowed to see you,' I said.

'She's calmed down now. Dad says she was stressed with work.'

'I heard Granpa say it was probably her *time of the month*.'

'Do you know what that means, Mary?'

'Like, her birthday?'

'You should ask your Granpa.'

'Okay. My birthday's in September, just in case you wanted to know.'

It was funny how much things could change overnight. I had lost Grace as a friend then got her back straightaway. I hadn't had much sleep that night because my brain couldn't turn off. It kept saying to me, "*Mary, that's Grace not your friend anymore*". It made me feel hot and sweaty and I kicked the covers off, but really I could never get to sleep without the covers. My legs didn't feel safe out there on their own.

Granpa came to the door to see what we were talking about.

'Uh oh,' he said. 'Ye're no being a bad influence again, are ye, Mary?'

He was smiling though, so I knew he was having a laugh. Grace understood.

'Ha ha,' she said. 'It was my idea to go to the hospital, anyway.'

'So *you're* the bad influence?'

'No, Mr-'

'Mr Sutherland.'

'Mr Sutherland, we didn't do anything bad.'

'I ken, hen, I'm only kidding ye on.'

I didn't like Granpa calling other people *hen*. That was his name for me. But I couldn't tell him he was only to call me it. He'd have had a right laugh at me. I supposed if it was only me and Grace, that was okay. Grace was my friend and not a stranger.

'Are you coming out then, Mary?' Grace said.

I looked at Granpa.

'Oh, ye're actually asking me? I thought ye went wherever ye fancied. Got yer phone?'

I pulled it out of my pocket, so he could see I had it. It was a blue Nokia. It wasn't as big as a brick, but it was definitely as heavy as one.

'Good girl. Be back for lunchtime.'

When we were going down the hill towards the village, we heard Iain shouting out the window.

'Look out! It's the Portree young team.'

Young teams were like gangs, but for people who weren't old enough or tough enough to get into a real gang. The young team in Stirling was the *Young Braehead Jungle*.

Being in a young team seemed to be mostly about writing the initials on things around town. *YBJ* was written on goalposts and fences and all sorts of things in Stirling. Portree was too nice to have a young team.

There were boys up the tower so we couldn't go inside. The tour lady was walking around with some tourists again. I heard her telling the people that the Apothecary Tower was almost destroyed by the wind once. All the bricks had come out and it had to be rebuilt.

'Is that true, Grace? Did the tower almost blow down once?'

'I don't know,' Grace said. 'Probably, if Michelle said so.'

Maybe Granpa had been right about the hurricanes on Skye. Only a hurricane could blow down bricks. The Big Bad Wolf couldn't do it, that was for sure.

We stood near the bottom of the tower, waiting for the boys to go away. They leaned over the side when they saw us. There were two of them and one was Lewis, the boy with the greyhound.

'Piss off, you two,' the other one said.

The boy had thick black specs, like old scientists wore, and he was definitely in high school. He was holding a can of beer. I guessed it was beer because it was a tall can, not like a regular juice can.

'Can we come up after you?' Grace said.

'No chance,' said Specs.

He had a bowl-cut. Someone had put a bowl on his head and cut the hair that poked out from under it. It was the worst hair-cut a boy could have.

'We're going to wait,' Grace said.

'You'll be waiting a while, Grace,' said Lewis. 'Oh, I know

her as well. Her name's Mary. She was slagging off Dad, Jamie.'

'Was she now?' Specs said. 'Well, she's definitely not getting the tower after us. No one slags off the Kerr's. Anyway, I've only just started my first tin.'

His name was Jamie and he was Lewis's older brother. That was where Lewis had got his annoying-ness from.

'Yeah, fuck off,' Lewis said.

It was so obvious he was trying to show off in front of his big brother.

'Prick,' I said.

The boys both laughed. I didn't even look over at Grace to see if she thought it was cool of me to say *prick*. I only said it because I knew they wouldn't come and get me. Even if I didn't like Jamie, I knew he wouldn't hit a girl so much smaller than him.

We decided to go to the Bowl while we waited for them to leave.

'Beer makes you tired,' Grace said. 'They probably won't be long.'

'My Granpa and Iain drink whisky and stay up most of the night.'

'My Dad has two bottles of beer then falls asleep on the couch.'

'Have you tried it?'

'Once. It's minging. I wouldn't drink it even if I was as thirsty as anything.'

'Me too. Whisky's even worse. It's like nail polish.'

'W.K.D's nice,' Grace said. 'It's tastes like juice. My mum gave me some last Christmas. Men don't drink it though, so Iain won't have any in the house.'

'Maybe I can have some at your house.'

'You would need to come at Christmas or New Year. I'm only allowed it at Christmas and New Year.'

'What if I came round for tea.'

'My mum might not like that.'

'Ask your Dad?'

'That's a good idea.'

People in my class were always saying how their dads were really in charge and if their mum said no to something they could ask their dad and maybe get a different answer. I was hoping Grace's dad would tell her mum that I was a nice girl. He hadn't met me, but he could probably guess. Then Mrs MacLeod would realise it too. She would see how I had good manners at tea, then everyone would forget about the hospital thing. It wasn't even an *incident*.

The grass was warm beneath us and it felt like a boy's spiky hair when I ran my hand through it. We lay on the grass and stared at the clouds.

'See that one,' Grace said, pointing. 'It looks like a big bowl of Angel Delight.'

It looked like a big splodge to me.

'What flavour is it?' I asked.

'Butterscotch, definitely. What do you see, Mary?'

I was struggling to come up with an answer. The clouds were too wispy.

'Well,' I said. 'That one there, sort of, maybe, looks like a pistol with a silencer on it. Like Pierce Brosnan uses.'

Grace squinted her eyes and put her hand flat over her eyebrows to have a good look.

'I don't see it, Mary,' she said. 'But that's okay. Everyone sees different things.'

I was relieved I hadn't ruined the game.

The boys were shouting from the tower so we thought

maybe they were leaving. When we went through the trees, we heard another boy at the top with them. It was Tom. He screamed like he was in pain.

'Thomas?' Grace shouted.

The boys leaned over our side again. Jamie had Thomas in a headlock. He didn't even need to try because he was so much bigger and stronger.

'I thought I told you two to piss off,' Jamie said.

'That's my brother,' Grace said.

'Grace,' Tom shouted, but it was hard to hear him in the headlock, 'Go and get Dad.'

I thought that would scare Jamie and Lewis but it didn't. They were going "*ooooh*" like they weren't scared at all.

'No, Thomas, I'm not getting Dad.' She crossed her arms. 'Let him go, Jamie.'

'He came up here,' said Jamie, 'Waving about a lethal weapon. We could go to the police.'

'Aye,' Lewis said.

Lewis held up the *weapon*. It was a screwdriver.

'I was trying to give *them* a fright,' Tom said, pointing at us. 'I thought Grace and Mary were up here.'

Jamie let Thomas go a bit, out of the headlock, and was only holding on to the hood of his hoodie.

'So this was just a big mistake?' Jamie asked.

'Definitely a mistake,' Tom said, nodding his head really quickly.

'A big mistake?' Lewis added.

'A big mistake, yeah,' Tom said.

'A *huge* mistake?'

'Lewis,' Jamie said, letting go of Tom's hood. 'Go and shut up, eh?'

Tom came down the stairs faster than I'd seen anyone

do it before. Grace still had her arms crossed and looked angry. I knew she wasn't annoyed with me, just Tom, but I didn't want her to be angry at anyone. She was much less of a laugh.

'What are we doing now?' Tom said.

'We're not playing with *you* if that's what you think,' Grace said.

'I didn't want to play with you, anyway. You were meant to be up there.'

'Well, we weren't.'

Tom turned back around and shouted up.

'Give me my screwdriver back.'

Lewis was twirling it in his fingers. Paul Reed from my class could do that with a pencil. He was such a show-off.

'What's the magic word?' Jamie said.

'Please,' said Tom.

'Nah, it's *Thomas is a fucking gimp*.'

Thomas turned to look at Grace. Grace flicked her hair and looked the other way.

'Thomas is a fucking gimp,' Tom said.

'It's changed again,' Jamie laughed. 'Now it's *Grace is a slut.*'

Grace made a disgusted noise and glared up at the boys. Tom stared at his feet.

'Thomas is a fucking gimp?' Tom said again.

'No, no,' Jamie said, 'You need to say the new one.'

Tom kept staring at his feet as he shook his head.

'That's a shame,' Jamie said.

Lewis passed the screwdriver to Jamie, then Jamie threw it over the side of the tower with all his might, into the trees and down towards the harbour. It would've taken a million years to find it in there. Jamie and Lewis did a high-five and gave us all the fingers. Jamie did his middle fingers and Lewis gave us the V's. I didn't do them back because I didn't see the point. The boys stopped leaning over and we couldn't see them anymore. Tom ran off down the hill.

'Do you think he's crying?' I asked Grace.

'He better not be. It's only a screwdriver.'

'I suppose I'll not be able to write my name in the tower now.'

'We'll find you something else, Mary. Don't worry.'

When I got back to Iain's, there was a strange man knocking at the door. He was banging away, but getting no answer. I wasn't sure what to do. Grace had gone home and I didn't even have someone who was ten to make the right decision for me. Maybe Granpa and Iain didn't want to talk to him. He was really tall and had on a black T-shirt and jeans. His T-shirt said *Queen*. I liked *Queen*, but Elvis was better. That was the only time the King was better than the Queen. I wanted to get a T-shirt with Elvis on so everyone would know how much I liked him.

The man was wearing trainers too. He was sort of dressed like a young person. Like he'd lost all his grown-up clothes and was trying to be an undercover young person to find out some important information from the young team so he could *crack the case.*

He saw me standing on the pavement.

'What are you looking at?' he said.

'Nothing.'

'On your way then.'

He knocked on the door again.

'I live here.'

He stepped away from the door and came down to the

pavement to stand in front of me. Then he crouched down because I was so small compared to him.

'Who else lives here?' he said.

He looked cross. I wished I hadn't said anything. I wished Grace had walked me back too. I told her I knew the way so not to bother.

'I'm not to talk to strangers.'

'You talked to me a second ago.'

He was right. I crossed my arms.

'My name's Gary Kerr. What's your name?'

'Mary.'

I didn't need to tell him my second name.

'Hello, Mary. You don't happen to live here with an old man do you? Your grandad or your uncle?'

'Why d'you want to know?'

'Do two old men live here, Mary? I'm not a stranger anymore so you can tell me.'

'I dinnae think I should.'

'I'll come back later if you don't tell me.'

'Okay, that sounds better.'

I wasn't scared of Gary Kerr. He had really thick eyebrows and smelled like a dog, but his arms were like twigs. I knew I could outrun him. I could outrun a lot of people. I was sure that if I met Usain Bolt, I could've kept up with him as long as he didn't show off about it.

'Do me a favour, Mary. Tell them Gary Kerr knows what they did. And I'm not afraid to get the police involved.'

He stood up and I heard his knees crack. He walked away down the street. I waited till he was completely out of sight before I went up to Iain's door.

I thought if Gary was angry at them then maybe they'd been hiding in the kitchen and they'd come out when they heard me. I went up to the door and said, 'It's me, Granpa. I'm coming in.'

The door was unlocked. Maybe Gary hadn't tried to get in, or was just too polite? I checked every room, but no one was home. I closed the front door over and went back outside.

The jeep was there, so they hadn't gone for a drive. I took my phone out so I could phone Granpa. I only had one bar of battery left. I was rubbish at remembering to charge it. It was my first time using it. The whole point of me having it was so that if I went missing, Granpa could find me. But instead, it was Granpa who'd gone missing and I was hunting for him. It was like I was the person taking care of him and someone had come and stolen him.

When you were the one phoning, it didn't go *ring ring*. That was only when you were the one getting phoned. When you phoned, you heard *brrr brrr, brrr brrr*. It made me shaky and a bit like I might be sick. Granpa would answer any second and then I'd need to talk. There was part of me that didn't want him to answer so I wouldn't have to talk. I could talk in real-life but on the phone, it was different.

'Mary,' Granpa said when he answered. 'I see the phone works.'

'Hiya, Granpa. Where are you?'

'We're at the pub having our lunch. Did we no tell ye? Sorry, hen. Ye awright?'

'I'm at the house.'

'Good thing I told ye to take yer phone, eh?'

I nodded.

'Mary? Ye there?'

'Granpa, there was a man looking for you.'

'A man? Quiet Iain.'

'His name was Gary Kerr.'

'Disnae ring a bell.'

'He was knocking on the door and looking for two old men.'

'Sounds like us.'

'He said he knows what you did and he'll call the police.' I heard him whispering to Iain.

'He didnae shout at ye, did he, Mary? He didnae threaten ye?'

'Naw, he wisnae scary.'

'Good. He's no still aboot is he?'

'He went away.'

'Right. Will I come and get ye?'

'I know the way, Granpa. It'll be quicker if I come to you.'

'If ye say so. Get yerself to the pub. And if ye see him again, cross to the other side of the road.'

Granpa and Iain had a big jug of beer in the middle of their table. I sat down and there was a cola for me on the table already. It had a pink straw, the way I liked it.

'Before ye ask,' Granpa said, 'There's nothing to worry aboot with that man. Iain kens him.'

'I beat Gary at pool last week,' Iain said. 'I took twenty quid off him. Now he's trying to say he didn't put the bet on. He's a right drama queen.'

That made me feel better. I had thought Granpa and Iain were in proper trouble. You couldn't get in proper trouble for winning a game of pool.

'What did you and Grace get up to?' Granpa said.

'There were boys in the tower so we did other things.'

'What's so special about this tower?' Iain said.

'It's ours,' I said.

'Was yer boyfriend one of these boys?' Granpa said. He laughed and nudged Iain with his elbow and Iain laughed too.

'He's not my boyfriend, but aye, Lewis was there with his big brother.'

'Ye cannae keep away fae him.'

'I can so. I wish they hadnae been there. They were both being nasty to us.'

'What age is the older brother?'

'Quite old. Maybe sixteen?'

'Should we pay him a visit, Arthur?' Iain asked. 'Show him what happens when you mess with a Sutherland?'

'Please dinnae,' I said.

'We better no, Iain. Dinnae want to make a bad impression in front of Mary's future parents-in-law. We've already upset one mother this week.'

Granpa loved to take jokes too far to embarrass me. I had already said twice that Lewis wasn't my boyfriend, but Granpa kept saying it because he knew I didn't want him to. It was *bad patter.*

'Mary,' Iain said. 'It's just come to me. You said the young lad's name is Lewis. Is the older brother called Jamie?'

'Aye, do you know them?'

'That man you met, Gary Kerr? He's their dad.'

No wonder Iain thought he was a drama queen. He wouldn't even let people pet his dog.

Grace came to the door the morning after. That was two mornings in a row. She was definitely my best friend.

'My mum says you're to come for tea tonight,' she said.

'I thought you were going to ask your dad?' I said.

'I did. But then my mum heard and she said she felt bad

and I was to make sure you come. She won't take no for an answer.'

'What if I said no then?'

'She wouldn't take it as an answer. She'd wait until you said a different answer.'

'Oh, that's okay, I was going to say yes anyway.'

♪

CHAPTER FOURTEEN

Granpa said it was fine for me to go for tea at Grace's house. I was to take my phone in case her mum started any of her *funny business* again. It hadn't been funny when she'd been shouting, but I knew what he meant. Granpa thought she was a bit mad. I did too, but I didn't tell Grace because secretly I wanted to be her sister and be able to go to her house whenever I wanted. I didn't want Tom as a brother very much. But if it was the only way to get Grace as a sister, then I would have him as a brother. Just as long as we could be sisters and best friends at the same time.

Granpa walked me to Grace's house. He had the address on a bit of paper that Iain had written out. *3 Coolin Drive*. Iain's street was *Coolin Hills* so Coolin was a popular name in Portree.

We had to walk past their back garden to get to the front of the house. It was a big long straight garden. Lots of grass and footballs lying about. A trampoline too, but no safety nets around it, so you could jump off right on to the grass which was better. There was a front garden too, and a shed at the side. There was more garden than house.

I went on my tiptoes to press the doorbell. Some doorbells, when you pressed them, you couldn't hear anything and you'd wonder if it was working or if you had pressed it hard enough. But this one was really loud and you could hear it chiming, even outside the door.

A man answered. He was wearing a light blue shirt with a tea towel over his shoulder.

'Mary,' he said. 'And Mary's Grandfather. Very nice to meet you. I'm Kevin.'

'Arthur,' Granpa said.

He gave Granpa a big proper handshake and then gently shook my hand so he didn't hurt me.

'Are you joining us, Arthur?'

'Och naw, I've a prior arrangement.'

That was a lie. He was going to the pub with Iain. That didn't count as a plan he couldn't cancel. He wanted to see Mrs MacLeod when he dropped me off to annoy her, but he didn't want to spend a whole night doing it.

'I just wanted to escort the wee lass. Probably a full house anyway, with the bairns and... yer wife?'

He was looking past Mr MacLeod to try and see Mrs MacLeod. She wasn't there.

'She's visiting the little girls' room,' Mr MacLeod said.

'Course she is,' Granpa said. 'I'll be back at half eight, right, Mary?'

It was five when we got there, so that gave us three and a half hours. That was quite a lot of time. If I got bored I could always secretly text Granpa and say I wanted picked up.

Granpa left and I went inside. They had wooden floors in every room. I hadn't seen that before. Every room. Imagine that. You'd need to make sure you had socks on all the time, or your feet would be freezing. No warm carpet to squeeze between your toes.

Mr MacLeod took me to the living room. Grace was on the couch and Tom was lying in front of the telly. I had hoped Tom wasn't going to be there. I knew he was part of the family, but I'd been hoping he was away for the night or something. They were watching a quiz programme. The man supposed to be asking the questions was laughing too much to be able to ask any questions. He had spiky, shiny hair. I hadn't seen the programme before.

'Come and sit next to me, Mary,' Grace said.

I did. It was a red leather couch. There were lots of little red things in the room to go with the couch. They had put a lot of effort into making everything match. They did it for guests and that was me. It had been worth it because I was impressed. Tom didn't say hello; he just kept looking at the telly.

I wasn't good at quiz programmes. It was always questions for grown-ups. Children had no chance to get the answers. But this programme gave you three choices, so maybe you could get it. Like, if you always guessed the middle answer, you would get some right eventually. You had to make sure no one noticed you were doing it, or they'd think you were cheating. I was doing it anyway. Grace and Tom were saying what they thought the answer was. Every time, I went for the middle one. I had to say it first though. When I said the same answer as Tom he said, 'Stop copying, Mary. That's my answer.'

'Mary's allowed to say whatever answer she wants,' Grace said. 'You can't steal the answer for yourself.'

Mr and Mrs MacLeod were in the kitchen getting the tea ready, so they couldn't spoil it by saying, "*No the answer is definitely C*". We'd never know until the right answer lit up in green. By the time I arrived, Grace was winning 2-1 against Tom. In the end, it was Grace 7, Me 4, Tom 3. But Tom said we were cheating and we had made up the scores and went in a huff.

'That's why no one likes you, Thomas,' Grace said.

That was nasty, but it was true. Even if I was a boy, I don't think I'd have been his friend.

We had our tea in the dining room. It was a separate room just for having meals in, not a table in the kitchen. All the chairs matched the table and everything was set up fancy. I wondered if they did that for every meal or because they were trying to impress me. But why would they want to impress me? I wasn't a grown-up. Maybe it was so I would tell Granpa how fancy it was later on. It was way too much effort to do all the time, so maybe it was for me after all. Candles in candlesticks, real napkins, instead of a bit of kitchen roll, different glasses for your water and your juice, two forks instead of one. But you weren't to hold them both at the same time.

Tea was chicken and peas and mashed potato. Stuffing too, which I thought was only for Christmas and New Year. I ate all the peas first, so I had only good tasting things left on my plate. *Best till last.*

'Are you enjoying Portree then, Mary?' Mr MacLeod said.

'Yes, Mr MacLeod, it's really different from home, but I like it.'

I was making sure to say *Yes, Mr MacLeod* and *Yes, Mrs MacLeod* so they'd know I was a good girl and Mrs MacLeod would forgive me for going to the hospital.

'Where is it you're from again?'

I had to make a decision. I could tell him the real answer, which was Stirling, or I could say Livingston, the fake answer Granpa had told Andy on the boat. My joke about Iain having a plane in the garage hadn't worked on Grace and I wanted another go at being good at kidding folk on.

'Livingston,' I said.

It was only after I said it, I realised that he might ask me where in Livingston and I'd have no clue what to say. Or maybe Grace would say, *"no, she's from Stirling"*. Grace was busy cutting her chicken and she didn't even notice.

'Never been there,' Mr MacLeod said. 'Is it nice?'

'It's okay.'

And Mr MacLeod was happy with that. I had totally fooled him. It was great. I had fooled everyone at the table.

Mrs MacLeod didn't say much. She was probably embarrassed about her shouting, but I'd forgiven her because she'd invited me to tea. I didn't want to say, *"I forgive you"* though, because she might've gone mad again. Grown-ups didn't like it when you were right and they were wrong. Mrs Lithgow gave Paul Reed detention once because he'd told her she'd written the wrong answer to a sum on the board. He'd been right, it was a different answer, but she still punished him so he wouldn't *question her authority.*

We had meringues and strawberries and cream for pudding. It was because Wimbledon was on and that's what they ate there. Andy Murray had beaten a man with a lot of 'K's in his name.

'Has Grace told you all about the dance next month?' Mr MacLeod said.

'What dance?' I said.

'Did I not tell you?' Grace said. 'There's this big highland ball in the Gathering hall. Everyone gets all dressed up. The men in their kilts and the ladies with long dresses. It's like something from a film.'

I knew where the Gathering hall was. We passed it every day on the way up to the Lump.

'It's a ceilidh,' Grace said. 'Do you know any ceilidh dancing?'

'We dinnae do it till P6 and P7 at my school. Does that mean I'm not allowed to go?'

'Well, Mary,' Mrs MacLeod said. 'It's an *invite only* dance. I don't think you and your Granpa will get an invite.'

'Why not?'

'Because you're only here for the summer, aren't you? The invites only go to the families with *roots* in the community.'

Me and Granpa hadn't had time to make *roots*. We'd only just been planted.

'Can I not go with your family?' I asked.

'It's very strict,' Mrs MacLeod said. 'There's only a limited number of places.'

She was trying to look like she was sorry, but I knew she wasn't. She liked me enough to invite me to tea, but not to go to the ball. I knew what happened at dances like that: that's where people became best friends for life. I needed to go.

'Maybe I'll get to go somehow,' I said.

Mrs MacLeod did a little smile, like she thought I had no chance.

'Here's hoping,' Mr MacLeod said.

Mr MacLeod was really nice. Why was he married to Mrs MacLeod? Maybe she had proposed to him and he was too nice to say no.

'Are all youse going?' I said.

'Youse isn't a word,' said Mrs MacLeod.

'It is really,' I said, so quietly she couldn't hear.

'Yes, we're all going,' Mr MacLeod said. 'Two boys, two girls. Saves us worrying about finding dancing partners.'

'I'm not dancing with Grace,' Tom said.

He had red all around his lips from the way he was sucking the strawberries dry before he chewed them.

'Yes, you will,' Mr MacLeod said. 'Unless you want to sit in the corner yourself the whole night.'

'I'd rather sit in the corner than dance with *her*.'

He said *her* like it was a bad word.

'And who says I want to dance with you?' Grace said. 'We have to, Thomas. We both need someone to dance with. If Mary was coming I would dance with her instead. They might not even let you in because of how smelly you are.'

'They'd let me in way before they'd let you in. They'd smell you coming from miles away and shut the windows and lock the door.'

'Very mature, Thomas.'

They were arguing but at least they were getting to go. It was so unfair. I decided I would find a way to go, no matter what. I would *put my mind to it.*

Mr and Mrs MacLeod cleared away the dirty plates and me, Grace and Tom went through to the living room.

'Arm wrestle me, Mary,' Tom said.

'Don't, Mary,' Grace said. 'He just wants to beat you.'

'Well, obviously. I wouldn't arm wrestle someone who could beat me.'

'What if you use your bad arm,' I said. 'That would make it fair.'

'Okay. I'll use my left.'

We both lay down on the floor on our stomachs. My top came up a bit and the wooden floor was cold on my belly. Grace lay down too so she could judge. Me and Tom went to join hands.

'Wait,' I said. 'This willnae work. We both need to use the same arm. So either we both use our good arms or both use our bad arms.'

'Good arms,' Tom said, excited.

'I dinnae want to anymore. I've got no chance.'

I stood up and went to the couch. Thomas kept lying on the floor. He looked annoyed for a second then jumped up singing, 'Champ-ion-ees, champ-ion-ees, oh way, oh way, oh way.'

'You didn't win, Thomas,' Grace said. 'You didn't even arm wrestle.'

'But Mary forfeited,' he said. 'That makes me the winner. That's the way it works. Even ask Dad, I'm definitely the winner.'

He was right. I had said I would arm wrestle then at the last minute pulled out. He was the winner. Those were the rules. I didn't say that though. No way would I tell him he beat me.

'Undefeated champion of the world,' Thomas chanted as he skipped around the room.

We were playing charades when Granpa arrived. The doorbell was super loud inside the house. Mr MacLeod went through to answer it. I could hear them chatting at the front door, Iain's voice too. They had both come to get me. I got my jacket on and went through to the hall. I said bye to Grace and Mrs MacLeod. I didn't bother saying it to Tom.

'How was yer tea?' Granpa asked.

'You shouldn't ask her in front of me,' Mr MacLeod said. 'She's too nice to say what she really thought.'

'Did you know you could have stuffing for tea even if it's not Christmas?' I said.

'I'll put it on the shopping list,' Iain replied.

'Come back anytime,' Mr MacLeod said.

'And tell your missus,' Iain said, 'We're trying our best to keep Mary's *bad influences* under control.'

'Ah, yes, she's sorry about that.'

'Then why's she not here to tell us?' Granpa said.

'She's tired from hosting.'

'Hosting an eight-year-old?' Iain said, looking at Granpa with his eyebrows raised. 'You're having a laugh.'

'We better be away,' Granpa said, shaking his head. 'It was nice of ye to have her over.'

'Like I say, anytime,' Mr MacLeod said.

I had to keep up with Granpa and Iain's fast walking again. They were talking quietly to each other about Mrs MacLeod. I knew because I heard them say *bint* and *daft cow*. It had to be her. I could tell they had been drinking. They had that funny smell about them. I was embarrassed that they were drunk in front of Mr MacLeod. It was fine when they were drunk in the house, just the two of them late at night, but I didn't want everyone to know they got drunk a lot. They would think Granpa was a bad granpa when he really wasn't. The drink was to help with his sore shoulder. Plus, it was our summer holiday. You were allowed to drink more on your summer holidays. That was the rule. Even I knew it.

♪

CHAPTER FIFTEEN

'Granpa, do you know about the ceilidh in the Gathering hall?'

He looked confused as he buttered his toast.

'Are you talking about the Portree Ball?' Iain said. 'Where did you hear about it?'

'The MacLeod's are all going. Could we go?'

'Probably not, Mary. You have to get an invite. I've not had one before. It's only the posh folk that get invited.'

'Are we not posh enough, then?' I asked.

'Maybe you are, but me and your Granpa aren't.'

I didn't think I was posh. But if I was, maybe I'd get an invite. How would the organisers know I was posh enough? Was there a test? I was friends with Grace and she was posh, so maybe it would be obvious I was posh too. If I said *alighted* instead of getting off, I thought that could help.

'Could you try and get one, please, Iain?' I said.

'Och, leave him alone,' Granpa said.

'I'll look into it, Mary,' Iain said, 'Only because it's you.'

If Iain managed to get me a ticket for the ball, I knew I would absolutely love him. I wouldn't tell him I loved him, but I'd make him breakfast in bed or something and that would be proof. Saying the real words out loud was too much.

'Who's the person that organises it?' I asked.

'That's something I'll need to find out, Mary,' Iain said. 'I'll try to pull some strings.'

Iain was going to pull a string and on the end of the string would be the person who organised the ball. Obviously, there were no strings on people, but I liked to picture it in my head. Imagine that. You could pull a string and the thing you wanted would come rushing to you.

Grace didn't come to our door that morning. I was disappointed she hadn't made it a *hat-trick* of visits.

'Grace no turned up, hen?' Granpa asked.

There was horse racing on the telly and Granpa and Iain were going to watch it all day. They had the horse pages of the paper all laid out. They were going to put bets on who would win. There wasn't a bookies in Portree, but Iain had a man he could phone who could bet for him. His own, personal *bookie*.

Horse races were all the same, but I liked the colours the jockeys wore and the funny names of the horses. There were little pictures of the jockeys' outfits next to their names in the paper.

'We didnae say we would definitely see each other today,' I said. 'She's probably with her mum and dad.'

'Ye ken where she lives noo,' Granpa said. 'Why don't ye go to her door?'

I hadn't thought of that.

'What if she doesn't want me to come?'

'Did she ask ye if ye wanted her to come round yesterday?'

'Naw, she just came.'

'There ye go. It's your turn to surprise her.'

Granpa was much more relaxed about me walking about

Portree myself. It was way safer than Stirling. Apart from that man Gerry getting beaten up in his house, but that was only because he'd had lots of money. We didn't have lots of money.

I passed the Co-op on the way to Grace's house. Craig was standing outside with his clipboard, asking people to do his handwriting project. Not many people were stopping to listen to him.

'Hiya, Craig,' I said.

'Awright there, Mary,' he replied.

'How's your project going?'

'Not so well, if I'm being honest.'

'That's a shame.'

'You're right there.'

He tried to stop a man but the man ignored him, grabbed a basket and walked inside the shop.

'What about the friend you were looking for?' I asked.

'I'm not so sure he's in Portree anymore.'

'I hope you find him. Having a friend is great. I'm going to see my friend Grace right now.'

'Thanks, Mary. I don't think I'll be around much longer, so if I don't see you again, have a good one.'

'A good what?'

'Eh, life?'

'Oh, you too.'

Diiing dooong went the bell. It was Mr MacLeod who answered.

'Hello Mary,' he said. 'I knew you couldn't resist more of my cooking.'

'I'm here for Grace, not for food, sorry. Is she allowed out?'

'I'm only having you on. Grace!'

He had a great voice. Not scary or angry. If you heard it from the other room, you wouldn't be worried about going through. You'd know he just had something to tell you - like Mary's at the door.

'Mary,' Grace said.

She still had her jammies on.

'Are you coming out?' I asked.

'I need to get a shower and get dressed. Come in.'

Grace went up to her room to get ready. I sat with Mr MacLeod in the living room.

'Do you get bored, Mr MacLeod,' I said. 'Not working during the summer?'

'Not at all, Mary. It's my favourite time of year. Do you?'

'I used to, but this summer's different. I'm glad it's so long.'

I used my foot to mess up the fringe of the rug on the floor then flatten it back down again.

'Do you teach Grace and Thomas?' I asked.

'No, no, no. They wouldn't like that. I'm always bouncing between years, so maybe one day, though. I have Primary 5 next year.'

'What are you doing today then?'

'I thought I might watch the racing.'

'I think Birdman will win.'

Mr MacLeod looked at me all surprised. I had heard Granpa saying that horse's name earlier. I remembered it because I pictured a bird, but with human legs. It wouldn't be much use as a superhero. I only said it for a laugh. I had no clue whether it would win or not.

'I didn't know you were so knowledgeable on horses, Mary.'

'My Granpa likes them. I watched a lot of horse racing when I helped him at work.'

'Where was that?'

Grace came through then.

'Let's go, Mary.'

She didn't even wait, running right out the front door.

'Bye Mr MacLeod,' I said.

I ran at full speed to catch up with her.

'You've made that up,' I said.

'No, it's really called that,' Grace said. 'They named it ages ago. It didn't mean that back then.'

Grace explained that there was a ceilidh dance called the Gay Gordons.

'Is it only for gay people then?' I asked. 'I'm not gay. I might be when I'm a grown-up, but not yet.'

'No, Mary. Don't keep going on about the gay part. You're just like the boys.'

We were at the Bowl. There was loads of space for dancing. Grace taught me the Gay Gordons dance. I had to be the boy though, that was the only way she could remember it. We did a normal dance forward and turned around, then she put her hands up and I held them from behind as we walked forward. Then I spun her round under me, which was hard because she was taller.

'Can we do the Dashing White Sergeant?' I asked. 'I've heard P7s talking about it.'

'You need lots and lots of people for that,' Grace said. 'We couldn't do it with just us two.'

'Can you not invite some of your other friends?'

'They're all away on their holidays. But hopefully they'll

be back home before you go. Sophie is great, wait till you meet her.'

'Are you not going anywhere?'

'Dad says maybe in October.'

I had gone to Portree for a holiday, but all of Grace's friends had gone other places because they were bored of staying in Portree all the time. I wondered if any had gone to Stirling. A holiday in Stirling would've been boring for me, but if I told Grace's friends I was having a holiday in Portree, they would've said the same thing back.

I was back at Iain's in time for tea.

'Did youse win?' I asked.

'I had a couple of winners,' Iain said. 'But your granpa backed nothing but donkeys. This is him who's worked in a bookies, too.'

'What can I say?' said Granpa. 'I went with my gut. Turns oot my gut is as clueless as my head for picking horses.'

People were always saying that. They *went with their gut*. Their gut made a decision for them. It was just a saying. It was only your brain that could decide things. You couldn't ask your belly what to do. It would only tell you if it was hungry or full. If my gut had tried to tell me something, I would've ignored it.

I had a microwave lasagne from the Co-op. Granpa did most of it for me, but shouted me through to poke the holes in the plastic. *Pop pop pop pop*. I did as many as I could before he took the knife off me and said, *"that's enough"*. I wanted to make sure there were plenty. To be safe. What if you put it in the microwave without piercing the film? I didn't even want to think about it. An explosion, probably.

I thought that would be a good booby trap. If you knew

there were robbers coming in the house, like in the *Home Alone* films, you could put a meal in the microwave and not pierce it. Then, when you knew the baddies would be walking past the microwave, you'd already set it for five minutes or something, then when they were in front of it: *BANG!* They'd be taken out by an exploding lasagne. I was keeping Granpa and Iain safe by piercing it so many times. Pierce was the word they always used on the cardboard packet. *Pierce the film several times.* How many was several? That was up to you. I thought it was loads.

Granpa and Iain played cards again while I played the keyboard. I had the volume turned down low, for when I was practising, then I turned it up when I wanted them to hear me play. They always said I had done a *grand job*, even when I made mistakes or didn't do the left hand properly. They couldn't tell I had made mistakes because they had their eyes on their cards.

We all sat together to watch the ten o'clock news. Granpa let me stay up late if it was to watch the news. Granpa said I was more up-to-date with *current affairs* than most grown-ups. *Affairs* meant the news, but also going out with someone who wasn't your husband. Mrs McArthur, my old P2 teacher, she'd had an affair with another man and her husband broke up with her and they got a divorce. Her P2 class didn't know about it, but the P6s and 7s knew and they told everyone. *Mrs McArthur loves the boaby.* A P7 boy was taken out of assembly for shouting that. Liam Davidson. But we had all heard it and everyone, even the teachers, all looked over at Mrs McArthur. She just looked straight ahead, but we could see her cheeks go red. Liam got sent home but all the boys cheered him when he came back the next day. Mrs McArthur changed her name to Ms Kennedy the month after, but we all still knew who she was.

Mrs McArthur loves the boaby. It meant she loved being with lots of men, and some of them were called Bobby. Having lots of man friends was okay, but if you were married, then it wasn't okay anymore. Her husband had left her, so she could go and get as many men as she wanted and that was allowed. I thought that would be the best way. If I ever wanted to be with a boy, I wouldn't want the same one all the time. Just like you didn't always want lasagne for your tea every night, but once a week was just right.

CHAPTER SIXTEEN

It was a Saturday morning when Gary Kerr came back to speak to Granpa and Iain. He woke us up with his banging on the front door. My clock said half past seven. I jumped out of bed, but when I got to my bedroom door, Granpa came in.

'You stay in bed, hen,' he said. 'Nothing to worry aboot.'

He waited until I got back under the covers then went away down the hall. As soon as he was out of sight, I went over to the window to watch. I left my window open at night and I could hear them really clearly. Mr Kerr was wearing his *Queen* T-shirt. He needed to buy more clothes.

'I'd appreciate you keeping it down, Gary,' Iain said. 'There's a wee girl trying to sleep in there.'

'And I'd appreciate not having people steal from my lobster creels, Iain,' Mr Kerr said. 'I know it was you and your new pal here.'

'Creel?' Granpa said. 'Ye'll need to enlighten me as to what that is.'

'You know very well what it is. It's illegal to steal from lobster traps, not that that stopped you.'

'Gary,' Iain said. 'We've not touched your creels.'

'My wife said she saw two men loitering about the harbour last week, right where my creels are on the pier.'

'And she says it was us, does she?'

'She didn't get a look at your faces, but she spotted you two at the pub the other night and she's ninety-nine percent sure.'

'I don't think you know what 'sure' means, Gary.'

Mr Kerr stepped right up to Iain and pointed his finger in his face.

'Don't be smart with me. If I catch you anywhere near them again, I'm phoning the police.'

'Well, this has been a huge waste of our time,' Iain said, moving Mr Kerr's hand back down to his side. 'Hasn't it, Arthur?'

'No completely,' Granpa answered. 'It's always nice to meet the locals. I'm Arthur, by the way.'

Granpa put out his hand for a handshake, but Mr Kerr stormed off. Granpa and Iain laughed and I jumped back into bed before they noticed me at the window.

Grace and me were sitting on a bench in Somerled Square. There were older boys, who looked about twelve or thirteen, doing tricks on skateboards. They were doing jumps over an empty can of Irn-Bru. I liked the sounds the skateboards made. The rumbling wheels and the *thwipping* sound when one of the boys tried to do a jump. They weren't very good at landing back on the skateboards after they jumped off though.

It was a bit scary to watch. They could fall and break their arms and legs any minute. None of them were wearing helmets or kneepads or anything. Grown-ups were all around and no one was stopping it, so obviously they were allowed. There wasn't a skate park in Portree, so the square was the main place you saw people skateboarding. I didn't go near the skate park in Stirling, because of all the *goths*. They looked like vampires, and even though vampires aren't real, I kept out their way.

I hadn't imagined skateboarders in a little place like Portree. The same with the motorbikes. Motorbikes were coming down the street every time you looked around. A lot with the *L plate* on, which meant they were still learning. In cars, when you were learning, you had the teacher in the seat next to you to tell you where to go and if you were doing things wrong. I had seen it on telly. But on the motorbike, it was just you, by yourself. You would have to keep stopping to talk to each other. I wondered if they had walkie-talkies. Or even better, those little earplugs spies had. You pressed your hand to your ear and it would look like you were talking to yourself, but really there was a voice in your ear telling you where the diamond vault was.

I noticed Craig sitting with a rucksack in the bus shelter. I told Grace I'd be back in a minute and went to talk to him.

'We can't seem to stay away from each other, Mary,' he said when he saw me.

'Are you leaving?' I asked.

'Aye, I'm waiting on the bus. Gave up on finding that friend of mine.'

'You shouldnae give up. Everyone should have a friend. I can help you if you want.'

'I appreciate that, but it's a grown-up thing I need help with.'

'I bet I can help. I'm really clever for my age.'

'You know what, why not? I'm leaving in five minutes, anyway. As long as you're good at keeping secrets?'

I locked my lips and threw away the key so he'd see how I knew the rules of secret keeping. He took out a bit of paper from his pocket.

'I can't explain exactly why,' he said. 'But I'm pretty sure whoever wrote this note is an old friend of mine. It's been so long, I can't recognise him by his face, so that's why I got people to write some of these words. Keep this between us, Mary, but I'm not even in university. If only I could find who wrote the bloody thing.'

The bit of paper said:

7. 34 to Perth
8.51 to Inverness
12. 55 to Kyle of Lochalsh
? – Portree bus

'Like I say,' Craig said. 'I've given up on finding him. Unless, by any chance, you know who wrote it?'

My whole body was shaking.

'Naw,' I said. 'I dinnae know who wrote that.'

He looked at me closely. I didn't know if he believed me. I hadn't been able to convince Grace there was a plane in Iain's garage, but I'd made the MacLeod's think I was from Livingston. Sometimes my lies worked and sometimes they didn't.

Craig smiled.

'It was a long shot.'

I blew out lots of air through my nose.

'Why do you want to find your friend?' I asked.

'He owes me something. And I owe him something, too.'

'Will you be okay if you dinnae get it back, then?'

'I'll have to be. My brother won't be happy though. He was looking forward to seeing him again, even more than me.'

'I better get back to my friend,' I said. 'Bye, Craig.'

'See you around, Mary.'

I ran back to Grace. I was sweating down my back and under my arms.

'Who was that?' she asked.

'Just a man I met,' I said. 'He's going away forever though.'

He would get on the bus and I'd never see him again. I don't know why he wanted to find Granpa, but I was sure it wasn't for a good reason. Granpa owed him something. Something to do with what happened in Perth. I had lost the note and he had found it. I thought maybe he had seen what Granpa had done. Maybe the lady Granpa had given his jacket to had found the note and given it to Craig. But why did he want to see Granpa so much?

He hadn't found him though. His handwriting plan hadn't worked. He had pretended he was doing it for university, but that had been a lie. He was leaving. And I got to stay in Portree with Grace and nothing needed to change. Everything would be fine.

Tom walked past us but he didn't say hello. He was trying to look like he didn't care about us. He walked up to the boys and asked for a go on one of their skateboards.

'No chance,' one said.

'Let him, Danny,' another said. 'It'll be a laugh to see him fall on his cunt.'

I couldn't believe he had said that. That was even worse than the 'f' word. I wouldn't even say the 'c' word in my head. I knew how terrible it was. But this boy had said it out loud for everyone to hear. I hoped he would fall and scrape his elbows and knees. The 'c' word boy was the one in charge because the other one, Danny, passed his skateboard to Tom after he was told to.

'Can Tom skateboard?' I said to Grace.

'He's never been on one in his life,' Grace answered. 'He's going to make a fool of himself.'

'Are you going to shout on him then?'

'Not after last time with Lewis and Jamie. He can't blame us this time.'

That seemed like something a bad sister would say. I didn't think Grace was a bad sister, but maybe she was tired of having to be the sensible one all the time.

I could tell Tom hadn't been on a skateboard before. He had one foot on it and was pushing with the other, but going really slow. The older boys were laughing and clapping and shouting things to make fun of him.

'Careful there, wee man. Speed kills.'

'Fuck me, it's Tony Hawks.'

'What a fud.'

Tom pushed as hard as he could with one foot, then he put both feet on top of the board. He looked okay for a second, but then he tried to turn and couldn't. He was about to go into the wall. He tried to jump off but it didn't work. The skateboard went shooting out from under him and crashed into the wall, and Tom flew up in the air. He landed hard. There wasn't enough time for him to get his hands down to stop himself. I heard him hitting the concrete. He was crying straight away. Danny ran forward to grab his skateboard back and the boys ran away. Me and Grace ran over to Tom.

I wished he'd been wearing long trousers. But he wasn't. He was in shorts so I could see the bone sticking out. I ran back to the bench and sat down. I felt like I was going to be sick. I held my hair back with one hand just in case, but no one came to check on me because it was Tom who needed help. There was a big crowd around him. Craig was there. He didn't get on the bus. The bus wouldn't wait for him. He was touching Tom's face and talking to him.

I made my mouth into an 'O' shape and breathed in and out. That way the air felt much cooler when I sucked it in. It helped to keep the sick down.

The ambulance came quickly. The square wasn't far from the hospital. It was probably the same ambulance Brian was in after he fell in the water. I stayed where I was. I didn't want to be in the way. The feeling of being sick had gone but it would come back if I saw the bone again.

Craig got in the ambulance with Tom. Grace went too. She didn't look back to see where I was or wave goodbye. She was doing such a good job of being a sister, she forgot all about me.

The ambulance went off without the sirens on. They must not have expected any traffic to have to scare it out of the way. When the ambulance left the square, it went right instead of left. The hospital was on the left and up the hill, next to the Lump. I didn't understand. Where were they going?

I ran all the way back to Iain's. Apart from the hill at the end. That was too steep to keep up the pace when I had already been running for over two minutes. I was a fast runner like Usain Bolt, not a long distance runner like Mo Farah.

'You look out of puff,' Iain said, as I came in the door.

'Awright there, hen?' Granpa said.

'Tom fell off a skateboard,' I said, running the tap till it was super cold and sticking my mouth under. 'I think he's broken his leg. He went off in an ambulance.'

'Jesus,' Iain said. 'Trouble's always at the back of you,

these days, Mary.'

'It wisnae my fault.'

'He's no saying it was yer fault,' Granpa said. 'Just that ye're having some bad luck. How'd it happen?'

I told them the story, but left out the bit about the bone sticking out of Tom's leg. I didn't want to talk about that ever again. And I definitely didn't say anything about Craig.

'But then they drove off to the right, instead of going up to the hospital.'

'They'll be taking the boy to Broadford,' Iain said. 'Probably can't deal with broken bones at the hospital here.'

'We came through there on the way here,' Granpa said. 'About half an hour away?'

'Less if you're zooming about like these nutters that drive the ambulances.'

I was glad Tom would get there fast. The sooner the bone was back in his leg, the sooner I would stop feeling so sick about it. If it was in the past it wouldn't be so bad. But I wished Craig hadn't gone with him. If I'd seen him get on the bus, I'd have known he was gone for good. He had given up on finding Granpa, but he was still on Skye.

'Granpa,' I said. 'You know that man who got you to write words down for his project?'

'Oh, yer pal,' he said. 'Whatshisface?'

'Craig.'

'Craig, aye, that was it. What about him?'

'Had you met him before that?'

'Cannae say I had, hen. Why?'

'Just wondering.'

He squinted at me but then he smiled and forgot about it. I had been right. Craig was lying and Granpa wasn't his old friend. Craig had lied about everything and wasn't to be trusted.

Grace phoned that night. Iain answered and passed it to me.

'Hiya, Mary,' she said. 'Dad said I was to phone and make sure you got home okay. I'm sorry I left you without saying bye.'

'That's okay. How's Tom?'

'Thomas is okay. His leg's broken. He got an X-ray and they decided he needs surgery. He has to stay overnight and they're doing the operation tomorrow. Dad's taking me home soon. Thomas has already chosen what colour his stookie's going to be. Guess what colour he chose?'

'Blue.'

'Aye.'

'I knew it.'

'I know,' Grace said. 'Such a boy. Anyway, he's not happy since the doctor says he won't get it off for months. He'll still have it on when we go back to school. So he can't run or walk properly all summer. He's to rest it for ages.'

'That's rubbish.'

'I know. But that'll teach him not to be so stupid.'

'He'll probably still do stupid things, anyway.'

'You're right. He'll never get less stupid.'

'Sorry I didn't stand next to him with you. I felt sick.'

'That's okay. Was it because of the bone?'

I pictured the bone again and shook my head to try and get it out of my head.

'Aye,' I said.

'That was horrible. I made sure I didn't look at it.'

'Did you go to Broadford, by the way?'

'How did you know that?'

'Iain guessed.'

'Oh. They can't fix broken legs at the Portree hospital.

If it's really, really bad they have a helicopter they can send out to pick you up.'

'What would be really, really bad?'

'Like if you got your leg chopped off and were bleeding too much.'

'Ew, let's stop talking about disgusting things.'

'This must be what boys talk about all the time.'

I nodded because of how right she was.

'Should I come and see Tom when he gets home?' I asked.

'I'll go and ask him.'

I could hear Grace going through to a different room and speaking.

'Thomas, do you want Mary to come and visit you when you get home?'

I didn't hear Thomas say anything.

'Mary, he says that's fine.'

'Okay... is that man Craig still there?'

'The man who came in the ambulance with us? No, Mum's away taking him back into town to get his bus. Mum and Dad were really grateful to him for making sure Thomas got to the hospital safe.'

My chest got less heavy. Craig was getting a different bus, but still leaving.

'I better say bye,' I said. 'The news is on soon.'

When I was watching the news I thought of something exciting. Tom wouldn't be able to dance at the Portree Ball because of his broken leg. And if he couldn't dance, then surely he wouldn't even go. You wouldn't go to a dance if you couldn't dance. I could go instead. I could go with Grace and we could dance together the same way we did at the Lump. But I would need to make sure Mr and Mrs MacLeod invited me and it looked like their idea. I didn't want them to think I was happy that Tom had broken his leg. Which I wasn't. They might even think I had made him break his leg on purpose. That didn't make any sense, but they might think it anyway because it's the kind of thing that happens in films. I hadn't done any *sabotage* on him. Mrs MacLeod would look for any reason I couldn't go.

She *had it in for me.*

CHAPTER SEVENTEEN

'Is it sore?' I asked.

'Quite sore,' Tom said. 'And it itches like anything. I'm taking tablets to stop it hurting.'

He was lying on his bed with his broken leg resting on some cushions. His duvet cover was a superhero one and I looked for Spider-man, but he wasn't there. He was the best one. His parents had died before he knew them, just like mine had. That made me as strong as Spider-man, apart from all the swinging and climbing up buildings.

Tom's chest of drawers had been moved right up to the end of the bed with the telly on top so he could see it better. I could tell that's not normally where the drawers were because the wires were stretched really tight from the plug.

'He wouldn't normally be allowed the telly so close,' Grace said. 'It's only until he gets the cast off.'

'Are casts and stookies the same thing?' I said.

'I think so,' Tom said. 'Mary, sign my stookie. The pens are on top of the drawers.'

'Do it in black,' said Grace. 'It's the only one you can see properly on the blue.'

I kneeled down to write my name. There was a really weird smell off the stookie. Like clean bandages, but sweaty skin too. I breathed through my mouth and wrote my name.

I did it in all capitals because there weren't any rules for how to write your name on a stookie. It was good practice for when I grew up. You had to have a signature or you weren't a proper grown-up.

The stookie said *Grace, Mum, Dad*. So Mr and Mrs MacLeod had signed it Mum and Dad instead of their real names. I didn't think I'd like to be called Mum. Loads of people were called Mum. If I had babies, I decided I would let them call me Mary. It was a much more special name.

'How long till you get it off?' I asked.

'The doctor said the end of August,' Tom replied. 'But I'm going to lie really, really still and that'll make it heal better.'

'It won't,' Grace said.

'It will. The less I move, the quicker it'll get better. I'm only getting up to go to the toilet from now on. I'll get it off before August.'

'You'll need to come down for your dinner.'

'Right, only going to the toilet and having my dinner then. Apart from that, I'm not moving a muscle.'

'Does that mean your mouth muscles too? So you'll shut up for a change?'

Grace looked at me and I smiled.

'Away you go,' Tom said. 'Dr Wales says I need my rest, so get out or I'll shout on Dad.'

'He's out in the garden, he won't even hear you.'

'Dad! Daaaad!'

He was shouting his loudest. Grace took my hand and we ran out.

It had been a week since Tom broke his leg. I hadn't seen Craig since then. He must've gone back wherever he normally lived. I wanted to tell Granpa that he'd been looking for him, but then he'd know it was my fault for losing the bit of paper with the train times on it. But Craig was gone, so I had got away with it. It had been a *close call,* but I'd survived. Just like James Bond. The bad guy had been defeated, so it was time to drink champagne with a beautiful lady then have all the actors' names come up on the screen. I wouldn't want to kiss the lady though, and I didn't want a man either. I didn't fancy anyone.

I still wasn't completely sure what Craig wanted. It was definitely something to do with what had happened in Perth. Maybe Craig just wanted to give Granpa his jacket back. That wouldn't have been so bad. But maybe it was nothing to do with the jacket. Maybe it was a bad thing. I tried to forget about it and only think about being best friends with Grace.

'What do you want to do?' Grace asked me.

Normally she just took us up to the Lump, but this time she was asking me.

'There's a wee waterfall near Iain's house that I thought looked nice. Can we go and see it?'

I had wanted to go from the first day I saw it, but I didn't want to go on my own. And then, when Brian fell in the water, that made me even more scared of falling in. But I knew if Grace came, then we would be fine. She was one of those people that you knew would never get hurt. I couldn't picture her name and photo being in the paper because she'd drowned at the waterfall. I could definitely picture Tom's name though. **BOY SADLY DROWNS BECAUSE HE WAS BEING SILLY AROUND THE WATERFALL LIKE A TOTAL BOY** would be the headline. But he was resting in bed so I didn't need to worry about him coming and trying to push us in for a laugh. That was a boy's idea of a laugh, trying to hurt you.

The water from the waterfall went under the bridge at the bottom of Iain's street. Instead of going over the bridge, we followed the stream to the waterfall. The path was muddy and right next to the water, which sloshed and rushed by. Grace went first and was going way faster than I thought was sensible.

'Grace, slow down.'

'Mary, you're such a goody-goody.'

'So what if I am, at least I'm not going to fall in like you.'

I didn't want to *try my luck*. I went slowly. I made sure one foot was down before I put the next foot in front of it. The mud was going up the sides of my trainers and sticking to my laces. I should've gone back to Iain's for my wellies, but it was too late and there was no way of keeping the mud from getting into my trainers.

The path didn't go all the way round to the waterfall. It stopped on the other side so we were facing it. Grace picked up a stone and threw it into the water. It didn't make a noise because it was already so loud. The waterfall was much bigger up close. The water came down like an avalanche instead of a trickle. The water never stopped. It was like the sound when Granpa ran me a bath. When the water slapped down into more water. Grace and me had to shout to hear each other.

'What now?' Grace said.

'I dinnae know. I just wanted to see it up close.'

'Okay. We'll go back then?'

Waterfalls were always bright blue on telly adverts. In real-life, they were grey and loud and you couldn't dive into the water underneath, unless you wanted to break your neck on the jaggy stones. Breaking your neck was the worst part of your body to break. If it broke, that was you dead. They didn't make stookies for necks.

We stood on the bridge looking down at the water.

'I've realised something,' I said. 'About Tom. He won't be able to dance at the ball.'

I was saying it like I'd only thought of it that second and didn't even care that much. *Acting*.

'You're right,' Grace said. 'I'll need someone to dance with. I'll ask Mum and Dad.'

'Ask them what?'

'Who I'm going to dance with instead.'

'Oh. I thought you meant maybe I could come.'

'That's a good idea. I'll ask them. But normally it's meant to be a boy and a girl.'

'But we've practised, so really it's perfect.'

'I'll say to them.'

'And I could use his ticket.'

'Right.'

'Unless it has his name on, but it probably disnae.'

'I'll ask,' Grace sighed. 'Don't worry.'

It seemed like Grace wanted me to stop going on about it. She wanted me to be a *silent partner*.

Balls were better than normal dances. I needed a proper ball gown though. It was to be a gown and not a dress. Granpa would need to buy me one and he wouldn't be happy about it. I would tell him that it was my birthday and Christmas *rolled into one* so then maybe he would say yes. If he still wasn't sure, I would maybe even say *two* birthdays and *two* Christmases' *rolled into one*. But that was too much, I thought. There would be nothing to look forward to for two years.

It would be like a fairy tale because no one would know who I was. People in Portree knew each other, but I was new. I would walk in to the hall and people would say,

'Who's that girl?'

'She's beautiful.'

'I want to dance with her all night long.'

And even if they didn't say it out loud, they would probably say it in their heads.

Some boys were coming down the road. One was Lewis. I didn't know the other two. They were passing a football between them, but it bounced off a kerb and came rolling down the hill towards us. It was white and red and had black lines going all around it. I picked it up.

'Here,' said one of the boys.

'Give us it back, Mary,' Lewis said.

'Don't,' Grace said. 'He didn't give Tom his screwdriver back.'

'It was Jamie who threw it,' Lewis said. 'And screwdrivers aren't worth anything. That's Jamie's new Premier League ball, he paid loads for it. If you don't give it back, we'll... we'll come and tank you.'

'I'm no hitting girls,' said one of the other boys.

The third boy nodded.

'We're going to the square,' the third boy said. 'Find us when you've got the ball back.'

And the other two ran off and left Lewis himself.

'Your friends didn't even back you up,' Grace said.

'Shut up,' Lewis said. 'Your brother's such an idiot he broke his leg on a skateboard.'

'Mary, chuck it over the side.'

'In the water?' I asked.

'Aye, fair's fair.'

'Don't dare,' Lewis said. 'My brother will tank the both of you.'

'He'll only tank you for losing it,' Grace said.

Lewis started running towards me and I didn't want to chuck it into the stream, but he looked like he was going to whack me. I chucked it up in the air so that maybe he could catch it. I wasn't good at throwing. It bounced off the railing and went over into the stream. It floated on top and started moving away from us. It was only a stream but the waterfall was pushing the water to the sea really fast.

Lewis's eyes went wide. He tried to punch us both, but we managed to get out the way. The ball was getting further away and he sprinted past us to catch up with it. He ran along the bank and stuck his foot out to try and stop it, but he had no chance. The ball got to the bit where the stream got wider and it bobbed off to the side. Lewis followed it and disappeared round the corner.

Grace smiled at me.

'Good throw,' she said.

'Oh, but it was his brother Jamie's ball,' I said. 'He's big. What if he's really, really mad?'

'He's twice your age, Mary. He'd go to prison if he hurt you.'

I felt better. Jamie wouldn't want to go to prison just because his football got a bit wet.

Granpa sent me to the Co-op to get milk. I loved doing little missions like that. The people at the shop would see me shopping by myself and think how grown-up I was. Granpa had given me the milk money, but the shop people wouldn't know that. They might've thought I had my own job and my own money. As long as it was still bright outside. Missions in the dark would be too scary.

When I got to the shop, Grace's dad was coming out.

'Mary,' he said. 'Just the person I was hoping to meet.'

'Hiya, Mr MacLeod. What is it?'

'Why didn't you tell me you were joining us at the school?'

'I dinnae know... what do you mean, *joining us*?'

'See, I thought I recognised your name when Grace first told me about you. Your last name is Sutherland, isn't it?'

I nodded.

'I really should've realised when you came round for dinner. Anyway, yesterday I was looking through my class list for next year and, sure enough, there's your name. Mary Sutherland, you're going to be one of my P5s!' Mr MacLeod smiled at me. 'Oh, don't look so upset about it, Mary. I'm a good teacher, I promise.'

I wasn't upset. I was confused. But maybe it looked like I was upset.

'Mr MacLeod, there must be a mistake. I go to Braehead Primary.'

'Was that your old school?'

'It's not my old one. I still go there. I'll be going back there in August.'

'Not according to my class list, Mary.'

'It must be another Mary Sutherland.'

'I don't think so.'

'It must be.'

I blinked fast to keep the tears from coming.

'Well, em, if you say so, Mary,' Mr MacLeod said. 'Maybe you should go and talk to your Granpa about it?'

'Aye. I will. I'll tell him there's another Mary Sutherland in Portree.'

'Yes, I think you need to talk to him, okay? I'll see you soon, Mary.'

And he went away with his loaf of bread under his arm. I rubbed my eyes with my sleeve. I didn't think any tears leaked out but Mr MacLeod might've seen anyway. Getting the milk wasn't as exciting as I thought it would be. The lady who served me said, 'Did your mum or dad send you for the milk?'

'Em, aye.'

I couldn't always be bothered explaining how my mum and dad were dead. I walked back really slowly. I was still confused about what Mr MacLeod had said and I needed to think about how to talk to Granpa about it.

When I got to Iain's, him and Granpa were playing Scrabble.

'Do you not like playing cards anymore?' I asked.

'Your Granpa was losing too much money,' Iain said. 'So we're on Scrabble till his funds have time to grow.'

'Or until Iain admits he's a cheating... so and so,' Granpa said.

I had been close to 50p there.

'Granpa,' I said. 'Mr MacLeod says I'm on his class list for next year. I told him there must be another Mary Sutherland in Portree. That's funny, isn't it?'

Granpa looked at Iain and not at me.

'I'm going to pop to the shop,' Iain said.

'But I just went for the milk.'

'Back in a bit.'

He got up, grabbed his jacket from the hook and was out the door quick.

'Sit doon, Mary,' Granpa said.

I sat in Iain's chair.

'Right, well, I was hoping to keep this a surprise...'

He still wasn't looking in my eyes. He was moving the Scrabble tiles about on his little green rack.

'What if I said we're no going back to Stirling in August? What if I said we're gonnae stay in Portree fae noo on?'

It had only taken him about five seconds to say that. Only five seconds and he had completely changed everything. My whole life. I had a million questions and I couldn't think which one to say first.

'So I'm really going to be in Mr MacLeod's class?'

That wasn't the most important one to ask, but it was the only one I could get my mouth to say.

'If ye're on his list then I'm guessing, aye. Ye're all enrolled to start in August.'

Mr MacLeod would think I was so stupid. I had told him there was no way that was true.

'And we're never going back to Stirling, ever?'

'The house is sold, Mary. We cannae go back. I've left the job at the bookies as well. But it's a good thing. Ye like it here, don't ye? Ye've got Grace and her brother to play with.'

'But what about Braehead? And my keyboard lessons with Mrs Stafford?'

'I'm sure they've got a music teacher here. I'll get yer lessons sorted closer to when the school goes back. And ye've got Iain's keyboard to play.'

Granpa shook the tile sack and took out a couple of tiles. I didn't know how he could be so calm.

'Did you get loads of money?' I asked him.

'Money? What are ye on aboot?'

'For the house. I know houses are worth loads. Is that why we left?'

'Well, hen, the house isnae really sold, so to speak. It

wisnae really ours to begin with. It belonged to the Council. I gave them the keys back.'

'It was. It was ours. It still is ours. You didnae even ask me.'

'Because it was a surprise, Mary. I knew ye'd like it here. It's better than Stirling.'

'But you didnae even check. If you gave away our house keys, you must've planned it ages ago. I didnae even bring my bronze swimming certificate. How am I going to get it back?'

'We needed a change, Mary. I thought it would be good to get ye away fae where the robbery happened.'

'You didnae care about that. You just wanted to spend all your time with Iain and drink. And you didnae even ask if I liked it here.'

'Ye're getting yersel in a tizzy. Ye should go to your room and calm doon.'

I was starting to cry, again. I didn't care. It was only me and Granpa and it didn't matter if he saw. It was good that he saw. He needed to feel bad about lying to me.

'And you lied about the robbers in Perth,' I said. 'You left me there alone and went away and didnae even tell me what happened.'

'Och, stop going on aboot that. I was making sure the people were safe.'

'I dinnae believe you.'

My voice was going all high.

'It disnae matter if ye believe me or no. It's the truth. Jesus Christ, Mary, I thought ye'd be happy.' Granpa shook his head. 'It's no like ye had any friends in Stirling anyway, after that Leona girl ditched ye.'

I swept the Scrabble board off the table. The tiles went

everywhere. Probably under the fridge even. Then I ran down the hall to my room and slammed the door. I thought about running out the house, but Granpa would've run up and caught me. My legs were wobbly and I only just made it to my room without falling down.

I lay on the bed and put my head under the pillows. I couldn't think properly because I had so many thoughts. They were all fighting inside my head and instead of being able to choose one, I cried instead.

Portree was my new home. I couldn't believe it. It didn't feel real. I was stuck living in Iain's house, forever. Granpa had known he would have a friend in Portree. He couldn't have known I would find Grace. He only cared that *he* would have someone.

I would have to go to a new school. I felt sick thinking about it. I would be the new girl that everyone made up stories about and no one would want to be my class partner, not even Grace because she would be in Primary 7 and she wouldn't talk to me during school time. The other Primary 7s would say, *"you're not hanging around with that Primary 5, are you?"* and she'd say, *"no, of course not"*.

That's why Granpa had made me take all my clothes and toys and everything from home. Because it wasn't home anymore.

♪

CHAPTER EIGHTEEN

I stayed with my head under the pillows till I smelled the tea cooking. I guessed sausages. I was hungry and crying made me thirsty. But I didn't want to see Granpa. He would make me say sorry and I didn't want to. If he said sorry to me, maybe that would be okay. But the house was gone and his job was gone too. It was done. He was the one in charge. There was no one to complain to. I would just need to get used to living in Portree, forever. But if he'd only asked me first, I might've felt better. I didn't have to forgive him. I could pretend to, but still be angry deep down.

The lights were on in the kitchen. It was still bright outside, but when they were making our tea, Granpa and Iain liked all the lights to be on. It was one of their funny grown-up things that they did every time.

'You all right there, Mary?' Iain asked. 'I want you to know that I'm a neutral party in all of this.'

Granpa was looking at the pan and not at me. I was right. It was sausages.

'I'm okay,' I said.

My mouth felt weird when I spoke. I had cried so much it felt funny to be talking again.

'Take a seat, hen,' Granpa said. 'Tea's nearly ready. Get the tomato sauce oot for me.'

I got the tomato sauce out the fridge. In Stirling, we kept it in the cupboard, but Iain kept it in the fridge. It was cold when you squeezed it over your sausages, but it still tasted the same. We weren't going back to Stirling; it would be cold tomato sauce, forever.

Granpa was acting like nothing had happened. I thought his eyes looked quite red, but that was probably from the steam off the frying pan. I couldn't see any of the Scrabble tiles. He must've picked them all up. I felt bad. His back would've been really sore doing it.

'Let me tell you a story, Mary,' Iain said.

I sat down next to him and listened while I picked off the label on the sauce bottle.

'In March,' he said. 'I was sitting at this very table looking at the Stirling Observer. I've got a cousin in Stirling who sends me his copies when he's done with them. There was a name I recognised. An old friend of mine I hadn't seen in a long, long time. Your granpa. Two idiots had turned over a bookies in Stirling and given him a right whack on the shoulder. So, with a little investigative research, I got your granpa's phone number.' Iain looked chuffed with himself. 'It was me who told your granpa how great it was here in Portree. Your granpa said, "*Would Mary like it? That's the most important thing*". I said, "*Of course, what little girl wouldn't love seeing those harbour houses every day?*" Mary, hand on heart, it was me who convinced your granpa to bring you here. I even offered up my spare room for you, didn't I?'

He took his hand off his heart and was rubbing his bald head and smiling.

'You promise it was you?' I said.

'Mary, if you should be angry with anyone, it's me.'

'It's okay. But you should've told me ages ago that I was staying for good. Both of you.'

'That's true. You can blame your granpa for that one.'

Granpa came over with the plates for all of us. I liked how he could carry all three plates over his arms and not drop anything. It was sausages and chips and beans, again.

'Sorry aboot earlier,' Granpa said. 'I lost my temper. Ye ken I didnae mean any of that. I've made ye my special dish. They're called "*Sorry Sausages*".'

I couldn't help but smile. That was the stupidest thing I'd heard in ages. But still quite funny. Because I laughed, he thought I'd forgiven him. I had a little, because it was Iain's fault as well, but not completely. He could've stood up to Iain and told him how I didn't want another music teacher. I liked Mrs Stafford and didn't want to change to a new person. The new teacher wouldn't know that I had smaller hands than most people and couldn't play 'C' and 'A' at the same time with my right hand. Mrs Stafford knew all the things I wasn't good at already. I didn't want to disappoint a new teacher.

'Iain,' I said. 'Have you pulled the strings about getting me a ticket for the ball?'

'I'm working on it, Mary. But I'll up my efforts since you've had the bad news of having to stay in my house permanently.'

'I might not need them. Grace might take me because Tom cannae dance with his stookie.'

'What an ordeal,' Granpa said. 'It's a bloody dance. Invite only, my arse.'

'It's a *ball*, Granpa, not a dance. And, and… I dinnae want to risk not getting in, like last time.'

'I ken, I ken. Disnae change, does it? No matter where ye

are. Rules, rules and more rules.'

'You know how these teuchters are, Arthur,' Iain said. 'They're set in their ways. They love the exclusivity of it all.'

'I say ye go, even if ye dinnae get a ticket,' Granpa said. 'Bloody teuchters.'

'But they'll stop me, Granpa.'

'Ye're only wee. I'm sure there's somewhere ye could slip in. I'll create a distraction for ye.'

'I dinnae like the sound of that. Oh, and you swore there. That's 50p you owe me.'

Plan A was going with Grace and Mr and Mrs MacLeod.

Plan B was Iain getting me a ticket.

Plan C was sneaking in. I really didn't like thinking about Plan C, but it was better than

Plan D: not going at all.

'That's amazing news,' Grace said.

'I suppose,' I said.

'It is. You don't have to go away at the end of summer now. We can hang around at playtime and lunch at school.'

'But then you're going to high school next year so you won't be able to.'

'I'll come down at lunchtime.'

'High school people don't hang around with primary school people.'

'Well, I will. I don't care that you're younger, Mary. You're the same age as Thomas, but you're like fifty times smarter than him.'

We were at the harbour. Grace had brought lots of bits of paper from her dad's printer. We were folding them up into planes and chucking them towards the boats. But

Grace didn't know how to fold them properly and I was copying her. None of our planes were getting very far. Some went straight down in a nose dive. Some went right to one side like the wind had taken it, even if there wasn't a wind blowing. Some gave the seagulls a fright.

I tried getting one on top of the pink house. I didn't have enough strength in my arms and the wind wasn't letting me, anyway. My plan was to get it to land on the pink house roof, then it would sit there for years and years. I could find it when I owned the pink house and say *those were the days*.

That was one good thing about staying in Portree forever. There was more chance of me being able to live in the pink house if I actually lived in Portree, just down the road. I would be there when the *FOR SALE* sign went up and I could tell them to take it down because I wanted it. They'd ask, "*How are you paying?*" and I'd say, "*Is money okay?*" and I'd open my briefcase filled with one hundred pound notes. They wouldn't need to count it because they trusted me and they could see the Queen's face staring out from all the notes.

'You're lucky you're not in Thomas's class,' Grace said. 'He's in the P5/6 this year. He's not happy having to go with the older ones. Dad said, "*Do you want to be with the older ones or be in my class?*" and he chose the joint class straight away. I would've too.'

'If he was your teacher, would you call him Mr MacLeod or Dad?'

'I dunno. Mr MacLeod I suppose.'

'I call him Mr MacLeod anyway, so that's fine.'

'You'll need to tell me whenever he gets something wrong and I can make fun of him.'

'He's a teacher, he willnae get anything wrong.'

Grace threw a plane which went all the way past the red buoy. Granpa told me I was allowed to call them *guirls* if I wanted to.

'You'll be one of the oldest in the school next year,' I said.

'It'll be good. I might be your wet playtime monitor. We can play Monopoly. As long as I'm the top hat.'

'Your dad probably thinks I'm a bit mad,' I said. 'When he told me I was in his class, I told him there was no chance.'

'I'm sure he'll just think it's funny.'

I walked Grace back to her house. I liked walking around Portree because it didn't take long to get to anywhere. I would need to get to know everyone since I was staying for good. The more walking about I did, the more people would see me and think, *"there's Mary walking past, wonder what she's up to? Probably being nice to people like usual"*.

I went into Grace's house for a bit. I wasn't staying for tea though. If Granpa made my tea and I wasn't back for it, he'd not be happy. Mr MacLeod told Grace to go through to the kitchen and wash her hands.

'Mary,' Mr MacLeod said. 'Is everything all right at home?'

I knew what that meant. That meant they thought Granpa wasn't looking after me properly. I had heard Mrs Lithgow ask James Hamilton the same question after home time one day. He had worn the same jumper every day for weeks. You could tell by the muddy patches on the elbows. It wasn't even a proper maroon Braehead jumper. It was a bright red one. It was *unofficial*. He was crying and he had to go to a *foster home* after that.

'Aye, it's fine,' I said. 'I was only pretending I didnae know about the school.'

He looked confused, like I must've looked when he first told me about the school.

'You were?'

'I was kidding you on. I'm looking forward to it, Mr MacLeod.'

'So you and your Granpa, you're all fine? Everyone's happy?'

'Aye, he's the one who taught me how to play jokes on people. I was only playing a joke on you, Mr MacLeod. Sorry if you got upset.'

'Not a problem, Mary. You were very convincing. You'll need to audition for the school play.'

Tom came down the stairs. He slid his crutches down before him and they made a big clatter once they reached the bottom. Tom went down the stairs on his bum, one at a time. *Bump bump bump.*

'Is Mary staying for tea?' Tom asked.

'Afraid not,' Mr MacLeod said. 'Get those crutches picked up, Thomas. Your mum'll be in soon and she'll go ballistic if she sees you launching them down the stairs again.'

He picked up the crutches and swung into the living room.

'Look who signed my stookie, Mary,' he said. 'One of your pals, eh?'

I crouched down to see, but not too close, I didn't want that strange smell up my nose again. The names on it from before were still there. *Mum, Dad, Grace, Mary.* There was one new name. *Craig.*

'I thought Craig went away?' I said.

'He was going to, but he missed his bus the night I broke my leg.'

'I think your mum's a little bit in love with him,' Mr

MacLeod said. 'She was very thankful for him taking care of Thomas after his accident. We both were.' He tidied up the magazines on the living room table and put the remotes in a nice, straight line. 'Turned out Craig had dropped out of university, so Linda got him an interview in the chippy at the harbour and he got the job. She set him up with Kelly too, a friend of hers from the hospital.' Tom made a face behind Mr MacLeod's back like he thought Kelly was disgusting. 'He's still staying at the hostel,' Mr MacLeod went on. 'But he's planning to save up and rent somewhere nearby. His whole life changed because he helped our Thomas when he was in need. It's a nice story, really. I should send it in to one of the papers.'

'I need to go,' I said. 'Granpa's waiting on me.'

All my worries came back. Craig wasn't going anywhere. He was in Portree for good and so were we. It was up to me to keep Craig from finding out Granpa was the man he was after. He wasn't looking for his friend. His friend was made up. He had already met Granpa and hadn't known Granpa was the man he was looking for. That meant it was okay for them to see each other walking through town. But that was the only worry I could get rid of.

I had to make sure he never saw Granpa's real handwriting. That wouldn't be too hard, but it was still a lot of pressure. I was only eight. But I had to handle it. It was my *cross to bear*. Instead of Jesus with his cross, it was me with Craig. He would've been way too heavy for me to carry, though.

If I thought about Craig and his bit of paper, which

was really *our* bit of paper, too much, I got stressed and wanted to curl into a ball on the floor. But I couldn't do that. It was still my summer holiday and I wouldn't let anything ruin it.

CHAPTER NINETEEN

Iain's back garden wasn't very big and didn't have the kind of grass you'd want to roll around on, but it was good for sunbathing. Iain had pulled out three of the kitchen chairs on to the grass for us. It was *taps aff* weather so Granpa and Iain weren't wearing their T-shirts. Iain had loads of chest hair like Sean Connery.

'Mr MacLeod asked if everything was all right at home,' I said to Granpa. 'Well, he said *home,* but I knew he meant Iain's house. Do I call Iain's house my home now?'

'Aye, this is home noo,' Granpa replied. 'What did ye tell him?'

'That I was only pretending the other day. That I really did know we were staying here. That it was all just a joke.'

Granpa opened one eye and looked over at me and smiled.

'Clever girl, and he believed ye?'

'Aye. He was saying I would be a good actress. I think I would be too.'

'I'm glad ye told him that, hen. D'ye ken why?'

'Because he would make me go to a foster home if I said I wasn't happy.'

Granpa leaned forward on his chair and looked over at Iain. They smiled at each other.

'I'm telling you,' Iain said, going back to reading the paper. 'She's far too smart to be related to you, Arthur.'

Granpa turned in his chair to face me.

'Ye're happy living with me, aren't ye, Mary?' he asked.

I nodded. I felt sweaty from sitting in the sun, especially at the bottom of my neck.

'And ye'll put up with Iain?'

'I suppose,' I said. 'But I dinnae like you not telling me the truth. You should always tell me everything, all the time.'

I hadn't told Granpa about Craig, but that was just to stop him being worried. That was allowed.

'And I will fae noo on,' Granpa said. 'Mary, if anyone thinks I'm no doing a good job looking after ye, they could take ye away fae me.' He stood up and paced up and down the square of grass we had. 'Ye get annoyed with me sometimes, but think how annoyed ye'd get with the people ye'd have to go and live with. Strangers who wouldnae even ken ye. Folk who dinnae watch James Bond films and hate Elvis.' He did his best Elvis pose, but I was better. 'Folk who'd think ye were making a racket with yer keyboard and never let ye play it again.'

That was true. Granpa wasn't perfect, but he was still the best person to take care of me. I thought maybe the MacLeod's wouldn't be so bad, but I still wasn't sure if I liked Mrs MacLeod. If it wasn't for her getting Craig a job and a girlfriend, he would be gone for good.

'Granpa, I told Mr and Mrs MacLeod I was from Livingston.'

'Why'd ye do that?'

He sat back down and picked up his beer bottle.

'You told Andy we were from Livingston,' I said. 'On the boat, he said, "*where are you from?*" and you said Livingston.

We're undercover, remember?'

'So I did. Well, if it comes up again, just say... just say ye were born in Livingston but ye moved to Stirling. Say ye got confused. Ye're a wee lassie, they're no gonnae think ye're a criminal mastermind.'

'Okay.'

'What a web of lies you two have concocted,' Iain said, folding his paper and leaning his head back. 'It's like being in a room with James Bond and M.'

I loved that idea. Even though he probably meant it the other way round; in my head I was definitely James Bond. Granpa was old like M, so that made sense. All that was missing was the gadgets. We couldn't afford them, but I would have money and buy us an Aston Martin when I grew up. That was the number one spy car. Pierce Brosnan drove one in *Goldeneye*. That was my favourite Bond film. I didn't want to go to Russia, but the hats they had there looked great and fluffy and warm. Daniel Craig drove an Aston Martin in one of his films, but he was too serious. Pierce would make jokes even when he was in trouble. That was how the *real* James Bond acted. Daniel Craig needed to cheer up a bit.

Me and Grace were watching telly at her house. *The Chase*. It was the same programme we had watched before, but I had learned its name. It was called that because you were getting chased by the people at the top of the screen. Not really though. They were mostly quite fat, so if it had been a real chase you would've won every time. Apart from when the black man was on. He was skinny and had a nice voice. Deep and manly. He always put up a good chase.

Everyone was home. I was always nervous when Mrs

MacLeod was about. She came in the living room and sat on the couch reading a magazine. Grace and me were on the floor, right in front of the telly.

'Back again, Mary?' Mrs MacLeod said.

'Hiya,' I said. 'We're guessing answers on *The Chase.*'

'Does your grandfather not worry about you?'

She was keeping her eyes on her magazine like she didn't care.

'He says it's fine as long as I'm with Grace.'

'I wish I could say the same about Grace. My children have a way of getting in trouble when you're around, Mary.'

Most grown-ups, even when they were angry, they were still nice to me because I was so young. But Mrs MacLeod didn't care that I was young. She treated me the same way as a grown-up. Only I couldn't talk back like a grown-up. I didn't know how. I hadn't learned enough grown-up words to make it a fair fight. I couldn't even guess answers on *The Chase* right.

'I didnae make Tom fall off the skateboard,' I said.

'Thomas,' she snapped back. 'Yes, well, you weren't much help after it happened, were you? I heard you ran off. It was lucky Craig was there.'

'Mum,' Grace said. 'Leave her alone. It was Thomas's fault.'

Mr MacLeod came through. He was making the tea. I was to let Granpa know if I was staying at Grace's for tea. I took out my phone to text him. Only one bar of battery again. Granpa told me to charge it overnight but I always forgot. I typed: *Coming home for tea.* I didn't want to be around Mrs MacLeod if I didn't have to.

'Mary,' Mr MacLeod said. 'My future pupil! Listen, one good thing's come out of Thomas's little accident. We've got a spare ticket for the ball if you'd still like to come.'

Grace looked at me. We were both smiling like mad. She hugged me. We were both lying down on the hard floor though so it was a bit sore.

'Kevin,' Mrs MacLeod said.

She didn't look happy. She nodded towards the kitchen and her and Mr MacLeod went through to talk to each other.

'I dinnae think your mum's happy,' I said.

'Who cares?' Grace said. 'If my dad says you're coming, then you're coming. It'll be the best night ever.'

She was right. I tried not to think about Mrs MacLeod. I'd done nothing wrong, she was being an idiot. I felt sorry for Mr MacLeod having to spend all his time with her. If he'd wanted to have an *affair* with another woman, I wouldn't have been annoyed with him.

When I was leaving, I shouted up to Tom in his bedroom.

'Bye, Tom!'

I shouted it as loud as I could so Mrs MacLeod would hear. I could call him Tom if I wanted. And if it annoyed Mrs MacLeod then who cared? Not me. She was a grown-up, but she needed to grow up.

When I got back, Iain stood up from the kitchen table. He was pretending to play a trumpet, doing the noise with his mouth and pressing invisible buttons.

'It's the Princess of Portree,' he announced. 'Miss Mary Sutherland.'

Then him and Granpa were clapping. It was only the two of them so it sounded a bit weird. Like how clapping sounded on the telly when the golf was on and you were allowed to clap but you weren't to get carried away.

'What's going on?' I asked.

'Ye're going to the ball, Cinderella,' Granpa said.

'Remember Gerry?' Iain said. 'The man who had a run-in with an intruder last month? He's still not up to dancing. He's very kindly letting you take his ticket.'

I didn't know what to say.

'Thanks, Iain,' I said.

Their smiles turned to frowns and they looked at each other.

'I'll admit, Mary,' Iain said. 'I thought you might be a bit more excited than this.'

'It's just…Mr MacLeod said I could go with them. Tom isnae using his ticket anymore.'

'Oh, right. Well then. No harm done I suppose.'

'But thank you so much anyway.'

I went up and hugged Iain, for the first time. Granpa was winking at me when I did it. He wasn't related to us, but he was sort of starting to feel like part of our family. Maybe like an uncle that you didn't know you had, then when you met him, you thought, *"he's fine, he can stick around"*.

'Arthur,' Iain said. 'Why don't you use Gerry's ticket?'

'Me?' Granpa answered, 'At a ball?'

'Oh, *pleeease*, Granpa.'

I hadn't even thought of Granpa coming. That would make it absolutely perfect. If the ball was an ice cream sundae, Granpa would be the cherry on the top. Imagine that. A person on the top of a sundae. Then the ice cream might melt and they could drown in the ice cream. That big an ice cream would be dangerous.

'I dinnae even have a kilt,' Granpa said.

'I dinnae have a dress either,' I said. 'But we can get them.'

'You can get kilts at the Aros centre,' Iain said. 'I'll take you in the jeep. And I can get Miriam in the paper shop to put together a dress for Mary. She's a bit sweet on me.'

I needed a *gown* not an ordinary dress, but convincing Granpa was the most important thing. I looked up at Granpa with my eyes shut tight and my mouth open to show all my teeth together. That was my best *'pleeease'* face.

'The things I do for ye, Mary.'

It was all settled then. I started dancing the Gay Gordons around the living room just myself. I didn't even need a partner. I had learned the steps so well. Nothing could stop me and Grace going to the dance together. Granpa would be there and if the lady at the door said, *"no, Mary, you're not coming in"*, Granpa would tie her up and leave her sleeping in the cloakroom and we'd dance all night long.

I was practising *Eight Days a Week* on the keyboard. The idea of the song was that the man from *The Beatles* wanted the lady's love so much, he wanted it eight days a week. That was a bit over the top. He wouldn't have time for any other important things, like sleeping or buying the milk.

Granpa and Iain were playing dominoes in the kitchen.

'Can't put if off any longer,' Iain said. 'Once you start playing dominoes, that's it. You're an old man. We're old men, Arthur.'

Something banged against the living room window.

'What the hell was that?' Iain said.

Another bang.

'Mary,' Granpa said. 'Come and sit in here.'

I sat in the kitchen while Iain and Granpa went to the front door to see what was making the banging. I wasn't worried. Nothing was coming through the windows, it wasn't bullets from a gun. You didn't get guns in Scotland.

'Hey, get back here!' I heard Iain shout.

'We've seen yer faces!' Granpa shouted.

They came back inside, but left the door open.

'What happened?' I asked.

'A couple of lads pelting the house with eggs,' Iain said. 'They took off sharpish when they saw us.'

Iain looked in the cupboard under the sink to get a sponge to clean the egg off the windows. He filled up a bucket from the tap and squirted some washing up liquid in. The foam bubbled up and went over the sides of the bucket. It dripped all through the living room when he carried it outside and made dark spots on the carpet.

'Did you see their faces, Granpa?'

'Naw, they had their scarves and hoods up. I shouted that to scare them. Looked like two boys. One tall, one short. Ye dinnae ken any lads who'd want to egg Iain's house, do ye, Mary?'

'Naw,' I said.

I was getting so good at lying, I could even kid Granpa on.

CHAPTER TWENTY

Granpa was shaking my shoulders. Normally he let me get up on my own, but he had come into my room without even knocking. The curtains were open.

'Wakey wakey,' he said. 'It's a braw morning.'

The light hurt my eyes so I went into squint mode. Squint mode stopped the light getting into my whole eye and waking me up. Granpa was standing by the window like he was waiting for something.

'Up ye get. There's something ootside for ye.'

He had on a big smile so I knew it was something good. Unless he was playing a joke on me to get me out of bed. I decided to trust him in case it really was something good. I went out without any socks on or anything. The ground was dry so it was fine.

On the drive, in front of the garage door, was my bike. My bike from home. I was so happy. I had completely forgotten about it.

'How'd you get it up here, Granpa?' I asked.

'I had it boxed up and delivered. It took a while since we're a bit oot the way up here.'

I got on it. It was as purple and sparkly as I remembered. My basket at the front was a wee bit bashed, but that was okay. I knew that wasn't Granpa's fault. I hadn't even thought about leaving it behind. And I didn't have to because the special bike van had brought it all the way to Portree. I couldn't have cycled it the whole way. Imagine that. My bum would've been way too sore and numb, and it wouldn't have felt like I had a bum anymore.

'Ye didnae think I'd leave it behind, did ye?' Granpa asked. 'That was yer birthday and Christmas combined last year. Arthur Sutherland disnae throw away money if he can help it.'

Even though I knew we were there in Portree for good, I kept thinking that I would see things from home again. That one day the holiday would end and we'd go back to normal. I was still getting used to Portree being where I called home. If I ever went back to Stirling, it would only be to visit.

I got dressed super-fast so I could go out on my bike. Granpa made me eat two bits of toast before he'd let me out the door. I ate it to keep him happy. Granpa made me my toast most of the time, even though Iain was better at it. It was Iain's toaster, he knew how to work it properly. He knew the best setting was half way between the 2 and the 3, but then a wee bit more to the 3. Granpa never took it out till it was starting to go black. He called Iain's toast *warm bread*.

Grace's bike was in the shed and she had to ask her dad to get it out for her.

'Finally,' Mr MacLeod said. 'I thought that bike wasn't going to turn a wheel all summer.

He had to get the shed key from a drawer in the kitchen. There were so many things in the drawer it took him ages. Scissors and a ball of string and lots of little black things he said were Alan's keys. There were so many, Alan must've had loads of sheds.

Grace's bike was behind lots of other things. Shovels and tins of paint and things so rusty I couldn't even tell what they were meant to be. Mr MacLeod was sweating and grunting a lot.

'Dad,' Grace said. 'Can we have some money to go to the shop?'

He looked in his pocket and gave us the change he had. £1.50. So that was 75p each for us to spend. I worked it out in my head really fast.

The chain had come off Grace's bike so Mr MacLeod had to sort that. There was black oil all over his hands, but he didn't seem to care. He kept on touching the chain, anyway.

'You girls are keeping me busy,' he said. 'I'm meant to be relaxing y'know.'

'Don't teachers get too much time off?' I said.

'Why d'you think that, Mary?'

'Granpa says teachers can't ever complain, because they got so many holidays. They've got it too good, he says.'

He was smiling and shaking his head. He used the hairy bit of his arm to wipe his sweat away from his forehead because he couldn't use his hands or he'd get oil all across his forehead.

Grace and me were jumping on the trampoline while we waited for the bike to get fixed.

'The other night,' I said. 'Two boys threw eggs at our house.'

'Eggs?' Grace said. 'I thought you only did that on Halloween. Did you see who it was?'

'Naw. Granpa and Iain chased them away. But Granpa said it was two boys and one of them was tall and one was short. I think it was Lewis and Jamie.'

'Why them?'

'Because of me throwing the ball in the water.'

I was getting out of breath from all the jumping.

'I forgot about that,' Grace said. 'Did you call the police?'

'I dinnae think they did. Iain and Granpa think it was just two boys doing it for fun. I didnae tell them about the football.'

'We should get them back.'

'I dinnae want to,' I said, getting off the trampoline for a rest. 'I dinnae want to make them any angrier. D'you think they'll leave me alone now?'

'Dunno. I wonder why they didn't egg our house too.'

'It was me who threw the football.'

'You probably shouldn't have done that.'

'It was you who told me to!'

'That doesn't mean you actually had to do it, Mary. I'm only ten. I'm not a grown-up.'

I spotted Tom watching us from his window. I waved. He ducked down and pulled the curtains together.

We cycled to the paper shop. They sold toys there which you didn't get in the Co-op. We left our bikes outside.

'I dinnae have my bike lock,' I said. 'They might get stolen.'

'We're fine,' Grace said. 'People don't steal bikes here. It's safe.'

I couldn't trust everything Grace said. It couldn't be completely safe if Craig was still around and looking for Granpa. I didn't think he would want my bike though.

There was a little bell that tinkled when you opened the shop's door.

'Hello, Grace,' said the lady behind the counter. 'Oh and is this your friend? I've seen you two running about.'

'This is Mary,' Grace said.

'Nice to meet you, Mary,' the lady said. 'I'm Mrs Jeffries.'

'Hiya, Mrs Jeffries,' I said. 'We've left our bikes outside. Is that alright?'

Grace had said it was okay but I thought it was a good idea to check with Mrs Jeffries. She might've been annoyed at people blocking her shop. We hadn't left them right on the doorstep or anything but I was nervous.

'Of course,' Mrs Jeffries said. 'They'll be fine.'

'Told you,' Grace said.

I was looking at the newspapers. Sometimes there'd be a bright advert on the front telling you about the vouchers inside. On the front of *The Sun* there was a bit at the top saying there was a voucher inside for a free trip to Legoland. That sounded amazing.

'Mary, come and look at the toys,' Grace said.

'I think I'm gonnae buy this paper,' I said. 'You get a free trip to Legoland in it.'

'I've seen things like that before. It's not completely free. I showed it to my dad and he said you need to save up loads of the vouchers and you still have to pay to get there. And it's really far away.'

I thought Granpa might take me anyway. If I asked especially nicely. He owed me for lying about moving away from Stirling. I could get loads of treats from him if I pretended I was still upset about staying in Portree. And I could use my pocket money from the Secret Pocket Money Spy Game.

I put the newspaper up on the counter.

'This and a 35p mix-up, please,' I said.

'Coming up,' Mrs Jeffries said. 'Are you being a good girl and getting a paper for your dad?'

'It's for me. I dinnae have a dad.'

I wondered if people would keep asking me about my mum and dad all my life. They were obsessed.

'Oh... right. It's good that you're taking an interest in the news. But don't believe everything you read in there.'

'Dinnae worry. I know you need to collect more than one voucher for the trip to Legoland.'

She looked like she didn't know what I was on about. She took one of the 30p mix-ups that were already made up and added another 5p worth of sweets to it. The bag had pink and white stripes instead of plain white, like at home. I gave Grace the change, but there weren't any toys for 75p so she got a Wispa Gold and a 25p mix-up.

We took our bikes up the Lump. It was a really sunny day, we didn't even think about going to sit inside. It was rubbish when you sat inside and it was roasting outside. We couldn't get all the way up pedalling our bikes though. It was too steep. We got off and walked them up the gravelly path. The tyres made a scraping sound against the stones and lots of grey dust swept up behind us. Grace wanted to go to the tower, but I wanted to look at my paper so we went to the Bowl. There was lots of space to spread open the newspaper and nice grass there to lie down on.

Page 3 had a pretty lady on it.

'My teacher last year,' Grace said. 'Mr Archibald, he always read *The Sun* at his desk. But he skipped this page.'

'Was he not allowed to look?'

'I dunno. I think men really like to look. But he didn't want us to see.'

The lady was only in her bra and pants. She was doing

her best smile to show off her white teeth. Her name was Sandy and she was from Wrexham.

'D'you think that's her job?' I asked. 'To get her picture taken all the time?'

'Maybe. She looks like she's enjoying it.'

'And it's really sunny where she is. There's a swimming pool behind her, look.'

'I wouldn't want people looking at me without my clothes on, though,' Grace said.

'Me too. Everyone would laugh at you because they'd seen you in the paper.'

'But if I wanted people to see me without my clothes on, then I'd do it, so I'd get a holiday.'

If you wanted a holiday, all you had to do was tell the paper that they could take your picture in your bra and pants and they'd send you off to somewhere sunny to get the photo taken. As long as you were really pretty. I wasn't worried about being pretty when I grew up because I didn't want to be in the paper and I didn't care about boys wanting to marry me.

The page with the Legoland voucher had little lines for you to follow when you cut it out. You had to do it with a pair of scissors.

'I can rip it,' Grace said. 'I'm good at it.'

'Naw, I'm going to wait till I get back to Iain's. In case it tears.'

I believed Grace was good at ripping, but I didn't want to risk it. I didn't have money for another paper. I didn't even know if they let you buy two newspapers in the one day.

Grace was bored with the paper and she was throwing her sweets up in the air to catch them in her mouth. If she missed, the sweets landed on the grass which was fine. If it had been concrete, then that would've been disgusting, but grass was okay because it was much cleaner.

Most of the pages had a serious story about *terrorists* or how Britain needed to get fixed, then a few little funny stories too. About people falling asleep when they shouldn't have or people dressed up as superheroes and climbing places they weren't allowed.

There was a story that made my heart go fast in my chest and I forgot to breathe.

ELVIS HAS LEFT THE BUILDING: THREE MEN STILL WANTED AFTER BOOKIES BASH-UP

I felt dizzy even though I was lying down.

'Grace,' I shouted, 'Come and read this for me.'

She lay back down.

'Why can't you read it?' she asked.

I was too scared, if it was going to say what I thought it would.

'The sun's getting in my eyes,' I said.

Grace put a fried egg in her mouth and started chewing.

'Fine,' she said. 'It says "*Police are still hunting three men following a heist-gone-wrong in Perth last month. Two men in ski-masks attempted the robbery in Ladbrokes on South Methven Street, on the morning of Thursday June 25th. They were interrupted by a third man, who witnesses claim was not a part of the robbery. The third man attacked the robbers whilst wearing an* **ELVIS MASK**, *before fleeing the scene with the money already taken from the till.*

"*The two injured robbers were able to escape before the police arrived. Security cameras around the shop were of little help having been covered in black spray paint. The police are encouraging anyone with any relevant information to contact them."* Why do you care, Mary?'

It was Granpa. It had to be. How many Elvis masks could there be in the world? I couldn't remember the name of the street, but it was Perth and it was a Thursday because my last day at school had been a Wednesday.

'I think they're talking about my granpa,' I said. 'The man that came in and attacked the robbers.'

'Don't be silly, Mary. Why would he have done that?'

'Because they hurt him. They hit his shoulder at the bookies at home. When we were in Perth, he went away for a minute without me and I never knew where he went. Does it say anything else?'

'That's all of it,' Grace said, flicking to the next page to make sure. 'No pictures or anything. It's been quite a long time since it happened.'

'You cannae tell anyone,' I said.

'I won't.'

'I mean it. I know you dinnae believe me, but you cannae tell your mum or dad or Tom. Especially not Tom.'

'Are you going to ask your granpa about it?'

'I dinnae know.'

CHAPTER TWENTY-ONE

The next few days, I thought about the story in the newspaper a lot. I didn't say anything to Granpa about it. I didn't even know how to begin.

I was happy that the robbers had been given a *taste of their own medicine*. But Granpa hadn't told me. He had lied. His last big lie, I let him off with it because I liked Portree. If I let him off with it again, he would keep lying forever and he wouldn't be like Granpa anymore. He would be some new person that had stolen Granpa's face and was wearing it like a mask and had left his body behind in Stirling. I needed *my* Granpa.

I knew who Craig was. I didn't want it to be true, but I knew it deep down. He was one of the robbers. He had robbed the bookies in Stirling and tried again in Perth. I didn't remember either of the robbers being called Craig, but I couldn't make any other story make sense. He didn't know us because he was Guard Robber. He didn't come near us like Desk Robber.

Craig was by himself though. He had told me about his brother and I guessed that was Desk Robber. He hadn't come to Portree for some reason. They wanted their money back. Granpa must've taken it. It was Craig's job to find Granpa, but he hadn't done it. He had failed. Guard Robber didn't know what Granpa's face looked like, but Desk Robber did. If Craig's brother came up to Portree we were *done for*.

Craig had decided to stay in Portree now that he had a job and a girlfriend. He didn't deserve either of them. It was all too much for me to think about. I got a headache whenever I tried to think of ways to keep Granpa safe.

Iain was taking Granpa to try on his kilt at the kilt shop. You didn't get kilts in normal clothes shops like Primark. They were too special and you were only allowed to sell them if you were an expert.

'And ye'll give me a text when you get to Grace's house?' Granpa asked me.

'Aye,' I said, as I closed the front door behind me.

'Ye sure ye dinnae want to join us?'

'Naw, Grace told me there's something she wants to show me.'

They drove off in Iain's jeep. The tyres made a crunchy noise when they were reversing over the stones. They were waving at me as they went down the hill. I got on my bike and cycled along with them for a few seconds, but then Iain *vroomed* up the car and they went off too fast for me to catch up. There was a great smell of petrol the car left behind. I could smell it all the way down the hill, but then when I got to where the waterfall was, the smell had disappeared and it was back to the normal smell of air.

I wasn't going to Grace's. I didn't care if I got in trouble because I knew I could bring up Granpa's lies about the robbers and I wouldn't be in trouble anymore. He would be in trouble instead. It was the *ace up my sleeve*.

I went back to the house. Iain always left the door unlocked. The house felt so empty without Granpa and

Iain. I was nervous but I knew they wouldn't be back for at least an hour.

Granpa's room was the smallest in the house. I was looking for the black bag he had taken out in Perth. I wanted to know what he'd taken with him and if it could be used as *evidence against him.* I was ninety-nine percent sure it wouldn't be a gun. You didn't get guns in Scotland.

His rucksack was under the bed. I didn't want to be a nosey parker so I closed my eyes when I opened it. I stuck my hand in and felt around for the slippery feeling of a black bag. It was like a game. I could feel a photo frame. That was his picture of Granny. Then I felt a bit of string. I went into squint mode. It was the string from my Elvis mask. It was poking out of a black bag.

I took out the rucksack and laid it on the bed. I pulled out the Elvis mask. There were spots of red on it. I tried to wipe them off but they were stuck. I used my fingernail and they popped off.

The other thing in the bag was heavy. It fell out and bounced on the covers. I didn't know exactly what it was. It was gold and had four holes. It sort of looked like a stretched out dog's paw. I picked it up and slipped my fingers into the holes. If it was jewellery, it was really sore to wear. You couldn't have worn it for long. It had red on it too.

Knock knock.

Someone was at the front door. I put the heavy thing back in the black bag and put it into the rucksack. I pushed it right under the bed as far as my arms could get it. I grabbed the Elvis mask and rushed through to my room and put it under my pillow. Granpa didn't need it. It was mine.

Knock knock.

I creeped through to the living room. Whoever was at

the door had opened the letterbox and was staring at me. It was too late to hide. I opened the door. It was Mr Ferguson, Granpa's boss from the bookies. His old boss. He looked nothing like he usually did. He wasn't wearing a shirt and tie. He was in a T-shirt, and he had a scratchy-looking beard.

'Mary,' he said. 'Is your Granpa home?'

'Hiya, Mr Ferguson. Did you come all this way to see us?'

'It's not like I've got anything else on these days. Is he in?'

I could tell he was angry and there was no chance of getting a smile from him. I wanted to close the door.

'He's away out,' I said.

'When's he due back?'

'I dinnae know. Is something wrong?'

'Don't act innocent with me, girl,' he said, pointing at me. 'I know it was Arthur who planted the money in those shoes you gave me. I know it was him who phoned in the tip-off and told the police right where to fucking look.'

I pursed my lips tight together to keep from crying. Mr Ferguson was staring over the top of me to try and look inside.

'I think you should go,' I said, but he wasn't paying attention.

'I spent weeks looking for him before I found out he was hiding up here like a fucking coward. It's lucky your old neighbour Malcolm is a gossip. You've got the money in there, haven't you?'

He tried to look inside but there was nothing to see. He stepped back to look round the side of the house and I slammed the door shut. He pushed against it but I managed to get the lock turned just in time. I could hear him shouting through the glass.

'Let me in, you stupid wee cow. Open up, you hear me? You've fucking had it.'

'Please go away,' I said.

I sat down with my back against the door. I closed my eyes and put my hands over my ears. I couldn't hear or see anything. I tried to think of good things, like when me and Granpa sang Elvis songs. *Marie's the Name (His Latest Flame)*. Granpa changed it to *Mary's the Name* when he sang it. It was like Elvis had written the song just for me.

I opened my eyes and ears. I could hear crying. It wasn't my crying. I had been brave and held it in. Through the glass, Mr Ferguson was leaning against the door, on the other side. He was crying like a P1 on his first day of school.

'I'm sorry, Mary,' he said. 'I'm so sorry.'

I left the door locked. It might've been a trick.

'Go away, Mr Ferguson,' I told him.

'I didn't mean to... I'm sorry.'

He stayed there for a while, sitting still and crying. I moved away from the door so he couldn't see me anymore. I wanted him to think I was away doing something else. Really, I was still watching him through the glass. He didn't say anything else when he stood up and walked away.

I pulled my phone out my pocket to phone Granpa, but it was out of battery. I connected it to my charger in my bedroom and as soon as it turned on again I phoned him.

'Granpa,' I said, when he answered. 'Mr Ferguson was here.'

He didn't say anything for a while.

'Right,' he said. 'What happened?'

'He was angry. He said something about the shoes we gave him and a tip-off. Then he started crying.'

'Is he away?'

'Aye.'

'Have ye locked the door?'

'Aye.'

'Stay there. We're coming home.'

It felt like forever till they got back. The clock in the living room knew I was paying attention to it and it ticked even louder than usual. I tried to get the little tail to stop swinging but it kept going back and forward when I took my hand away.

I was watching from the window when the jeep pulled in. Granpa had a kilt bag with him. I was glad they had bought it before they came back. Granpa couldn't go to the ball if he didn't have his kilt.

Granpa came in and dumped his bag on the couch and Iain put the kettle on.

'Tell me everything he said to ye,' Granpa said.

I did my best. I couldn't remember every word. I said *effing* instead of *fucking*. Granpa couldn't have been mad if I had said it, I was only copying Mr Ferguson. But I didn't want to say the *'F' word*. Swearing didn't feel good coming out of my mouth, even if Grace could do it without caring. That was something we didn't have in common. We had different *personalities*.

'Mary, I've no idea what he's talking aboot,' Granpa said. 'He must've got sacked after we left and he's blaming us for some reason. D'ye remember what I told ye about Michael Jackson before he died?'

'He went daft?' I said.

'Exactly. Mr Ferguson's gone daft the same as Michael Jackson did.'

Granpa phoned the police. It wasn't 999, but some other number which let them know you didn't need them to rush right away. He told them all about Mr Ferguson and how he had *terrified his granddaughter*. Terrified, that was a good word for how scared I'd been. But I'd kept him out of the house. I was quite proud of that. I was strong. The lock on the door was strong too. We made a good team.

'I remember the days,' Iain said. 'When you never would've trusted the police, Arthur.'

'What am I supposed to do?' Granpa said. 'Hunt round Portree for this nutter? We're settled here, Iain. We dinnae need any more trouble.'

I was glad Granpa didn't want to beat up Mr Ferguson. I hoped he didn't beat up anyone ever again. I hoped *those days were behind him* and he'd never turn around to see them.

I wasn't allowed out the house for the rest of the day. The police were keeping an eye out for Mr Ferguson and so were we. When we needed something from the shop, it was Iain who went. I was to be *within earshot* of Granpa at all times.

I got a lot of keyboard practice done. And the weather wasn't that sunny, so I wasn't desperate to go outside. Granpa kept asking how I was and I always said "*fine*". I wasn't scared like he thought I would be. I couldn't tell him, but I knew he had beaten up the two robbers. It was the very last thing I wanted to happen, but I was sure Granpa could win in a fight against Mr Ferguson. Mr Ferguson's belly was big and when he wore a shirt at the bookies, it was stretched tight and looked like the buttons were going to pop off. Every now and again I could see little bits of his hairy belly. It was horrible.

The police phoned in the morning. Granpa tried to shoo me away to the other room, but I stayed so that I could listen. Iain was allowed to stay, so why did I have to get out? I could only hear Granpa's part of the chat.

'Mark Ferguson, that's him,' Granpa said down the phone. 'Ye're kidding... Christ... I understand... I'd really rather no, pal, she's still shaken up... we'd rather forget the whole thing... naw, no wife or kids... please, dinnae tell this sister of his what happened yesterday, no need to drag his name through the gutter... thanks again for letting us ken.'

Granpa put the phone down and sighed.

'Did they get Mr Ferguson, Granpa?'

'They did.'

'So we dinnae need to worry about him coming back?'

'Aye, the police gave him a good scare. It's all over, Mary.'

I smiled at Granpa. He went into the kitchen and had a drink of whisky. Iain wasn't having one with him though.

'Too early, even for me,' Iain said.

I guessed Granpa's shoulder was really hurting.

The only good thing about Mr Ferguson turning up was that it took my mind off the robbers and what Granpa took from them. I knew no matter what I said to Granpa, he would have an excuse. He always did. I thought maybe I should wait till the summer was over to tell Granpa what I knew. That would give me enough time to come up with a good way to tell him. And I didn't want to do anything that might stop me from going to the ball.

After lunch, I went out for a walk to have a think. I told Granpa I was meeting Grace, but I wasn't. He didn't check or say, "*I'd better walk you, Mary*". Maybe I was getting fantastic at kidding people on, or he was too busy drinking whisky to care.

Going to the top of the tower wasn't the same without Grace there. The views weren't as fun if I couldn't tell Grace what I saw. There were a lot of people on the Lump. More than usual. It was a Monday and it was usually quieter because people were at work. A lot of people stood at the gap in the trees where the path went round to the Bowl. I came down from the tower and walked towards them.

People were standing and chatting to each other. Not in a hurry to get anywhere. I went round the outside of the group, through the gap so I could get to the Bowl. I heard people saying,

'Terrible.'

'This kind of thing doesn't happen in Portree.'

'He wasn't from here, was he?'

When I got to the front of the crowd, two policemen were blocking the way. A piece of blue and white tape was stretched between two trees to keep everyone out. I tugged at the bright, yellow jacket of one of the policemen.

'Why can't we go round to the Bowl?' I asked him.

'Hello there, wee one,' he said. 'I'm afraid this part of the hill is off limits today. But it might be back open tomorrow.'

'Why?'

'You'd be better to go and play somewhere else today. Okay, darling? Great.'

He smiled, then stood back up straight and looked around like he was on guard.

'What happened?' I asked.

He was pretending as if I wasn't even there. I waved my hands but he still wouldn't look down. I wondered if he'd look down if I gave him *the finger*. But I wasn't brave enough for that.

I went to the harbour and left my bike up against the rails. I peeked into the chippy to see if Craig was working. He wasn't. I was glad. The thought of seeing him again made me nervous.

I watched the seagulls. Sometimes on telly, when people needed to make a big decision, they'd go and sit by themselves and stare at some hills or water and then they'd realise the right decision to make. I wondered if watching the seagulls and the water would work, but it wasn't helping. The seagulls were doing their weird things like normal and when I watched them I forgot about everything else, which felt good.

I heard Andy's voice. He was in the chippy talking to the men behind the counter. They were laughing and talking quite loudly. *Banter*, that was the word for it. Men liked to have *banter* which was like what Granpa and Iain did, making fun of each other and things. Grace and I didn't make fun of each other, only men liked banter. Girls didn't see the point and preferred being nice to each other instead.

Andy came out of the chippy and I ran to catch up with him.

'Hiya, Andy,' I said. 'Do you remember me?'

He was drinking a bottle of Irn-Bru and he got a bit of a fright because I came out of nowhere and some of the juice squirted out his mouth.

'Oh, hi,' he said. 'Don't tell me... starts with 'M', right?'

'Mary.'

'Mary. Of course. How goes it, Mary? Are you winning?'

'Winning what?'

'It's just a saying. How are you?'

'I'm okay. Have you seen any dolphins since me and my Granpa came on the boat?'

He took a bite of his Mars bar.

'Eh... one fella said he did, but I think he was just trying to impress the Sheila he was with. I'll tell you what, though, no one's fallen in since that bloke did. That's all I'm worried about.' He moved to walk by me 'You take care, Mary.'

I stepped into his path so he couldn't walk unless he was going to stomp on me, which I knew he wouldn't. He was too nice.

'Can I ask you a question, Andy?'

'Have I got a choice in the matter?' he said.

'If someone you knew lied to you, then said sorry and that they wouldn't lie to you ever again, but then did lie again, what would you do?'

'Well, it depends how well I knew this person. And if I thought maybe they were lying to protect me. Sometimes grown-ups use these things called *'little white lies'*, which are okay.'

'Lying's never okay,' I told him.

Andy took another bite of his Mars bar and chewed while he thought of how to answer.

'Mary, let me give you an example,' he said, finally. 'I proposed to my girlfriend last year. I took her over to Raasay and she was totally surprised. I told her we were going for a hike and a little picnic. I told her a *little white lie* so I could surprise her. Y'see? Don't you think it was okay for me to lie then?'

'I suppose so. Did your girlfriend like it?'

'She bloody loved it. It's about the only romantic thing I've ever done. She never saw it coming. That's also why I tell that story to anyone who'll listen. Makes me seem like a decent bloke. Right, Mary?'

I nodded.

'I hope I've been of some help, darl,' he said, and he took a big swig of his juice, 'And I hope you patch it up with whoever's been lying to you.'

He walked past me and down towards his boat. He had a bit of a strut like cocky people did because they thought they were cool. But he actually was cool so it suited him. I let him off with it.

I went to Grace's to tell her what Andy had said. No one answered for ages, then Tom came to the door.

'Is Grace in?' I asked.

'No,' Tom replied. 'Her and Dad are away to Inverness for the day.'

'She didnae tell me about that.'

He shrugged like he didn't know what to say.

'I thought you werenae getting out of bed for anything,' I said.

'But you kept ringing the bell!'

'Sorry, I wanted to ask Grace something. Tom, if you found out someone you knew was a really big liar, what would you do?'

He scratched inside his stookie while he was thinking.

'I'd tell them to piss off,' he said, sniffing his fingers. 'And I'd never be friends with them again.'

'Really?'

'Too right. And then I'd karate chop them in the face.'

'I didnae know you could do karate,' I said.

He tried to do a karate pose but almost fell down and had to grab on to his crutches.

'I haven't had proper lessons,' Tom said. 'But Dad says I'm a natural. I could get to black belt in like, a week, if I wanted to. But I can't be bothered.'

'That sounds really good,' I said. 'Maybe you should be bothered and then you'd have a black belt.'

He rolled his eyes.

'It's not about having the black belt, Mary. I don't even want it.'

'Then how will anyone know you're good at karate?'

'Because I karate chop people who lie to me. I do it in front of everyone at school, so everyone knows not to lie to me.'

'Right,' I sighed. 'By the way, Tom, I want to say sorry for not staying with you after you broke your leg. I felt sick when I saw the bone sticking out.'

'That's okay. I just wish someone had taken a picture of it so I could show it to people at school.'

'When you got hurt, I realised that I want us to be friends, Tom. Is that okay?'

He went a bit red and started scratching the back of his neck and looking away.

'I suppose. Thanks, Mary.'

'Maybe you can come and play with Grace and me next time.'

He made a disgusted face.

'Maybe,' he said. 'As long as Grace has a shower first.'

Andy thought I should be okay with Granpa lying. Granpa was only doing it so I wouldn't get upset. Tom thought I should karate chop Granpa in front of everyone, but I didn't have any karate training. They were both boys though and I knew I would get a better answer from Grace —or maybe even Mrs MacLeod.

'Tom,' I said. 'D'you know anything about the police being up at the Lump?'

'Dad said something about that this morning before he left.

He said a man's hanged himself.'

'I'm being serious.'

He looked upset like I'd called him a liar.

'So am I!' he said. 'How much d'you want to bet?'

I walked away. Tom was obsessed with hanged men. He wasn't good at fibbing like me and Granpa were.

CHAPTER TWENTY-TWO

Granpa's kilt was purple. He had chosen it because he knew I liked pink and purple and you couldn't really get a pink kilt. The plan was that I was to get a pink or purple dress to go with it.

'Try it on,' I said.

'Naw, hen, it takes an age to get on,' he said. 'Ye can just imagine it for noo.'

Him and Iain were watching *University Challenge*. Neither of them had got an answer right the whole programme.

'But what if it disnae suit you?' I asked.

'The lass at the shop said I was awfie handsome in it, as it happens.'

'Are you going to ask her to be your girlfriend?'

'She's half his age!' Iain laughed.

'She was only being nice,' Granpa said. 'Trying to make a sale.'

'Was it a little white lie?' I said.

'That's exactly what it was, hen. Who telt ye about little white lies?'

'Grace.'

That was a little white lie.

'I think ye've picked a good yin in her,' Granpa said. 'I

was thinking aboot it, you two running aboot the hospital, that's the kind of thing me and my pals used to get up to at your age. I'm glad ye've got a pal here.'

It was hard to stay mad at Granpa. He never seemed that worried about anything. Even though the paper had said the police were looking for him, he was all smiley and not at all serious. Maybe he *was* scared of the police and he was really good at hiding it. He wasn't scared of the robbers, but that was because he didn't know one of them was in Portree. I couldn't ask him if he was scared, that was a weird question to ask for no reason.

'The Leaning Tower of Pisa!' Granpa shouted at the telly. 'A-ha! One-nil, Iain.'

'I'm not having that,' Iain said. 'This must be a repeat.'

I wasn't going to tell Grace about Mr Ferguson. I didn't want her mum and dad to think Granpa had an enemy. *With friends like these, who needs enemies?* That was a famous saying that Granpa taught me. No one *needed* enemies, but sometimes they appeared anyway.

Grace's parents would've stopped letting her see me for sure. The police had promised us that Mr Ferguson was never going to come back anyway. I don't know what they did, but they must've *put the frighteners* on him.

Sometimes me and Grace sat for hours in her back garden, lying in the grass, playing the cloud game. I was sure I would've been better at it back in Stirling. The clouds moved too fast in Portree.

'Did you ask him yet?' Grace said.

'Did you go to Inverness yesterday?' I asked her back.

She looked annoyed that I'd not answered her question. 'Aye, with my dad. Why?'

'Just wondered. Why didn't you tell me?'

'Sorry, Mary. Dad decided in the morning. Did you want to come?'

'Not really. But I thought you would've told me about it. By the way, I decided not to say anything to Granpa.'

'Why not? Will he not get caught? What if he doesn't know the police are looking for him?'

'I cannae be bothered with him shouting at me.'

'He might not shout at you.'

I sat up and leaned back on my elbows.

'He definitely would,' I said. 'It's obviously a secret because he thinks only grown-ups can hear about robbers getting punched and things. I bet he's told Iain.'

'It's a good place to run away to though. Portree, I mean. We're ages away from anywhere.'

I thought Grace was right. I remembered that Iain had lived in Portree for years before we came. Granpa hadn't run away to Portree on purpose. The police weren't looking for us when we left Stirling, only after what happened in Perth. The Perth thing had been an accident. We got lucky that Portree made a good hideaway.

'It's my fault,' I said. 'If I hadnae seen the robbers van, then Granpa wouldnae have gone and beat them up.'

A dog barked from somewhere far away.

'But you didn't tell your Granpa to go and beat them up, did you?' Grace asked.

'Naw, but I'm glad they got beat up.'

'Were they really scary?'

I nodded.

'I was so scared,' I said. 'I thought I might pee myself.'

Grace laughed.

'That would've been funny,' she said. 'The robbers

could've slipped in it.'

I was going to tell her they couldn't slip in it because I did it on the carpet bit behind the desk, but then I didn't. I didn't need to tell Grace I'd peed myself. That was the kind of thing, when people found out, they stopped being friends with you. There was a rumour Ewan Halliday had to move to Bannockburn Primary because he'd pooed himself in front of his P3 class and no one would sit next to him from then on.

'It all worked out then,' Grace said. 'The robbers got beat up, which is good. Me and you are friends now, which is good. Your granpa told fibs, which isn't good, but adults are always telling fibs. That's normal.' She stood up. 'Let's practise our dancing for the ball.'

'Okay,' I said. 'And you willnae tell your mum and dad and Tom about what Granpa did?'

'My mum already doesn't like your Granpa. I wouldn't tell her anything else bad about him. We need everyone to get on at the ball.'

'We could make a plan so that my granpa and your mum become friends?'

'Good thinking.'

I had come up with the idea and Grace had agreed. It counted as *my* idea. It wouldn't be much fun if we were swapping partners during the dancing and Granpa and Mrs MacLeod were giving each other *evils* the whole time. The ball could get ruined for everyone that way. If the ball was perfect, there was no way Grace would stop being my friend. I had made friends with Tom, so surely Granpa and Mrs MacLeod could be friends too.

'We should find out something they both like,' Grace suggested. 'Then they can talk about it and they'll forget about hating each other.'

'What do your mum and dad like?'

It was hard to talk and dance and think at the same time.

'They like their programmes on the telly,' Grace said. 'Does your Granpa watch any of those adult programmes with the guns and detectives?'

'I dinnae think so. It's mainly football and horses he watches. We like watching the news, but everyone talks about that.'

'We'll make something up.'

I spun round under Grace's arm. I was getting better at ducking my head down.

'But I dinnae like lying,' I said.

'It's not like proper lying.'

'It is little white lying? I'm good at that.'

'What we'll do is, you find out something your granpa really likes, then tell him my mum loves it too. And I'll find out something my mum really likes, then tell her your granpa loves it.' Grace gave up on proper dancing then and started spinning with her arms out. 'They'll never think we're lying and they'll think the other one isn't so bad because they like, oh I dunno, Robbie Williams.'

'I dinnae think Granpa likes Robbie Williams.'

'It doesn't need to be Robbie Williams. That was just an example.'

'I dinnae think Granpa would even know who Robbie Williams is.'

'He probably would. Robbie Williams is ancient now. He's like my mum's age.'

Grace knew all about the robbers. The only thing I didn't tell her, was that Craig was one of them. I didn't want her to know everything. I'd have to tell her about the bit of paper and how it was my fault Craig had it. I never wanted anyone to find out about that. My neck went hot whenever I thought about it and not even ice cubes could cool it down.

Craig was going out with her mum's friend. If I said he was a robber, Grace would've definitely told her mum. I couldn't risk it.

'Guess what's happening next week?' Grace asked.

'Tell me,' I said.

'It's the Skye Highland Games. At the Bowl on the Lump.'

'Will thousands of people be there?'

'Maybe.'

'Do they let everyone have a go at the games?'

'Only the strong men.'

That wasn't fair. I knew I could've given the strong men a *run for their money.*

It was chicken and chips for tea. They had invented chips called *sweet potato fries,* but I hadn't been brave enough to try them. And I would need to call them chips, not *fries.* I always had to be careful about saying American things around Granpa and Iain. I called a pound coin *a dollar* once and they made a big fuss about it.

'Dollar is it?' Granpa said. 'Just dinnae put it in the garbage can.'

'The garbage can?' Iain added. 'Is that out on the sidewalk?'

'Yeah, dude. Right by the mail box.'

'Are you having a nice vacation, Arthur?'

'It's a grand vacation. Pity there's no any soccer on the tube.'

'Would you like some French fries with your dinner?'

'That would be ace. Then we can have some candy.'

They went on like that for ages.

Granpa and Iain had brown sauce with their chips but I had tomato. Brown sauce was an old person's sauce. Just like whisky was for old people.

'Grace and me were talking today,' I said. 'About our favourite things in the world.'

'And what are yours then?' Iain said.

'Em, James Bond, Elvis, playing with Grace, and playing the keyboard.'

'Keyboard should be yer number one, Mary,' Granpa said, squirting a big dollop of brown sauce on his plate. 'Ye're gonnae be a concert pianist, remember?'

'I bet there's not many others your age,' Iain said. 'That are into James Bond and Elvis.'

'That's because she learned fae the best,' Granpa said, looking proud with himself. 'Had a good role model, didn't she?'

'I still would've liked James Bond if you hadn't told me to watch it, Granpa.'

'We'll never ken for sure.'

Iain got up to knock on the window. He said there was a fat seagull which was always sniffing around his garden. I'd never seen it.

'Away you go,' he shouted at it.

'So what are your favourite things?' I asked.

'Let's see,' Iain said, sitting back down. 'Taking your granpa's money at poker, taking your granpa's money at pool. Any activity where I can take your granpa's money, really. It's an ever-growing list.'

Iain laughed loud and Granpa shook his head.

'What about you, Granpa?'

He popped a chip in his mouth and thought about it.

'Football... having a wee flutter... reading the paper... Hemingway books... and the King, of course.'

The King was Elvis. We both knew exactly who he was talking about.

'Who's the Heming person?' I asked.

'Hemingway? He was an American writer. The greatest.'

America was where all the best things came from. It didn't matter if you were Scottish and you did something amazing. There would be someone in America who did it better than you. Apart from if you were J.K. Rowling or Andy Murray. They were the best Scots we had. Well, J.K. Rowling wasn't properly Scottish, but she liked Scotland so much I let her off with it.

Even if I got really fantastic at the keyboard, a girl in America would probably be twice as good. I would need to try my best to catch up with her.

There weren't any clouds to watch, so Grace and me played with her hula hoops. One was Tom's, but he wasn't going to be able to use it for a while. It was blue, but that was fine. Tom would come to the window sometimes and stare at us.

'Does he not go out at all?' I asked Grace.

'He says it's too sore. Dad wants to take him places but he won't go. Dad says he's just feeling sorry for himself.'

I felt sorry for him too. I knew once the stookie was off he'd probably get annoying again, but I'd told him I was his friend so I had to keep being nice to him, no matter what.

'Did you ask your mum about her favourite things?'

'Oh, aye,' Grace said. 'She said... Stephen King, he's a writer.'

'Is he American?'

'I think so.'

'I knew it.'

'What else... *Game of Thrones*, *Buffy the Vampire Slayer*, and *Doctor Who*.'

'I dinnae like *Doctor Who*. It's too scary.'

Grace shook her head and laughed.

'I don't think it's scary at all. My dad says my mum's a big geek for watching those programmes.'

'She should buy a T-shirt with *geek* written on it then no one could make fun of her for it. If it's on a T-shirt, it's cool. I dinnae think your mum would believe my granpa likes all those geek programmes.'

'Okay, tell her the writer then.'

'What was his name?'

'Stephen King.'

'Stephen King.'

That was another name I had to remember.

'So what does your Granpa like?'

I couldn't remember the writer he'd said. All I could think of was Elvis because I liked him too.

'It'll need to be Elvis,' I said. 'He's all I can think of.'

We did the hula hoops for a while longer. Grace was way better at it than me. I didn't care though. I liked watching her. Hula hooping wasn't even an Olympic sport so who cared?

Mrs MacLeod came out to bring us diluting orange juice.

'Here you are, girls,' she said. 'You'll be thirsty, I bet.'

When we were drinking the juice, I caught Grace's eye. Then she started drinking it super-fast like she was racing me. I stopped drinking. I didn't want to race. I wanted to enjoy the juice and not ruin it. Diluting juice on a hot day was one of my favourite things. It was even better than fizzy juice because it didn't make you burp. Burping was horrible, but if you did burp it wasn't really your fault. You just had to say, "*pardon me*" as quick as you could so everyone would know you weren't disgusting.

'Mrs MacLeod,' I said. 'Do you like the writer Stephen... em...'

'Stephen King?' she said.

'Aye, him.'

'Yes, Mary, he's my favourite author. Was Grace telling you that?'

'Granpa was reading one of his books last night. He has loads of them. I bet he probably has all of Stephen's books.'

'Oh, I didn't expect your grandfather to be a horror fan. Hmm, people surprise you don't they.'

She smiled. Grace and me looked at each other. The plan had worked on Mrs MacLeod. We could tell from the way she'd smiled. She was going to be nice to Granpa next time she saw him.

'Mrs MacLeod,' I said. 'Is your friend still going out with Craig?'

'I had forgotten you knew him, Mary,' Mrs MacLeod said. 'Yes, him and Kelly are quite smitten with each other. Did you know him before he came to Portree?'

'Naw, I met him not long after I got here.'

'I see. Only, Kelly says he won't talk much about his family or, well, what he used to do before he came to Portree. A mystery wrapped in an enigma, that one.'

I had no clue what that meant and I just smiled. If Craig wasn't telling Kelly the truth, maybe she would dump him. On telly, girls were always getting upset with their boyfriends because they weren't being honest enough. I hoped Kelly was the same way. Craig deserved to be dumped a million times over. No one watching would feel sorry for him.

CHAPTER TWENTY-THREE

'She's a big fan, aye?' Granpa said.

'Aye, she has all his songs on her laptop,' I said. 'She was playing him when we were having our lunch and she was loving it.'

'That's a turn-up for the books. Maybe she's got some sense in her head, after aw.'

It was so simple. I told Granpa that Mrs MacLeod liked Elvis and all of a sudden he seemed to like her. The plan had worked exactly like me and Grace thought it would. I decided any time in the future, that if two people I knew didn't like each other, I'd use that plan again. All I had to do was make them think they like the same thing and all the hate went away.

I went round for Grace to let her know the plan had worked. She answered the door as if she was a grown-up and it was her house.

'Hiya Grace.'

'Hiya.'

She said it kind of sulky.

'What's wrong?' I asked.

'Are you angry at me for not telling you I was going to Inverness?' Grace said. 'I said I was sorry.'

'Naw. What are you on about?'

'I didn't lie to you, if that's what you think.'

'I dinnae think that. I never cared that much.'

I got the feeling Grace wasn't going to let me into the house till I made her calm down.

'Thomas told me you were asking him questions,' she said. 'Like what to do about knowing a liar. He told me you were asking because I had lied to you about something. I guessed it must be the Inverness thing because I couldn't think of anything else.'

'I was meaning Granpa was the liar. Not you. That's Tom being an idiot.'

She took her sulky face off and was back to being normal Grace.

'Oh. That makes sense. I was wondering why you'd think I was a liar.'

'I'd never say that about you. You're not annoyed with me anymore?'

She hugged me. Our hair got a bit tangled up but it pulled apart easily.

'Nah,' she answered. 'Now I'm annoyed with Thomas. I'll need to get him back.'

'We can make a plan together. Our last one worked. Let's not be mean though.'

We went inside and sat on the couch. The telly was on but I didn't know the programme. Probably a fancy programme you only got on *Sky*.

'Did you tell your granpa that my mum likes Elvis?' asked Grace.

'Aye, I was going to say. He believed it. He thinks your mum has sense now.'

'My mum's always had sense.'

'I know, she's a grown-up. You have to have sense to be a grown-up.'

'Great, now there's nothing to worry about for the ball. Except that you've not got your dress yet.'

Grace called it a dress and not a *gown*. I let her off with it. Everyone was allowed a wee mistake.

'It's fine,' I said. 'Iain says he knows a lady that can make me one.'

'Made just for you?'

'Aye.'

'Like a celebrity?'

'I suppose so. I'm not special like a celebrity though.'

'There's plenty of time for us to be celebrities when we grow up.'

'Do you think being a famous pianist counts as being a celebrity?'

She put her finger on her chin while she thought about it.

'I think so,' she answered. 'As long as you still dressed amazing. Anyway, Let's get Tom back.'

We went up the stairs as quietly as we could. But when you're trying to be quiet, that's when it feels like everything is way louder than usual. That's when you step on every creaky bit of the stairs, even when you never even noticed they were creaky before. I waited out in the hall and Grace went into Tom's bedroom. I could hear everything they said.

'I didn't say you could come in,' he said.

'Thomas, the hospital just phoned,' Grace said.

'I didn't hear the phone.'

'I had the phone outside. They say you need another operation.'

'No, they didn't. They wouldn't tell you that. That's something they'd only say to Mum or Dad.'

'They did, because they wanted you to know straight away. They say you need to wear your stookie until after Christmas.'

'You're lying. Mu-uum!'

He was shouting on Mrs MacLeod, but she wouldn't hear him out in the garden.

'You're the liar, Thomas,' Grace said. 'You told me Mary was annoyed with me, but she wasn't. You're just a big stirrer.'

It wasn't part of the plan for Grace to say that. She was meant to say they only had pink casts left at the hospital so he would need to wear a pink stookie till Christmas. That was what made the whole thing funny.

'Well, she's not happy with someone,' Tom said. 'And she's always with you. I'm her friend now, by the way. I was trying to help her.'

Grace stormed out his bedroom and I followed her downstairs.

'Sorry I forgot to say that bit about the pink stookie,' she said. 'I'm just so annoyed with him.'

'I understand.'

I wasn't annoyed with Tom but Grace was. Sometimes not all your friends got on with each other. I had forgotten how hard it could be having friends. The famous saying came into my head again. *With friends like these, who needs enemies?* Whoever wrote that, I knew exactly what they meant.

The next day, I came back from seeing Grace and there was a dress bag hanging from the hall door.

'Ask and you shall receive,' Iain said. 'Your dress, m'lady.'

'You don't even know my size,' I said.

'Let me guess… size eight-year-old girl?'

'Of course,' Granpa said. 'With the rate ye're growing, it might no fit ye by the time the ball comes round.'

That was him being silly and saying an old person thing. The ball was less than a week away and I wasn't going to grow that fast.

I pulled down the zip to see what the dress looked like. It was dark pink. It had lacy bits at the shoulder but it wasn't sleeveless like a real grown-up dress. That was a wee bit disappointing, but I kept it to myself. You were never, ever to complain about things you got for free.

'It's amazing,' I said. 'Can I try it on now?'

'Why no?' Granpa said.

I grabbed the hanger and ran to my room. I was trailing the dress behind me like a bride. It was quite heavy because of the bag. but I managed it. When I went back through wearing it, Granpa and Iain were going over the top and being silly.

'Oh my goodness,' Granpa said, putting his hand on his forehead, like he was fainting.

'You look fabulous, darling,' Iain said. 'Who are you wearing?'

'I dinnae know,' I said. 'Granpa, who am I wearing?'

'Miriam fae doon the road.'

We all laughed at that. On the red carpet at the *Oscars*, women had to say what famous designer had made their dress so people would be impressed. Miriam from down the road wasn't famous, but I was still impressed.

'This is all some palaver,' Iain said. 'All these kilts and dresses for one night. And you can't even have a few beers, Mary.'

'It's not about the beers,' I said.

'Just you wait till you're older,' Iain smirked. 'What's it about then? The dancing?'

'Naw, it's about...'

It was about making sure Grace really did want to be best friends. Balls and dances, that was when you found out who your *true* friends were.

'I cannae tell you what it's about,' I said.

'Mary has a secret, does she?' Granpa said. 'Are ye meeting this boyfriend of yours on the dancefloor?'

'Lewis isn't my boyfriend. I don't like him at all.'

'It's sort of like a forbidden romance, especially with Lewis's dad thinking we pinched his lobster.'

'I wouldnae ever go out with him.'

'And why no?'

'I'm not saying.'

'Another secret.'

'It's not a secret.'

'Tell us then.'

'You'll be angry.'

He looked over at Iain and smiled.

'What could ye tell me about a wee boy that'll make me angry?' Granpa asked.

I decided to let one of my secrets slip.

'He's the one who egged the house.'

Granpa looked confused. Iain put his hands on my shoulders and walked me through to the living room. We all had a seat.

'Talk me through this,' Iain said. 'You think Lewis did it?'

'I think so,' I said. 'And his big brother. I accidentally threw their football in the sea so it makes sense that they'd want to get me back.'

'Accidentally?' Granpa said.

'I chucked it in the air and it bounced and went in. I didnae mean it, not really.'

'And is that the end of it?' Iain asked. 'No more eggs?'

'That's… probably it. I dinnae think they're mad anymore.'

'Mary, tell the truth,' Granpa said. 'He's no been bullying ye or anything? Because I'll go and have a chat with him right noo and he'll no know what's hit him.'

'Please, Granpa, please dinnae hit him. We just dinnae like each other. I hardly ever see him. I dinnae even know for sure it was him that did it.'

'What d'ye think, Iain?'

'If it was a one off,' Iain said. 'No harm done, I suppose. But next time you see him, Mary, tell him I prefer my eggs scrambled.'

I wondered if Iain knew how bad his joke was or if he really thought he was funny.

Grace and me went to the Lump, again. The excitement of going there had *worn off* ages before that. But Grace always made up new games and tried to keep it fun. The only time I had decided where we should go, I ended up throwing a football in a stream. It was safer to let Grace choose.

Before we went up the tower, she told me to close my eyes and put my hands out. I did it because I knew she wouldn't push me over or hit me. I felt something cold in my hands. I opened my eyes and it was a screwdriver.

'My dad's got loads of them,' Grace said. 'All different sizes. He'll not miss it. He never even missed the one Thomas lost.'

'I like the green handle,' I said.

Green wasn't as good as pink or purple, but it was still good. I couldn't think of any colours I didn't like. Orange was a good one. Brown could even be good on a nice, tall tree.

'I thought you could write your name in the tower with it,' Grace said.

'As long as you think we willnae get in trouble.'

'Me and Thomas have never, ever been in trouble. No one has. Look how many names are on here.'

She was right. There were hundreds of names scratched all over the inside. Nobody had been scared to write their name.

'What if I write someone else's name?' I said. 'Then no one will be sure it's me.'

'As long as you don't put your second name,' Grace said. 'Then it could be any Mary.'

I decided to do it at the entrance, on the right hand side. Someone had written *MAZ* two times. Maybe folk would think me and the *MAZ* person were the same person and blame *MAZ*.

It was harder than I thought. I had to push the screwdriver in with all my might. My arms were sore after. The wall got a bit crumbly when I did the 'y' and it looked a bit like 'Maru' instead of 'Mary'. That was okay. I knew it said Mary.

'Will I do my name next to yours?' Grace said.

'Have you not done one already?'

'I can do another one next to yours so everyone will know we're best friends.'

That was the kind of thing Leona used to say.

'Can you wait until after the ball?' I asked.

'Why?'

'It'll give us something to look forward to.'

'Oh, okay.'

That wasn't the real reason, but Grace believed me anyway.

Two people came up the hill. One of them was Craig. He was holding hands with Kelly, the lady who'd shouted at us at the hospital. I crouched down as soon as I saw them.

'What are you doing, Mary?' Grace said.

I put my finger on my lips. I hoped she knew the finger on the lips code. I tried to pull her down but she wouldn't move.

'Grace!' I heard Kelly shout, 'You up there yourself?'

'Em,' Grace said. 'Yes. Hi again, Craig.'

'Hiya, Grace,' he said. 'How's your brother's leg? Healed up yet? I heard he hasn't budged from his bed in weeks.'

'It's not healed yet, no,' said Grace. 'What are you two doing?'

'Out for a walk. I remember the first time I came up here with the walking tour, they almost left me behind.'

'Come on, Craig,' Kelly said. 'We better get a move on if we're going out for tea. See you later, Grace.'

I waited below the turrets till Grace said they were well away from the tower.

'What was that about?' Grace asked.

I didn't know how to explain it; all I could do was shrug.

'You're really weird sometimes, Mary.'

'Is that okay?'

She thought about it for a minute.

'It's fine.'

CHAPTER TWENTY-FOUR

Grace came round for tea. Haggis, neeps and tatties. All through the meal, I was worried she would say something to Granpa about the story in the paper. I thought about telling her not to, but maybe she had forgotten and it would be best not to bring it into her head again. She would only get me in trouble by accident.

When we were finished our tea, Grace was allowed to stay and play in my bedroom. I showed her the keyboard. I had been using it so much, Iain had moved it into my room. It was a *special privilege*.

I played Grace, *Eight Days a Week.*

'You're really good,' she said. 'You could definitely be a celebrity pianist.'

'Thanks. I've got another dream too.'

'What is it?'

'I dinnae know if I should tell you.'

'Why not? We're best friends, Mary.'

I hadn't even asked her to say that. She had said we were best friends all by herself. That was a good sign.

'Well, okay. You know the pink house in the harbour? I want to live there one day.'

There was a few seconds of silence where she didn't say anything.

'That's a good dream,' she finally said. 'Because it wouldn't be as hard as being a famous pianist. Would you keep the pink house as a hotel?'

I told her all about my plans for the pink house. I was so happy she didn't think it was a stupid idea. I would've *died of embarrassment* if Grace had started laughing.

Someone knocked at the front door. They came in the house before I could look through the window and see who it was. If Iain had let the person in, I knew it must've been a friend. But not my best friend. She was already in my room.

'Only four sleeps till the ball,' Grace said. 'Are you excited?'

'Mega excited. Do you want to see my dress?'

'Nah, it should be a secret.'

'Oh. Right. Is that a rule?'

'There aren't any rules, but it'll make it more exciting on Saturday when we see each other's dresses.'

'Good idea.'

I went through to the kitchen to get us a glass of milk. Iain and Granpa were sitting playing cards and drinking whisky with the man who'd come in. It was Craig.

'Mary,' Craig said. 'Long time no see. How's it going?'

I didn't want them to see how worried I was. My chest went up and down so fast and I couldn't stop it and the thumping echoed all round my head and heart and ears.

'Okay, thanks,' I said. 'How are you?'

'Great, thanks. I met Iain here at the pub last week and he said I should come round for a game of Rummy.'

'He told me,' Iain said. 'He had ditched that silly handwriting dissertation he was doing. I thought since he'd come to his senses, we should have him round.'

'That's nice,' I said.

'I know it's a bit horrible to say,' Craig said. 'But that young boy Thomas breaking his leg was the best thing that ever happened to me. If I hadn't gone with him to the hospital, I never would've met his mum, who never would've got me the job at the chippy. I never would've met Kelly. University never really suited me, anyway. Funny how things turn out.'

Craig winked at me. I knew his university secret and he trusted me. But I knew loads more of his secrets.

'I'm sure young Thomas is just as chuffed as you are,' Granpa said.

They had a laugh at that.

'I've been really lucky,' Craig said. 'And I should thank you as well, Mary. The first friend I met here in Portree.'

I smiled. I decided not to get the milk. I just wanted to be away from him. I turned around and Grace was coming down the hall.

'Look what I found in your room, Mary,' she said.

She was wearing my Elvis mask. She pushed past me into the kitchen. I tried to catch her, but she was older and stronger and wriggled out of my hands. Iain was laughing.

'Are you giving us a song?' he said. 'That's a cracker. I never knew you had that, Mary.'

Granpa looked confused.

'I thought that was in my...' he said. 'Never mind. I got it at a car boot sale a few years ago, Iain.'

Craig wasn't laughing. Craig wasn't saying anything at all. He put his cards face up on the table and stood up. He had three Kings and was just waiting for another heart to finish his straight. Grace was dancing around with the mask on and no one else saw Craig's angry face.

'Where was it you and Mary are from, Arthur?' Craig said.

Grace spoke before me or Granpa could.

'They're from Stirling,' she said. 'They thought they were only staying for the summer, but now they're staying for good.'

'Is that right?' Craig said. 'And when did you get here?'

'When was it,' Iain said. 'Let me check the calendar.'

'Dinnae,' Granpa said.

'Don't be silly. It'll only take a second.'

Iain went over and flipped the pages down on his wall calendar. Granpa was squinting at Craig, like he'd figure it out any second. I was trying to get him to look at me, but he wouldn't.

'It was was June 25th,' Iain said. 'I had it circled, Arthur.'

'Tell me, Arthur,' Craig said. 'You didn't make a stop on your way up here, did you? Maybe you got off the train at Perth and thought you'd put a bet on?'

Granpa stood up to look Craig in the eye. Iain flipped the August page of the calendar back to the front. August's picture was a man on a desert island with sharks circling him. I'd never looked close enough to read what the joke was.

'It's getting late, son,' Granpa said. 'Maybe ye should be on yer way.'

'I think that's a good idea,' Craig said. 'I tend to lose my temper when the cards don't go my way.'

Craig finished his whisky in one gulp and went to the door. He was staring at Granpa while he put his jacket on. He opened the door, slammed it, and I could hear his steps on the stones in the driveway as he walked away.

Granpa and Iain stared at each other. It was quiet for ages.

Grace lifted the mask up and rested it on the top of her

head. She whispered to me.

'Does Craig know something about the robber your Granpa beat up?'

'Do you promise?' I said.

'Mary, I've said it twice,' Grace said. 'I won't say anything to my mum and dad.'

'We'd appreciate it, hen,' Granpa said, helping Grace put her jacket on. 'It's really nothing. Just grown-ups being silly. I think Craig might be away for a wee while noo, so if anyone asks...'

'I've not seen him in ages,' Grace said.

'Good girl.'

Granpa still didn't know Grace knew *everything*. But he didn't want Grace telling her mum and dad she'd seen Craig recently. It was all getting too confusing in my head. Grace was ten so she could handle all the information better. I decided I wasn't ready to be a spy yet. Or at least a double agent. I could maybe handle being a single agent.

'Are you and Mary still going to the ball?' Grace asked, as she stepped outside.

'We wouldnae miss it,' Granpa said.

I was so glad to hear that. I couldn't let the robbers ruin the ball for me.

While Iain took Grace home in his jeep, Granpa and me sat at the kitchen table. He had put away the cards.

'Do you know who that man was?' asked Granpa.

'One of the robbers.'

He nodded slowly.

'I've no been honest with ye, Mary. And for that, I'm sorry. Really sorry. Ye're smarter than I ever gave ye credit for.'

He took off his specs to wipe his eyes. It was only the second time I'd seen him cry in my whole life. It made me want to cry too.

'It's okay, Granpa.'

'Naw, it's no. All I had to do was leave it alone. But I couldnae help myself back in Perth. It's my fault we're caught up in all of this.'

'I've known about what happened in Perth for a while, Granpa. I saw it in the paper.'

He snorted and shook his head.

'Jesus. Why'd ye no tell me?'

'I didnae know what to say. Did you beat them up, Granpa?'

He put his glasses back on and nodded.

'It was only because of what they did to me, hen. To us. They deserved it, ye see?'

'I know it's not right, Granpa, but I was glad you beat them up.'

A laugh came out his nose.

'What am I laughing at? A wee girl's no meant to say something like that. Mary, I didnae leave it at that. I took their money. The money they were stealing fae that bookies. I dinnae ken why I did it. It was just… an impulse.'

'Can't you give them it back now?'

'Well, that's what we're gonnae find oot, I suppose. Listen, I'm no gonnae let them hurt ye, ye understand? Ye dinnae need to worry aboot him or the other one. I can handle them.'

'I believe you.'

Granpa put his hand on mine. He was finally telling me the truth. *The truth, the whole truth, and nothing but the truth.* It felt so good to have it not be a secret anymore. It was time to get my last, biggest secret out. Then I would be free.

'Granpa, it's my fault the robbers found us.'

'How's that?'

'The bit of paper with our train times on it. I put it in your jacket pocket. I didnae want to lose it.'

He wiped his eyes again and smiled.

'That's awright. That's no yer fault, hen. At least I know how they found us noo. Craig - that'll no be his real name.'

'Are the police going to come?' I asked. 'Will Craig and his brother phone them?'

'I dinnae think so. If they phone the police on me, the police will want to talk to them as well. They willnae fancy that.'

'So what happens now?'

'Noo, we go to bed. I'm sure I'll have a plan in the morning. Remember, there's nothing to worry aboot.'

I picked up the Elvis mask from where Grace had left it on the floor. Granpa took it off me.

'Ye better let me keep that, hen.'

CHAPTER TWENTY-FIVE

I slept *like a log* that night. I knew I should've been scared, but somehow I wasn't. I was so glad to have told my secret, and that Granpa had been honest with me. It was like most of my worries had been swept away by a broom. I knew Granpa could handle whatever Craig - or whatever-his-name-was - tried to do. He had already beaten him up once. It was 1-0 to Granpa and I hoped that was the full-time score.

When I woke up in the morning, Granpa was in my room, packing my bag.

'Are we leaving, Granpa?'

'Sort of,' he said. 'It's our final spy mission. We're going to lay low for a wee while.'

'Whereabouts?'

'D'ye remember that place just off the square ye saw the first day we were here? The big yellow house?'

'The hotel for smelly people, with bunkbeds?'

'Bingo.'

Iain took us in his jeep. It was to save us carrying our bags all the way to the hostel. I made sure that I took one of my Harry Potter books because Granpa said we might be staying there for a few days. It took me ages to read *Harry*

Potter. J.K. Rowling made up so many words to keep me *on my toes.*

'We'll definitely still be able to go to the ball?' I asked.

I wanted to make sure. Granpa had said yes in front of Grace, but she wasn't there anymore. It could've been a little white lie. They were happening all the time.

'Hen, I wouldnae let ye miss it for the world. I promise.'

Granpa and Iain were annoyed at each other on the drive to the hostel.

'I can't believe you didn't tell me,' Iain said. 'Taking their money? What a bloody stupid thing to do.'

I didn't like him talking to Granpa like that. I stared out the window and pretended I wasn't listening.

'I ken, Iain,' Granpa said. 'But it's done noo.'

'You were greedy, that's all it was. You had enough from Stirling, but no, you needed a fucking boat fund. Silly bastard.'

Granpa didn't argue back. Iain was right and he had been wrong. I didn't know if Iain was serious about the boat though. I wouldn't have said no if Granpa wanted to buy us a boat. A boat would've let us sail away from all our troubles for a while.

The man who checked us into the hostel was really nice. His catchphrase was *I love it when a plan comes together.* He said it about five times while we were at the desk.

'We have a very spacious kitchen, free Wi-Fi in the common area, tea and coffee facilities.'

The common area was where the front desk was. There were couches and a telly and old videos to watch. Not even DVDs. But I did like the clacky sound videos made when you slid them in the video player's mouth. When you wanted to watch a video, but you'd forgotten to rewind it last time: that was so annoying.

There were three floors and our room was on the same one as the entrance and the kitchen. I got top bunk. We had to put on our sheets ourselves. Granpa did the mattress for me, but I did my pillow. I knew it wasn't a good reason we'd gone to the hostel, but I was still trying to have fun. I'd never slept in bunkbeds before.

'Are we allowed to leave the hostel, Granpa?'

'You needing to be somewhere?'

'It's the highland games today, remember.'

'I'd forgotten aw about that. I suppose... he's no going to risk doing anything in front of that many folk. Okay, we'll go for a bit.'

Granpa was annoyed that there wasn't a safe or somewhere to lock up our *valuables*. He took his rucksack with us when we left. I guessed that was where he kept Craig's money. It was important it didn't go missing. It wasn't really Craig's money, or ours, but I didn't care if the bookies got it back. Craig and his brother could have it, as long as they left us alone. That was what I thought, anyway, and I was sure Granpa thought the same.

The Lump was the busiest I'd ever seen it. Loads of people were coming and going up the gravel path towards the grass bowl. It was raining, so everyone was in their waterproof jackets. I saw a woman in flowery wellies. They were nowhere as good as my green farmer ones.

There were hundreds of people around the outside of the bowl. There was orange netting all round it too, to stop you getting too close to the men in the middle. Maybe some years, thousands of people went, but not as many people had turned up this time. It was too wet. People must've thought, *"Oh, I'll go next year, I don't want to get soaked"*. I didn't mind getting soaked. It would make getting my bath feel even better later on. And then I remembered that the hostel only had showers, but that was okay. I guessed they wouldn't be busy because the smelly people who stayed there didn't use them much.

There were food vans. The smell off them was amazing. Burgers sizzling and chips frying. I had no idea how they got up there. There was only the little gravel path. It was just for people, not for vans. And how did they know they'd have enough burgers for the whole day in the van? What if they ran out? I wouldn't have been happy if I'd queued for ages in the rain and not got a burger.

We squeezed our way to the front. People didn't get annoyed because I was only wee and I was allowed at the front. Sometimes, we had to tap people on the shoulder because they had their hoods up. Everywhere I looked, someone was wearing a different colour of jacket. When I spun around quick, it felt like being inside a kaleidoscope. We had one in our class but Paul Reed broke it, the idiot.

The first thing I saw down in the Bowl was a man swinging a heavy ball on the end of a stick. He was wearing a kilt, but only a T-shirt on top. A proper kilt came with a nice white shirt and black jacket. But this was a kilt for doing sport in.

He stood with orange netting all round him apart from at the front. He spun round and round then let go of the ball and it went flying through the gap. If he'd thrown it anywhere apart from the gap, it would've hit the orange netting and not got far. He knew exactly what to do. The ball landed far away, taking a big chunk out of the ground.

An announcer man said,

'*Good opening hammer throw there from Gordon,*'

Everyone clapped. The hammer the man had thrown was much bigger than the ones the robbers had used.

'Can I get a burger, Granpa?'

'They'll be an extortionate price,' he answered.

'But please?'

'Fine. But I'm having a bite.'

The burger was three pounds and fifty pence. The bun was covered in flour which went all round my mouth when I took a bite. The bun was cold, but the burger was red hot. I held it in a napkin because you didn't get plates. I felt it warming my whole body when I took a bite. Granpa took a huge bite, like half the burger. It still only counted as one bite, but it was like five of my bites. He'd cheated.

We got back to our little space at the front. It was a different event. Instead of chucking a heavy ball on a stick, it was a big heavy weight. Like something the Road Runner would drop on Coyote's head. In the cartoon, it would give him stars round the top of his head. In real-life, it would probably kill you. Or maybe it would push your head down so much your neck would disappear.

When one man got it really far, the judges walked out and put a red flag in the ground, to show the rest of the men what they had to beat. Sometimes, one man would get it so far you expected the other men to give up. But none of them put down their weights and said, "*That's you won that one. Next game.*" They always gave it a go, even if they were rubbish. Everyone always clapped anyway, even when one man slipped over and chucked it sideways.

'We better get back, Mary,' Granpa told me.

'Oh, but what about the event with the big log? I want to

wait for that one.'

'The caber? I heard someone say it was right at the start. We missed it, hen.'

The *caber* was the best one and we'd missed it. It was no one's fault so I couldn't be annoyed with Granpa. I decided I would go back the next year and be the first person in the queue. I was glad I was staying in Portree for good. I could look forward to loads of things in the future.

On our way back to the path, I noticed a pile of stones that hadn't been there before, on the edge of the Bowl. It was definitely new because Grace and me had been up there loads and I knew exactly how it usually looked. All around the stones were flowers, fancy ones you'd get from the shop. It was pretty, even though it was wet with rain.

'What's that for, Granpa?' I asked.

'That's a wee cairn they set up for...,' Granpa paused, 'The games. They'll give out the flowers to the winners later.'

'Isn't that quite girly? To give the big strong men flowers? Maybe I'd be allowed to take some.'

'Naw, dinnae go near it. It's tradition, hen.'

It looked like there was a picture of a man's face at the bottom of the cairn but we were too far away to see who it was.

I hoped people would throw flowers when I became a proper piano player. I'd finish my piece and I'd stand up and the audience would throw flowers at my feet. Just underarm throws, they didn't want to hit me with the flowers. Maybe I'd catch a bunch and smell them and they'd actually smell nice for once. One time at assembly, Mrs Lithgow gave our class a flower each to throw to the front when Mrs Black announced she was retiring. The boys started whacking each other with them and mine didn't even make it past the P2s.

I spent the rest of the day in the hostel's common area. I had the first Harry Potter with me, but I mainly talked to the man at the desk or to the people who were sitting around. Some of them couldn't speak English properly, so I just smiled at them.

'Have you booked with us?' the hostel man said. 'Yes? Excellent.'

I watched films on the telly too. I was allowed my choice of all the videos they had there. They didn't have any James Bond, but I watched *A Bug's Life* three times in a row. When I rewound the tape, the film went backwards at a hundred miles an hour. It was a completely different story backwards, where the ants start happy and then go back to serving the grasshoppers at the end.

Granpa left to get us food from the Co-op. He took the rucksack with him. I wasn't to leave the common area. I didn't mind. The only thing I missed was seeing Grace. I hoped I'd see her at the games, but we didn't stay very long. I didn't like the idea of her going to Iain's and me not being in. She might never come for me again. Best friends were supposed to know where the other one was at all times.

When Granpa was away, Mrs MacLeod's friend Kelly came into the hostel. I picked up my book and hid behind it and hoped she wouldn't see me.

'Hiya, Simon,' she said to the desk man. 'Is Craig in? He was meant to come over to mine for tea and he's not answering his phone.'

Simon looked a bit worried.

'Sorry, Kelly,' he said. 'Craig checked out last night, said he was catching the last bus. Took everything with him.'

'What? I don't understand. Where was he going?'

'He didn't say. He went in a hurry, though.'

'Oh. Maybe a family emergency or something?'

'Perhaps.'

Kelly looked quite upset. She stood for a few seconds, not moving.

'Give me a phone if you see him, will you?' she said.

She walked out like a zombie. She shouldn't have felt bad, he was a no good robber.

The kitchen in the hostel was massive. Maybe not as big as the canteen at school, but still huge.

'Granpa, Kelly was in when you were away.'

He poured some orange juice for me.

'Kelly who?' he asked.

'Craig's girlfriend. She was looking for him.'

'Looking for him here? Christ, is this where he stays? Is he still here?'

'Simon said he left last night and got the bus. He took all his things with him.'

He was chewing on a bit of bread and thinking.

'Right,' he said. 'That's fine. We're safe here, Mary. Plenty of folk aboot.'

He was right. The kitchen was full of people from all over the world. I didn't know why more hotels didn't use bunkbeds. You could get double the number of people in that way. And you could meet new people and tell ghost stories at night.

'How did this Kelly take the news of Craig leaving?' Granpa asked.

'She looked quite sad,' I said.

'Stupid bint.'

Our room had a mix of boys and girls in it. It was a *family room*. But I was the youngest. There was a high school aged girl, but she slept all through the day so I couldn't talk to her. The dads snored all through the night. I wanted to put pegs on all their noses to shut them up. No one was even telling ghost stories. I thought about the ball and tried to remember all the steps in the Gay Gordons till I fell asleep.

The showers in the hostel were a bit scary. There wasn't a lock so anyone could come and look at you. Granpa stood outside my cubicle till I was done. The towels they gave us were quite scratchy and didn't dry you very well. They obviously didn't have enough money to spend on more towels. They couldn't even afford DVDs.

When we were walking through to the kitchen to have breakfast, Iain was sitting in the common area.

'Iain,' Granpa said. 'What's the word?'

'Craig phoned this morning,' Iain said. 'He wants to talk to you.'

Iain had a number written on a bit of paper. Granpa typed it into his mobile. People were busy checking out while Granpa talked on the phone. I could only hear what Granpa said so I had to guess what Craig was saying.

'It's Arthur... ye can have it... I dinnae ken if I even have that much... give me some time... tomorrow? Fine... I'll find it... I understand... see ye then.'

We checked out of the hostel that morning. Granpa had agreed to meet Craig and his brother in Inverness the next day to give the money back. There was no chance they would come to try to hurt us anymore. I was glad to be going back to Iain's house. Bunkbeds were fun but sleeping in my own bedroom without a load of snoring men was better.

It was good to be back at Iain's. I wasn't ready to call it home yet, but it was definitely starting to feel like it. My Elvis mask had been put in the bin, but I didn't complain. It got us into trouble. It was cursed.

'Is it okay if I go and see Grace?' I asked Granpa

'That's fine,' he said. 'Let me ask ye something before ye go out though. D'ye ken what *hypothetical* means?'

'Aye.'

'What does it mean then?'

'A word that you made up right now.'

'Ye're on the right lines. Hypothetical means, well, sort of made up. If I tell ye a hypothetical situation, it means that it could happen, no that it definitely will happen.' Granpa sighed. 'I've no explained that very well. Let me give ye an example. Say, I had to go away for a few weeks. MI5 call me up for one last mission.'

'You've never been in MI5.'

He curled his finger at me and I leaned in close so he could speak right into my ear.

'That ye ken of,' he whispered and smirked, then leaned back. 'Anyway, I have to go away for a few weeks. Where would ye want to stay while I was away, here at Iain's house or with Grace and her mum and dad?'

'I dinnae know.'

'It's no a trick question. I willnae tell Iain.'

'You promise?'

'Cross my heart.'

'I think I'd want to stay with Grace.'

'See, that wisnae hard was it?'

'But I really do like it here, Granpa. You're not going away for a few weeks are you?'

'Course no, Mary. That was all hypothetical. Can ye say it?'

'*High-po-thet-icul*?'

'Good girl. Remember, dinnae say anything to Grace about me seeing Craig tomorrow.'

I locked my lips and threw away the key. Granpa picked up the key and put it in his pocket. There wasn't really a key. He was just playing along. He knew the rules.

Grace answered the door.

'We should go out,' she said. 'Kelly's here and she's crying.'

Mrs MacLeod shouted from the living room.

'Who's at the door, Grace?'

'It's just Mary. We're going out.'

Kelly came out of the living room.

'Mary,' she said, walking towards me. 'You knew Craig, didn't you?'

She had lots of tissues in her hands, but they were for crying, not for snotters.

'Sort of,' I said.

'He didn't talk to you about leaving, did he? Tell you where he was going?'

'I didnae know he was away.'

'Oh. Right then. You girls go out and enjoy yourselves.'

She went back into the living room to cry some more. When we were a bit down the road, Grace said, 'You were really good there, Mary. I believed you for a minute.'

I was becoming an expert at kidding people on. If there was a type of spy who only needed to kid people on, and didn't have to go into dangerous situations, I'd be that type of spy.

'I came round for you yesterday,' Grace said. 'So we

could go to the games, but Iain said you and your Granpa were away on a trip.'

'We were at the hostel. Sort of like a sleepover.'

'But you're back home now?'

'Aye. We dinnae need to worry anymore.'

'Have you actually heard from Craig, by the way?'

'Naw, not even once.'

I thought maybe I was getting *too* good at kidding people on. MI5 would want me to join them and I wasn't ready for that. I kept checking my mobile in case they rang though. I needed to remember to charge it. MI5 wouldn't let someone in if they always only had one bar of battery.

♪

CHAPTER TWENTY-SIX

'You promise you'll be back tonight?'

It was the day before the ball and Granpa was going to Inverness to meet Craig and his brother. The rucksack with the money was going with him.

'I promise,' Granpa said. 'Noo, I better go or I'll miss my bus. I'm on a tight schedule, hen.'

He kissed me on the cheek and got in the jeep with Iain. I waved and waved till my arm was sore. I wasn't scared for Granpa. If he said he'd be back, he'd be back. I wondered what Iain and him would talk about on the way to Somerled Square. Maybe Iain would call him a bastard again. I was glad I didn't need to hear that.

While they were away, I got things ready for the ball. I checked my dress was still in its bag and not stolen. I laid out Granpa's kilt for him, all the different bits of it. There was a knife thing called a *ski-and-do* which you were to put in your long socks. That was quite weird. No other outfits came with a knife. It was an old-fashioned thing and people kept going along with it. I might have wanted to say, "*Isn't it a bit dangerous, to have a knife with your kilt?*" but I wouldn't, because people would've thought I hated Scotland. I didn't say anything and stuck the knife in Granpa's sock and made sure to say *loch* and not *lake*. I didn't want a knife in my dress. What if I stabbed myself?

Iain came back before long.

'Did Granpa get on the bus okay?' I asked him.

'He did,' Iain replied. 'He'll be back before we know it.'

I went to Grace's to take my mind off Granpa being away. She showed me how to make these special bracelets. *Loom bands*, that was the proper name. You took all these tiny little coloured plastic rings and wrapped them round this plastic case which looked like a board game and at the end you had a bracelet or a necklace. They weren't as good as real bracelets from a shop, but they were special because we'd made them ourselves.

When Grace went to the toilet, I popped upstairs to see Tom. I knocked on his door and all I could hear was his telly. I knocked again.

'Go away, Grace,' he called.

I opened the door. It was all dark, even though it was lunch time and still bright outside. Tom had the blinds and curtains closed and it didn't smell very nice. He was lying on top of his covers like usual. He put the volume on the telly down, but not all the way.

'Hiya Tom,' I said.

'Hiya Mary.'

'Do you not get bored sitting in here all day?'

'Obviously. But I need to stay still to get my leg better. I can watch anything I want on Netflix though. Mum doesn't know I can turn the parental lock off. Wait till I get back to school and tell my friends how much *Daredevil* I've watched. They'll be jealous.'

I didn't know why you'd be jealous of how much telly

someone had watched, even if it was special telly like Netflix. I had watched the Pierce Brosnan James Bond films about a hundred times each, but I never told anyone. It wasn't fair that he'd only been allowed in four films.

'Grace said Lewis and Jamie egged your house,' Tom said.

'Maybe,' I said. 'I dinnae know for sure it was them.'

'Lewis used to be sound, but he only hangs about with Jamie now. He does whatever Jamie tells him to.'

'It's funny how they get on really well, but you and Grace dinnae.'

'Because she's ten and thinks she's queen of the world. She's not.'

'There's no such thing.'

'I know.'

'They wouldn't let Grace be queen of the world. It would probably be an American lady.'

Tom pushed his telly remote into his stookie to scratch his leg.

'Are you going to get Lewis and Jamie back?' he asked.

'Naw, that's it done now,' I said. 'We're even-stevens.'

'You shouldn't let them away with it, Mary. I can help.'

He sat up and did one of his karate poses.

'Why do you want to help?' I asked.

'Aren't we friends? Didn't you say that?'

'Aye, but I thought you had to stay still in bed to get better?'

'I do. But forget about that. I could get up one time. My leg's starting to feel much better, actually.'

'Dinnae get up for me, Tom. You need to get better.'

He laid back down and started drumming on the wall with his knuckles.

'Okay, Mary.'

I had thought he might get up anyway. Stand up slowly and wobble a bit, but manage it and say, *"let's do this"* or *"the Kerr boys are going down. Downtown."* like in a film. Instead, he put the sound on the telly up and I went back downstairs.

Tea wasn't the same without Granpa. I didn't know what to talk to Iain about.

'Are you looking forward to this ball then?' he asked.

'Aye.'

'And you'll be starting school soon.'

'Aye.'

'Would you like more tomato sauce?'

'Aye.'

After tea, we watched the telly and Iain taught me a new card game. We used cards, but you could've used anything. He put a hat on the floor and gave me half the deck. You had to try and throw cards into the hat. There was a special way of throwing the cards sideways that Iain was an expert at. Mine didn't get very close. The best bit was tipping the hat over at the end and counting how many you'd managed to get in. It was a surprise because you were throwing so fast you couldn't count, but sometimes I tried counting and if my number matched the cards in the hat, I was chuffed. Not *chuffed to bits*, just chuffed. I wasn't that happy.

I woke up when the front door closed. Granpa was back. I had fallen asleep on the chair with the cards all over me. I stood up and they scattered everywhere. I didn't care. I ran and gave Granpa a big hug.

'Watch my back, hen,' he said. 'Calm doon, I told ye I'd be back.'

'I know but I'm just glad you didnae get hurt.'

'Those two couldnae hurt a fly.'

Iain poured Granpa a whisky.

'All go to plan?' he asked. 'They were happy with the money?'

'They seemed awright,' Granpa said, taking a sip. 'Happy might be stretching it.'

Granpa didn't have the rucksack anymore.

'Did you not take your rucksack back once they'd taken the money out, Granpa?'

'It was easier just to let them have it,' he answered.

'Rucksacks dinnae grow on trees,' I told him.

He laughed. He was always telling me things didn't grow on trees. But giving away the rucksack was fine because we were all safe now. It was a fair trade. The rucksack + the money = the robbers leaving us in peace. There was nothing to worry about.

'Guess what, Granpa?'

'What?'

'One sleep till the ball.'

Our ticket was on fancy card and said:

The Portree Trust presents
The Portree Annual Highland Ball
Portree Gathering Hall, Bank Street
7.30pm
Saturday 8th August 2015

The writing was in gold and when you ran your fingers over the letters, you could feel it was a little bit higher than the card. It was like writing for blind people. The man we'd got the ticket from, Gerry, had written his name on it already but we were still allowed to use it. His writing looked quite like Granpa's. I hoped the people at the hall would let us keep the tickets. I wanted to keep mine forever.

Grace and me cycled around to pass the time until the ball started. Granpa and Iain were at the pub to watch the football. It was the first proper football of the season since the male footballers all had the summer off. Sometimes, countries would play summer football but this summer they decided not to. There had been Scottish football on the week before, but Kilmarnock's game hadn't been on the telly. Granpa said English football was *of a much higher quality*. He didn't support England when they played as a country though, that was against the rules for a Scottish person. Secretly, I supported Scotland, England, Wales, Ireland and other Ireland at everything, but I didn't tell anyone. They were all together at the Olympics when they were team GB and not a lot of people remembered that. People had reasons to hate other countries, but I hadn't found any yet.

We went past the Gathering hall. There were some cars outside all parked close to each other, and people going inside the hall with all sorts of things. Chairs, tables, balloons and big carrier bags full of things I couldn't see.

'Dare you to run inside,' Grace said.

'Naw,' I said, 'They could ban me.'

Grace rolled her eyes but she didn't run inside either.

We went up the hill and stood our bikes outside the tower. It was a Saturday so a lot of people passed by. The lady taking the tour was there again. She must've got so bored saying the same facts day after day. I wondered if she ever made up a fact to kid people on. Like those two girls up the tower are actually ghosts, who died hundreds of years ago, and they haunt us and chase people on their bikes. We could've made ghost noises to give people a laugh. Instead, she did her facts over and over and the people nodded and did sounds like they were interested. *Hmm* and *mmm* and *ooh, is that right?*

Granpa came through to the living room all done up wearing his kilt.

'What d'ye think, Mary?' he said.

I felt the kilt. It was nice and soft and a bit fluffy round the edges.

'You look like James Bond,' I said. 'But older. Like James Bond's dad.'

'Who would James Bond's dad be married to?' Iain asked from the kitchen. 'Jennie Bond?'

I didn't know anyone called Jennie, but it made Granpa laugh. I had only seen James Bond in a kilt once, and he wasn't even Scottish in that film.

Granpa's kilt was purple for the main skirt bit. Then he had a black jacket and white shirt and white socks. His knife was tucked in and he had these things called *flashes* around the tops of his socks. Men didn't usually have lots of fiddly bits like that, but kilts were different. It wasn't manly to have lots of fiddly bits, but kilts were a special treat for men. His tie was purple but you didn't call it a tie, it was called a *cravat*.

'Can girls wear kilts, Granpa?'

'Sometimes,' he said. 'Like professional highland dancers. Ye must've seen them at the games the other day? Would ye like to wear one?'

'I think so. I like all the different bits.'

'How aboot ye take these then?'

He took off his flashes, lifted up my dress, put them round my legs and pulled them tight. When he dropped the dress back down you couldn't see them because my dress went all the way to the floor. I liked the feel of them.

'But no one will know I've got them on.'

'When ye're dancing,' he said. 'Ye're dress will come up a bit and ye can *flash* yer *flashes*.'

That was a clever way to say it. I lifted up my dress and they were still there. I decided I would do a curtsy when I saw Grace and then she'd see them too.

'Let's get a picture of you two,' Iain said. 'I paid all this money for this thing, may as well use it.'

He took out his big black camera.

'I've told ye to stay off QVC,' Granpa said.

'It was Bid-Up TV, actually,' Iain said.

'Jesus, that's even worse.'

It didn't even have a digital screen on it to look back over the photos you'd taken. But Iain said it was still worth a lot of money. Maybe it was an antique like on *Antiques Roadshow*. But probably not, it was mainly vases on that programme.

Granpa got down on one knee and put his arm around me and I said *chips and cheese* instead of just *cheese*.

Granpa carried my jacket for me. It was warm and I didn't even need it, but I had to take it anyway. *Just in case.* Granpa never worried about anything but the weather. He was really relaxed about everything else, apart from if he'd need a jacket or not. It was such an old person thing to worry about.

Iain came to the door to wave us off and take more

pictures of us walking away. We weren't even looking at the camera. It was a fancy kind of photo but really everyone knew the best photos had people's faces in them. I thought he might print out the photo and hang it in the living room. I wanted one for my bedroom, too. It was my home and I needed to make it look that way.

'What's he like with that camera?' Granpa said. 'Thinks he's David Attenborough.'

'David Attenborough disnae take pictures, Granpa. He's always in front of the camera, talking about the animals.'

'Well, I was speaking metaphorically, of course.'

He used that word whenever he was trying to be right about something.

'Tell me what it means?' I asked.

'Never. It's the only way I can win an argument with ye.'

We got there at twenty past seven. Granpa's phone said so. Loads of people were standing outside. Ladies in amazing dresses and men in their kilts. All different colours, everywhere you looked. Some men wore normal suits, but most were in kilts. I recognised a lot of them from around the village. I didn't know their names, but that was okay. I could introduce myself and I'd know all their names the next time I saw them in the village. And we would already have something to talk about because we'd been to the ball together. Because some of the dances meant you had to swap partners, all the people outside were really my dancing partners.

'D'you see anyone you want to dance with, Granpa?'

'How aboot that old bird?' he said.

He pointed at an old lady in a black dress and green cardigan. She was using one of those walker things you leant on to help you walk.

'That's just mean, Granpa.'

'Well, come on, what's she doing at a ceilidh. At least I've still got some spring in my step. She's only got winter in her step.'

He looked at me with his eyebrows up like he was waiting on me to say something.

'Ye get it? Like spring and winter the seasons.'

'Oh,' I said. 'That's not even funny.'

'I swear ye were born withoot a funny bone.'

'It's right here.'

I showed him the knobbly bit next to my elbow. The funny bone was one of the sorest bits on you to get hit. I was glad I was a girl and boys weren't allowed to hit me. I was glad I was a girl for more reasons than that, but that was a good one. The full list would've been too long to write out.

It was nice standing outside waiting to go in. Everyone was talking non-stop and seemed to be as excited as me. Apart from Granpa, but I thought he was pretending not to like it because that was the way he was. He didn't get excited over much, apart from when he had a bet on a horse and it looked like it might win. He'd get really close to the telly and would whip behind him with his hand like he was a jockey, only he didn't have a real whip.

I spotted Grace and her mum and dad. They were a bit further up the hill near where the church was. I grabbed Granpa's hand and ran towards them. I was pulling my hardest, but Granpa didn't come any faster. It was like he was an old horse who couldn't be bothered anymore.

'Giddyup, horsey,' I said.

'Neigh chance,' he said and started laughing.

Grace was wearing a silver dress and had her hair done

in a side ponytail. I wished I had thought to do my hair in a side ponytail. If Grace had told me, we could've matched. But then what you were going to look like, that was a secret at fancy balls, so maybe she wasn't allowed to. There weren't any real rules but it was an *unwritten* one.

'Grace,' I said and then hugged her. 'You look beautiful. I love your hair.'

'That dress is amazing,' Grace said. 'I couldn't wear that. I don't suit pink.'

That was nice of her to say. I was better at wearing pink than she was. I didn't even know I was good at wearing pink before she said it. I would wear pink all the time, every day, when I lived in the pink house.

Mr and Mrs MacLeod were still talking to another couple and I felt bad because Granpa didn't have anyone to talk to.

I did a curtsy for Grace to show off my flashes.

'What are those?' she said.

'Flashes. They're my granpa's. They look nice, eh?'

Grace went right over to her dad and started taking off his flashes. His kilt was yellow with red lines on it. It wasn't as nice as Granpa's. He was still talking to the other people and was looking down at her and laughing and shaking his head. She had them off super-fast and put them on herself.

'See, Mary,' Granpa said. 'Ye're a trendsetter.'

Grace and me both lifted up our dresses so people could see our flashes. Maybe they weren't looking but if they did, they must've thought we were experts at fashion. Especially since I was so good at wearing pink.

The people Mr and Mrs MacLeod were talking to went away and then they turned and looked at me and Granpa.

'Hello, Mary,' said Mr MacLeod. 'Hello, Arthur.'

'Hello MacLeods,' Granpa said. 'Ye've been to this shindig

before then, I take it?'

'Oh yes,' said Mrs MacLeod. 'For years now. It's become a tradition.'

'Shame yer lad couldnae make it. Dangerous things those skateboards.'

'Too right,' Mrs MacLeod said. 'We've never let him have one. It was those boys who hang around in the square. What teenager gives their skateboard to a wee boy? I have half a mind to have a word with their mothers.'

'I dinnae envy them, I've seen ye in action.'

I was worried when Granpa said that. He was meaning when Mrs MacLeod shouted at him. That was the last thing I would've ever mentioned at the ball. But Mrs MacLeod rolled her eyes and laughed a bit. She wasn't even angry anymore and it was okay to joke about it.

'So Mary says,' Granpa said. 'We've a shared love of a certain artist. The King?'

'Oh? Oh, yes,' Mrs MacLeod said. 'Took me a minute there. The King, that's a good way of putting it. I've always thought he's so... unpretentious? And there's plenty of his work to get through.'

'Aye, definitely. I got Mary into him as soon as I could.'

Mrs MacLeod looked confused. I hadn't thought they'd actually talk to each other about it.

'Really, Mary? You seem very young for his work.'

'Och, no really,' Granpa said. 'It's fairly family-friendly stuff.'

Mrs MacLeod looked really confused but didn't say anything else. The plan could fail if they talked anymore about it. But would they? It was a *cliffhanger*.

♪

CHAPTER TWENTY-SEVEN

We all got in the queue. The man in front of me had really hairy legs. Normally I couldn't see men's legs but with loads of them wearing kilts I could get a good look. Lots of the men's legs were quite chubby and not as nice to look at as the ladies'. The muscles on the backs of the ladies' legs were a nicer shape. They got to wear high heels since they were mostly smaller than the men and the heels made things a bit fairer.

Grace and me were in front of the grown-ups.

'Is Tom at home by himself?' I asked Grace.

'No, Louise is babysitting him,' she answered. 'She's at the high school. Mum pays her ten pounds just to sit and watch our telly. Thomas is up on his bed anyway; it's not like he can make a nuisance of himself.'

Ten pounds just to watch telly. Imagine that. That could be part of my plan too. I could live in the pink house and have people over for cakes during the day, then babysit for people at night. The ten pounds would go towards the cakes. But ten pounds wasn't enough to live on, Granpa's wages had been a lot more than that.

I spotted Lewis and Jamie Kerr in the queue. They were with their mum and dad, who were both tall and skinny. It was strange to see Mr Kerr not wearing his Queen T-shirt.

He was wearing a blue kilt and his shirt looked like it needed a good iron.

Lewis and Jamie had kilts on too, and if I hadn't known they were idiots, I would've thought they looked quite nice. They were both wearing the boring red tartan kilts you saw everyone in. Lewis spotted me and nudged Jamie and they were both looking. I looked away before they could give me the fingers, which I guessed they probably did.

We were almost at the front of the queue. There was a man and a lady taking the tickets. I could hear them telling people which side to sit on. It was all about your number. I had my ticket ready. I was letting Grace go first so I could see exactly what to do. If there were any extra things to get, like a stamp on your hand or a wristband, I would be prepared.

'And here's Grace MacLeod,' the man said. 'Who's your friend?'

He looked at the lady and seemed a bit worried because he didn't know who I was.

'This is Mary,' Grace said. 'She's just moved here. She's going to the primary school after the holidays.'

School was coming up and there were things I needed to get. New pencils and a rubber and a pencil sharpener because they might not have one next to the teacher's desk. I was waiting till the ball had been before I thought about school. I wanted to enjoy myself and not worry about it.

I had been really wee when I went to school for the first time. I wasn't even that good at putting my thoughts together back then, but I remember it being scary. I had done it before, but this was different. All the other boys and girls were already used to the school and I had to learn everything all over again. Teachers' names were the hardest to learn and you needed to know them to be able to ask them questions or if you could pop to the loo.

The lady was looking through her bit of paper which was on a clipboard. Her pencil was attached with a bit of string. Granpa stepped in front of us.

'Hello there,' he said. 'I'm Arthur Sutherland, Mary's granpa. Her ticket's under Thomas MacLeod. Mine will be under Gerry O'Toole.'

The lady flicked over to another bit of paper.

'Oh, is Gerry not coming?' she asked.

'Remember,' the other doorman said. 'The lad who broke into his house.'

'Okey dokey,' the lady said, then did a couple of ticks on the list. 'Arthur, Mary, you're 67 and 68, right hand side of the hall, table six.'

Granpa walked in, but I waited in the little hall bit where people were hanging up their coats. We got in ahead of Grace by mistake.

'Come on,' Granpa said.

'I want to make sure Grace gets in,' I said.

Granpa opened his mouth like he was going to say something then didn't. Instead, he took off his glasses, breathed on them then wiped them with his special glasses hankie.

Grace and her parents came in after us. Their tickets were twenty-something and they were on the other side of the hall.

'Dinnae worry,' Granpa said. 'The numbers are so they can keep track of folk. Ye can move aboot aw ye want once the dancing starts.'

'Grace,' I said. 'Promise we'll dance together when the dancing starts?'

She nodded.

The hall was beautiful. White fairy lights were hanging everywhere. There was a big band on the stage and a wide open space for the dancing in the middle. Round tables with white tablecloths were up and down each side and silver balloons had been dotted around. The balloons had a little bag at the bottom of their strings to keep them from floating away. There weren't any names on the balloons and I didn't know if you were allowed to keep them. On the left, just as we went in, was the bar for drinks. It was busy with grown-ups getting champagne. But there was orange juice too so that was lucky. I hadn't tasted champagne but I guessed it wouldn't be *my cup of tea*. Tea wasn't *my cup of tea*, either.

The clock on the wall said 7.35pm and it hadn't started yet. The ball was running late.

'We should sit down in case it starts without us,' I said.

'It disnae really work like that,' Granpa said. 'The band will play for a bit, then the buffet will open, then the band plays again.'

It seemed as if you didn't really need to sit down at all. It wasn't important; that was great news.

'Ye see him there,' Granpa said, pointing at a great big fat man who was sitting down. 'He'll be our main rival at the buffet. He's got plenty of experience.'

'Is the buffet a competition, Granpa?'

'Sort of. It's aw aboot getting as much as ye can on yer plate. Then, if ye're an expert, like him, ye go up for seconds, or even thirds.'

'Is there a prize?'

'There is... a full belly.'

Then he tickled my belly and I ran away, right across

the hall, over the dancefloor. He didn't chase me though. I thought he would but he stood waiting for me to come back. I galloped like a horse back across, making loud tappy sounds on the wooden floor.

Dances for people my age were always during the day and nice and bright, but grown-up dances had to be at night and everything had to be dark. But it was still bright outside because it was summer, I liked that. Night time was when grown-ups were allowed to drink alcohol, so that was important. Dances had to be at the same time as they were drinking alcohol.

There were two ladies serving drinks behind the bar. The bar was really one long table with glasses of champagne and orange juice on it. If you wanted something different you had to ask.

'Any Talisker?' Granpa asked the lady.

She had blonde hair in a ponytail and was wearing a black waistcoat and a white shirt, like a butler or maybe even a James Bond baddie. It was unfair she had to dress like that when everyone else got to dress in bright colours.

'We do, sir,' she said.

'And is it, eh, included in the ticket price?'

'It's all complimentary, sir.'

She smiled and Granpa smiled even bigger.

'These teuchters are growing on me, Mary.'

We went and sat in our seats. It was all grown-ups except for me. Granpa started chatting to a curly haired lady straight away and I was looking around. I pretended I was a cameraman and I was recording everything in my head, so I could play it back for myself later on. People queued up to get their drinks, men stood in a circle in the middle of the dance floor having a chat, the band were getting ready by playing their instruments nice and quietly, to make sure they were in tune. You didn't have to tune keyboards, so I never had to worry about that.

I could hear Granpa's phone vibrating in his sporran. He unclipped the clasp and took it out.

'Who's phoning?' I asked him.

He stared at the screen and frowned.

'Whoever it is,' Granpa said, turning to me. 'They'll need to try again some other time.'

His frown turned into a smile and he switched off his phone.

I saw Grace at her table. She looked really pretty. Then another girl came and started talking to her. Grace looked surprised and they hugged each other. I didn't understand. I didn't know who the girl was. I was Grace's best friend. I needed to go over there, fast.

Something tapped on the window to my right. I got such a fright. It was Tom. He was looking right at me and waving for me to come outside. I looked around, but it was definitely me he was waving at and no one else had noticed him. He was smiling and waving his hand non-stop.

I tapped Granpa on the shoulder.

'Granpa, I need to go.'

He turned to me.

'Do ye ken the way or ye wanting me to come?'

I knew the way but it didn't matter because I didn't need to pee. That was just my *cover story*. I went out to the entrance hall and looked back to check no one was following me. I went outside and round the side of the hall to find Tom.

He was down the tiny alley on the right side. He was on his crutches, swinging himself back and forth.

'Tom, what are you doing here?' I asked. 'Should you not

be in bed?'

'I'm sick of my bed!' he shouted.

'Okay, calm down. But I thought your leg was too sore to move around?'

'It's sore, Mary, but I can get around okay. Look, I've come all the way from the house on my crutches and I've been fine. It's just… I was so annoyed at missing summer with this *thing* on.' He swung his stookie out. 'I didn't want anyone feeling sorry for me.'

I walked up to him and put my hand on his shoulder. I had seen people do it on telly, when people talked about their feelings, they liked someone to put a hand on their shoulder. If Granpa had been there, he would've told Tom he'd been *feeling sorry for himself.*

Instead, I said, 'It's okay to want to be left alone sometimes.'

'I knew you'd get what I was saying,' Tom nodded. 'Now, come on. I need to show you something.'

I needed to get back inside to stop Grace forgetting about me and going off with that other girl.

'Tom, I need to go back inside. The dancing's about to start and I cannae miss it. I thought you had a babysitter looking after you?'

'Louise didn't even notice me going out the door. Mary, you've *got* to see this. Come on, it'll only take a minute.'

'A minute?'

'Promise.'

'Fine. What is it?'

'Follow me.'

He was faster on the crutches than I thought he'd be. Zooming over leaves and stones like he'd been born with a stookie leg. He really had been faking all summer. We went up the hill towards the Lump but took the right hand path towards the beach, where the old shed and all the nets were.

When we were going down the steps towards the old shed, I saw what Tom wanted me to see.

'Oh, Tom,' I said. 'How did it get here?'

'Funny, isn't it?' he replied. 'The front door wasn't locked, I just went in and took it.'

Nippy, the Kerr's greyhound, was walking around on the dirty sand. She was sniffing at things and didn't even know she'd been stolen. We went down the steps and I patted her on the head.

'How did you manage to lead her on your crutches?' I asked him.

'It wasn't hard,' he said. 'I wrapped the leash around one of my crutches. She's the slowest dog on the planet.'

Nippy tilted her head to one side like she knew we were talking about her. I picked up the handle of her leash from the ground.

'You didnae even tie her up, Tom. She could've ran away.'

'I did so. She must've got loose somehow.'

'Why did you even take her?'

'Because they deserved it. They egged your house, Mary, so this is what they get back.'

'What are you going to do to her?'

'I'm not going to hurt her. When they get home from the dance, they'll think she's run away and then they'll get a fright. Then I'll let her go tomorrow and she'll run home.'

'But what if you get caught? Or she disnae get home okay?'

'Don't worry so much, Mary. I did it for you. We're friends.'

Boys had the weirdest way of showing they liked being

friends with you.

'Take her back, Tom,' I told him. 'Take her back now.'

'I thought you'd be happy I got them back for you.'

'I'm not happy. This is such a stupid thing to do. Take her back.'

'No.'

'You better.'

Then he started going back up the steps.

'Come back and take her,' I said.

'You do it.'

'I have to go back to the ball.'

'Tough.'

He got to the top and disappeared into the trees. It was just me and Nippy. She did a wee whine and lay down with her front legs out and her head leaning on them. I felt like doing the same.

I needed to get back before Granpa got worried, but I had to make sure Nippy got home safe. It was the kind of problem that James Bond would have, but then he'd come up with a genius idea to fix it and get the girl. I had to get Grace, but not like that.

'I'll be back soon,' I said to Nippy.

She squinted at me with sleepy eyes.

My arms were tired from lifting my dress up to keep any mud from getting on it. I thought I would pass Tom, but I didn't. He must've gone a different way.

I was out of breath when I got back to our table. The dancing hadn't started.

'I was starting to worry, hen,' Granpa said. 'Ye awright?'

'I had diarrhoea,' I said.

'Oh. Ye wanting me to get ye some tablets?'

'Naw, it's all out now, Granpa.'

Diarrhoea was the best excuse. Granpa never wanted details when I said I had diarrhoea. It was disgusting and no one would ever lie about having diarrhoea. That's what made it the best fib I could tell.

Grace was still talking to the other girl. I was about to go over when the leader of the band started talking on the microphone and told people to get up for a dance.

'First up is the Gay Gordons,' the man said. 'I think you all know this one.'

No one was laughing about it being called Gay Gordons. Grown-ups were good that way.

I had to be with Grace because the Gay Gordons was the one where you stayed with someone the whole time and I couldn't let it be the other girl. It was hard because Granpa was walking behind me slowly and I couldn't see Grace because of everyone in the way. It was rubbish being so short compared to the grown-ups. I couldn't see over them, even if I tiptoed.

'Mary,' Grace said.

She had been following me the whole time. She smiled and I knew for sure we were going to be partners. Her mum was with her, but not her dad.

'Who was that other girl you were talking to?' I asked.

'That's my friend Sophie,' she said. 'I told you about her, didn't I? She's just back from America today.'

'Are you not going to dance with her then?'

'No, Mary. You're my best friend.'

I almost started crying, even though I was the opposite of sad.

'Right,' said Granpa. 'I'll go and prop up the bar while you two show me how it's done.'

And he went to walk away, but Mrs MacLeod put her

hand on his arm.

'Actually, Arthur,' she said. 'Kevin's had to step out for a bit. We've had a call from the babysitter that Thomas has gone walkabouts. So...'

She had her arms behind her back and was raising her eyebrows at Granpa. She wanted him to ask her to dance but he didn't understand.

'Oh,' Granpa said. 'Where's my manners? Would ye like to join me at the bar, Linda?'

She laughed. Grace and me looked at each other like *what an idiot*.

'What if we danced together instead?' Mrs MacLeod said.

It was the smiliest I'd ever seen her. She had definitely turned into a friend. It was all because of our brilliant plan. Granpa thought Mrs MacLeod loved Elvis and she thought Granpa loved Stephen King. As long as they never talked about it ever again, they'd never find out.

'I'm afraid I'm no much of a dancer,' Granpa said.

'I'll keep you right,' Mrs MacLeod said.

She took his hand and led him on to the dancefloor, even though it should've been the other way around. I was so glad we didn't have any enemies to worry about anymore.

Granpa and Mrs MacLeod went in front of us in the circle. He was making her laugh loads and she was waving her hand at him like *oh, stop it you* but still laughing.

'Grace,' I said. 'I need to show you something after this dance.'

'Is it the little sausages wrapped in bacon?' she asked. 'I've seen them already. I'm definitely getting them when the buffet opens.'

'Naw, it's on the other side of the Lump.'

'Can't you show me tomorrow?'

'It needs to be soon.'

Most people knew how to do the Gay Gordon's. The only person who kept getting it wrong was Granpa, but he wasn't getting angry. Him and Mrs MacLeod were having a laugh and not caring that people were staring and getting annoyed when they stumbled and bumped into them.

I was out of breath. It went on for ages. Every time I thought the music was going to stop, the accordion man kept going. When the band did stop, everyone clapped and some people clapped each other. I ran up to Granpa.

'Grace and me are going to the toilet,' I said.

'Ye sure ye want Grace to go with ye?' he said. 'If ye've got an upset stomach...'

I nodded and ran back to Grace. I grabbed her hand and led her to the front door. I wasn't telling her what Tom had done until she saw it with her own eyes in case she thought I was kidding her on. But I was so good at kidding people on, she probably wouldn't have guessed.

When we went outside, there was a group of people arguing. It was Mr and Mrs Kerr, Lewis and Jamie's mum and dad. They were shouting at Iain and Mr MacLeod. Iain had hold of Nippy's leash. I had no idea why Iain had Nippy or how he had found her.

'Explain yourself!' Mr Kerr shouted.

He grabbed the leash and took the dog from Iain. Iain didn't try to fight him.

'I've told you,' Iain said. 'I was having a walk up the Lump, and I came across this pup wandering around. Are you accusing me of stealing her or something?'

'There's no way she got out the house by herself,' said Mrs Kerr. 'And it's not like you've not got previous. I know it was you I saw fiddling with my husband's lobster pots.'

'Why would he steal your dog?' Mr MacLeod said. 'Think about it.'

'Stay out of it, Kevin.'

'I'll speak my mind if I like, Liz.'

'Don't speak to my wife like that,' Mr Kerr said.

Grace leaned in to me.

'Is this what you wanted me to see?' she whispered, 'The grown-ups shouting?'

I shook my head. It was all Tom's fault.

'You think I pinched your dog from your house?' Iain said. 'Then took it a walk past the hall where the ball's happening? Some dog thief I am.'

'Then how else did she get loose?' Mr Kerr asked.

I walked up and no one saw me coming because they were all shouting over the top of each other, like on *Jeremy Kyle*. When I started talking, they looked down at me and shut up.

'Maybe it let itself out?' I said. 'Because it wanted someone to pet it.'

The Kerr's looked at me like I was an alien with ten heads. Iain and Mr MacLeod were smiling and trying not to laugh. I hadn't meant to make a joke. I really did think Nippy wanted a clap.

'It was you then, what's your name again?' Mr Kerr said.

'No, Mary was with me dancing,' Grace said. 'Hiya, dad.'

'Hello, angel,' Mr MacLeod said. 'Did I miss much?'

'The Gay Gordons.'

'Aw, I like that one.'

'Excuse me,' Mrs Kerr said. 'Can we get back to the real issue here? One of you has tried to steal our prize racing dog. And whoever this girl is, she's a friend of the MacLeod's.

They're all in it together.'

Granpa and Mrs MacLeod came out to join us.

'Iain!' Granpa said. 'What're ye doing here?'

'Well…' Iain said.

'This wee idiot's tried to steal my dog,' Mr Kerr said, nodding at me. 'And if I hadn't caught them at it…'

Granpa tried to rush at him to hit him, but Mr MacLeod stepped in the way and Mrs MacLeod pulled him back. Iain tried to get round Mr MacLeod too, but Mr MacLeod was younger and stronger and he could hold them off.

'Arthur, leave it,' Mrs MacLeod said. 'He *really* isn't worth it.'

Granpa was fuming. If it had been a cartoon, smoke would've been coming out of his ears.

'Let's go back inside, Mary,' Granpa said. 'Some people cannae enjoy a good night oot. We'll see ye later on, Iain.'

Iain gave me a wink.

'Good idea,' Mrs MacLeod said to Grace, and we all started going inside.

Then Mrs MacLeod said, 'Wait a minute. I forgot something.'

She walked up and slapped Mr Kerr across the face. The sound of it was so loud and it must've stung like anything. Mr Kerr's face went red from the slap and the embarrassment too. The Kerr's were so shocked, they just stood there and shut up, finally. Mrs MacLeod took Grace's hand and led her back inside like nothing had happened.

'I've always liked that woman,' Granpa said.

He put his hand out and I took it. As we walked back inside, I said as loudly as I could, 'Can we have lobster again soon, Granpa?'

I turned to see their faces. They couldn't have looked

any madder.

'By the way,' Granpa said, turning round too. 'Yer two lads egged our house a few weeks ago. I'd hate to have to get the police involved.'

We both laughed. When we got back in the hall, Granpa asked me, 'D'ye ken what Iain was doing with that man's dog?'

'I dinnae know, Granpa. What d'you think?'

'I've no got a clue,' Granpa said. 'But I cannae wait to find out later.'

We saw Mr and Mrs Kerr grabbing Lewis and Jamie by their ears and dragging them outside. We didn't see any of them the rest of the night. That *case was closed.*

♪

CHAPTER TWENTY-EIGHT

We were getting along like one big family. The MacLeods and us all sat together in between dances and Granpa talked to Mr and Mrs MacLeod like old friends. When it was time for the Dashing White Sergeant, Granpa said me and Grace were to go up ourselves because he wanted to talk to Mr and Mrs MacLeod about something.

'Why am I not allowed to listen?' I asked.

'It's a grown-ups only thing,' Granpa said. 'But it's something good, I promise.'

'Give me a clue.'

'It's a secret, Mary. And what do good spies no do?'

'*Divulge their secrets.*'

Granpa and Mr and Mrs MacLeod came to the dancefloor and joined in when it was time for Strip the Willow. That was the most knackering dance of the whole night. After it was finished, Grace and me fell into our chairs, we were so tired.

'Dare you to drink the champagne,' Grace said.

'No way,' I said. 'It could kill me.'

'It won't. Alcohol only kills you if you drink lots of bottles then choke on your own sick.'

'Granpa says because I'm small, alcohol is about a hundred times worse for me.'

'That's just him trying to scare you.'

'I still dinnae want to, it's probably horrible.'

Grace didn't drink any either. I had seen boys do stupid things because other boys dared them to. But Grace and me were smart, so we only did things we wanted to do. If I didn't want to do a dare, I didn't do it. It was that easy.

Grace's friend Sophie came over to talk to us.

'Hiya, Sophie. I'm Mary.'

'Grace was telling me about you,' Sophie said.

'Did she tell you I play the keyboard?'

'No, she said about the pink house.'

'Shh,' Grace said. 'You weren't to say.'

I felt sick. I didn't want everyone knowing my dream. It was only meant to be me and my best friend. Your best friend was supposed to keep your secrets. That's what being a best friend was.

'My dad says those houses cost a fortune,' Sophie said. 'Even he couldn't afford one of them and he's rich. He says he'd paint the pink house blue. It sticks out too much.'

'It's only a dream,' I said.

'I'm just saying. It probably won't happen.'

'Stop it,' Grace said. 'You were meant to keep it a secret. She's going to cry.'

I was going to cry. The DJ had started and he was playing a song way too loud and we were sat right next to a speaker and it was all too much.

'I'm not going to cry,' I said. 'I need to go outside for some fresh air.'

'Do you want us to come?' Grace asked.

'Naw, leave me alone.'

I needed to get outside before I started crying. But it was hard with all the people in my way. I had to dive under a woman and she nearly spilled her glasses of champagne.

'Slow down, young one.'

I got through the lobby bit and into the night air. The tears were hot as they ran down my cheeks. I tried to cry as quietly as I could. I didn't want anyone asking how I was. I didn't want to hear anyone say, *"oh dear, oh dear, oh dear, what's happened?"*. I wanted to be left alone. I wanted Granpa to take me home and listen to Elvis and forget all about how horrible friends could be.

The fresh air was helping; it felt good to breathe it in. I took my flashes off and threw them into the dark. Grace had stolen my flashes idea and she could keep it. She could try and steal my dream, but I wouldn't let her.

When I lifted my dress, the cold air swooped over the backs of my knees. The sweat went cold and it felt good.

It was dark. We'd been dancing for ages. I took my phone out my pocket to check the time. The lady who had made my dress had sown one on the front for me. *10.33pm*. I only had to get through the last twenty-seven minutes, then we could go home. I'd forgotten to charge my phone properly, again. It blinked with the low battery sign then switched off.

Some grown-ups appeared from the left-hand side of the hall where the church was. They were putting out their cigarettes and going back inside.

'Hello, dear,' a lady said. 'Are you coming back in for the last dance?'

'Two minutes,' I said. 'I'm getting some fresh air.'

'Quite right, it's stuffy inside.'

She blew out some cigarette smoke then went inside and closed the door behind her. I guessed to keep the heat in. Grown-ups were fussy about trying to keep the heat inside of places. Like the cold was a monster always trying to come into your house and haunt you with the chills.

It was quiet and I could hear the water down at the beach. *Slosh shhh, slosh shhhh.* I went round the side of the hall, so I could lean over the railing and look over the tops of the harbour houses. I wanted to see how bright the pink house was at night, or if you could even see the pink in the dark. So what if it was expensive? So what if Sophie's dad couldn't afford it or didn't like the colour? It was my dream and if other people knew it and made fun of it, I didn't care.

At the side of the hall, I could hear men's voices. It was hard to see because it was so dark. There were three men. Two were standing with their backs to me and one was facing them. I stepped slowly on the stones so they wouldn't hear me.

The two men sounded angry at the other man. I got closer and still no one knew I was there.

'What did you think was going to happen, Arthur?' someone said. 'Did you think we would just let you off with it? We didn't want to have to come here. Johnny gets carsick on long drives.'

It was Craig. I knew his voice. His brother was the one next to him. Johnny. Granpa was the one furthest from me.

'We waited a long time for you yesterday,' Johnny said. 'We're no waiting anymore. We know the money's no at the house. We've already been to see your pal Iain tonight. Where is it?'

'Where is it, Arthur?' Craig said. 'Let's end this, here and now. I need out of here tonight. If Kelly sees me... You need to tell us.'

'That money's for my granddaughter, boys,' Granpa said. 'And I'll be damned if I'm handing it over to thugs like you two.'

'Have some fucking sense,' Craig said. 'Johnny's not as patient as me.'

Craig looked over at his brother. Johnny took something out of his pocket.

'Ye do whatever ye need to,' Granpa said. 'The money's gone. Ye'll never find it.'

'What the fuck does that mean?' Johnny said.

'It means ye're too thick to ken where to look, ye inbred eejit.'

Johnny rushed towards Granpa. He swung the thing in his hand near Granpa's face but Granpa dodged out the way and whacked Johnny in the ear. Johnny stumbled back, then came forward again. I wanted to shout or to run for help but when I opened my mouth, nothing would come out, and my legs wouldn't work.

'I was amateur boxing champ of Ayrshire in my day,' Granpa said, breathing hard and fast. 'Ye dinnae scare me.'

'That's not going to help you here, Arthur,' Craig said. 'You stupid bastard.'

'You're fucking dead, old man,' Johnny said.

This time Johnny's swing got Granpa. I heard the thud echo and Granpa fell to the ground. Johnny got on top of him and grabbed his cravat. He punched Granpa over and over. All I could do was watch and feel my heart breaking in my chest. The punching seemed to go on forever. Somebody needed to jump in and *save the day*, but I only had Granpa and he wasn't fighting back.

'Easy, man, easy,' Craig said. 'We need him to speak, for fuck's sake.'

Johnny let go of Granpa and stood up.

'There's something wrong with him,' he said.

'You're beating the fucking life out of him,' Craig said.

'What d'you expect?'

'No that. He's no breathing right. Might be a heart attack.'

'Fuck me. I told you to ease off.'

They stood over Granpa and it was silent except for a gargly noise, but it wasn't the sea. I tried to take my phone out but my hands were shaking too much and I didn't have any battery, anyway.

'The state of him,' Craig said, 'We better go, Johnny.'

'What about the money?'

'You heard him, it's gone. If he was going to tell us, he'd have told us. Not that he fucking can now. We need to be gone before this dance ends and the place is hoaching with folk.'

I felt my tears dripping to the ground and I finally managed to force out a wail. Craig and Johnny turned round.

'Who's that?' said Craig.

They both started walking over to me. My whole body felt heavy when I turned. It felt like there was warm toffee in my body instead of blood and I was moving in slow motion.

'Mary?' Craig said. 'Mary, come here.'

I ran straight into the street. I should've run inside the hall and they couldn't have followed me there. But I was already past it and had to keep going. I went downhill. My dress was getting muddy at the bottom but I didn't care anymore. I raced down the steps towards the harbour. I jumped the steps, five at a time. I had always thought about trying it, but had been too scared. Now I was scared, but not of the stairs.

I ran down the harbour street. Past the blue house, the green house, the pink house. My chest hurt and I had a stitch. I was getting slower. The men's footsteps were getting closer and I knew one of them one going to grab my leg and pull me down any second.

'Andy!' I shouted. 'Andy!'

I wished so hard that he would pop up from somewhere and whisk me away. His boat wasn't there and neither was he. I shouted but I wasn't sure if any noise came out. I needed someone. Andy, or Iain, or Granpa. Anyone. But no one came. They were all too far away, especially Granpa. He was having a heart attack and I needed to help him. Someone needed to help him.

I was so out of breath from the running, I was ready to fall over. They were going to catch me and I didn't know what they'd do to me. There was no way I could go back to Granpa. And I couldn't go any further. I had run past all the oil tanks and was already halfway down the pier. My feet were loud on the wooden slats. It was a long thin pier but soon I was at the end. It was just the water in front of me.

I couldn't hear any other steps on the pier. They must've got lost. Or maybe I was too fast for them. I had run like a superhero because my body had given me super speed and I was safe. I had won. I turned around so I could use my super speed to get back to Granpa and save him.

Craig and Johnny were waiting for me at the start of the pier. They came forwards, slowly. I couldn't even hear their steps. I tried shouting for help, but I had run too far past any houses and my voice was sore and too quiet. My heart was pounding in my head so I closed my eyes to try to make the noise go away. I felt dizzy. They were almost at me. They weren't running because they didn't need to. I was wrong; they had won. There was nowhere for me to go. I crouched down and put my hands over my head and was ready to kick them in the shins when they got close. I wasn't a boxer like Granpa, but I could make them feel pain.

Johnny was right in front of me and Craig had stopped a little bit behind.

'Johnny, stop,' Craig said. 'What are you even going to do? Just leave her, man.'

'You're Desk Robber, aren't you?' I said.

My lips were shaking and so was my whole body.

'What are you on about?' Johnny said.

'You're Desk Robber and he's Guard Robber.' I pointed at Craig.

'Fuck. See, Duncan, I told you. She knows too much.'

Craig wasn't Craig. Craig was Duncan. It didn't matter.

I thought of my bronze swimming certificate. I didn't bring it to Portree with me and if the old house had new people living in it, I probably wasn't going to see it ever again. But it was mine and I could picture it and remember all the swimming I'd done to get it. I was a good swimmer. It was pitch black, but I knew the other bit of Skye wasn't too far across the water.

Johnny reached his hand out towards me. I jumped off the pier. I was underwater before I could even take a breath.

♩

CHAPTER TWENTY-NINE

It's Tuesday and I have to do my talk in front of the class.
Everyone needs to do it. It has to be two minutes long and
be about your best friend. I wrote mine last week, but now
I need to think of someone else because Leona Turnbull isn't
my best friend anymore.

We stopped being friends on Friday. We were meant to
be going to the end of term disco at the church hall together.
When we got there the lady in charge said,

'I'm sorry, Mary, the disco is only for Brownies. You're not
one, are you?'

'Naw,' I said. 'But no one told me. Can I not come in
anyway?'

'Well, that wouldn't really be fair to the other girls.'

Leona is a Brownie and she went into the hall. She didn't
say sorry or come back to check on me. The lady in charge
had to phone Granpa to pick me up. We only live down the
road, but it was past school time so they wouldn't let me walk
home alone. I didn't want Granpa to find out.

He wasn't happy about me not getting in.

'But her pal's in there,' he said.

'Yes, I understand, sir. But it's Brownies only.'

'Ye can stick yer disco up yer arse.'

He took me to the shop on the way back so I could get a

sweet. He owed me 50p for swearing, but he gave me a whole pound instead. I got a Kinder Egg. The chocolate was good but you didn't get much of it. I tried to show Granpa the little princess toy that came with it, but he was going on about how annoyed he was with the Brownies. Saying random things, just talking to himself really.

'Ridiculous way to treat a wee girl... could've whacked that snooty woman... Granpa in the jail, that'd be good.'

'Can we do something tomorrow, Granpa? Like go to M&D's?'

'No tomorrow, hen. Too expensive. Maybe for yer birthday?'

'I was wanting a bike for my birthday.'

'Might need to be yer birthday and Christmas combined.'

'It's not till September, anyway.'

'It'll come sooner than ye think. What age will ye be again?'

'Eight.'

'Eight going on twenty-eight.'

'What does that mean?'

'That ye're the cleverest girl I ken.'

On Saturday, I went to Leona's house. Her mum said, 'Sorry, she's away out with Hannah.'

I went back again on Sunday.

'Sorry, Mary, she's at Hannah's again. She stayed over last night.'

Leona had always said that her mum didn't let her stay over at other people's houses. It wasn't safe.

Yesterday, Leona did her talk on Hannah.

'Hannah Hunter is my best friend,' she said. 'Because we get on really well and have brilliant sleepovers. We have our

own dance routine we did at the Brownie's disco last week and we both got our dancing badges.'

After the bell went, I said to Leona, 'D'you want to come round to mine for a sleepover?'

'Naw,,' she said. 'I'm just hanging around with Hannah now. We're both only hanging around with each other and no one else is allowed.'

Now it's my turn to talk. Everyone's staring. Mrs Mills is nodding at me so I need to start. I look at my paper and I'm ready to read out my talk about Leona. Then I think that doesn't make sense. To be best friends, both of you need to think it.

'My best friend,' I say. 'Is my granpa. His name is Arthur Sutherland. He was born in Kilmarnock.'

People are laughing. Your best friend can't be your granpa. It's silly, but I keep talking. I try to think of all the things there are about Granpa that makes him my best friend.

'Granpa's looked after me my whole life, mostly. He's really nice and sometimes we build dens in the living room and play castles. If he says a swear word, he has to give me 50p. It's our game.'

I've run out of things to say. There are other games Granpa and me play, but no one even smiled when I said about the swearing game and they'll think the other games are stupid too.

'Mary,' Mrs Mills says. 'Are you and your granpa doing anything during the summer?'

'We might be going to M&D's.'

People are laughing even more. Leona is laughing and whispering to Paul Reed about something, probably saying that M&D's is rubbish.

'Are you going away anywhere on holiday?' says Mrs Mills.

'We dinnae really go on holidays.'

'That's all right. Does anyone have any questions for Mary about her best friend?'

They're all just looking at the floor and no one wants to ask me anything. Paul Reed puts his hand up.

'How can you be best friends with your granpa?' he says. 'Your granpa doesn't count. Did you no have anyone else?'

Everyone bursts out laughing. Leona is laughing. Mrs Mills stares at Paul and points outside and he gets up and goes out to the corridor. My face is hot and I want to take off my jumper to cool down. I'm going to cry and I want to sit down. Mrs Mills nods and starts clapping.

'Well done, Mary,' she says. 'Who's up next?'

I sit on the floor with my legs crossed. The carpet is old and I pull at it instead of listening to the next person's talk. I can feel tears going down my cheeks, but I don't wipe them away. If I wipe them away, then people will notice, but if they dry themselves, people might not know.

I won't talk to Leona, ever again. I hate her and I'm glad she's not my best friend. Granpa says hate is a strong word, but I mean it. She's only friends with Hannah Hunter because she went to the disco and I wasn't allowed. That is the stupidest reason to be a person's friend. My best friend can be anyone I want it to be. It can be Granpa if I say so. No one can tell me who my best friend is.

It's later on and we're having a chippy for tea.

'Did ye hear, hen?' Granpa says.

'Hear what?'

'There was a big fight at the chippy tonight.'

'Oh, dinnae, Granpa.'

'And d'ye ken what happened to the fish?'

We say it together.

'They got battered.'

He's chuffed to bits with his stupid joke. His specs are fogged up from the steam off the chips.

'How did yer talk go the day?' he asks me.

'Aye, fine.'

'What was it aboot again? Yer best friend?'

'Actually...'

He gets the tomato sauce out the cupboard and sits it next to my plate. He knows I like to squeeze it out myself.

'Aye,' I say, 'My best friend.'

♪

CHAPTER THIRTY

The water was the coldest thing I've ever felt. It shot up my nose and took the breath from my mouth and I didn't have any more air. It was so dark I couldn't see which way was up. My arms and legs were stiff and my dress was heavy and pulled me down towards the deepest place. I wanted to swim away, but it sooked me down.

It was nothing like swimming in a pool. I was so tired from running away from the robbers and my body wasn't strong enough to get back up to the surface. I stared up and thought I saw the moon through the water. I tried to reach out for it, but I couldn't get my arms to do what I wanted. I could feel my heart get slower and the moon got smaller.

I opened my eyes. The moon was bright and full and there wasn't any water in the way. I put my head to the side and threw up salty water. Some sick came out too. I sucked in all the air I could. My chest hurt every time I breathed, but I did it anyway because I needed to stay alive. I tried to wiggle my fingers and toes but they stayed still.

'Thank God,' said a voice.

It was Craig. His real name was Duncan, but I was used to calling him Craig.

He ripped my dress off. It was soaking but it would've

dried. I tried to tell Craig not to ruin my dress, but I couldn't get the words out. I didn't want him to see me without any clothes on. I wasn't a woman in the newspaper. Something else was being wrapped round me. His jacket. It was dry and black and smelled of aftershave. He was trying to be a gentleman. Only gentlemen gave their jackets to a lady. But they didn't rip the lady's dress off first. Granpa was a gentleman. Craig was still a no good robber.

He picked me up. He was running and it made my body shake. I tried to keep my head up, but my neck was too tired. The whole world was bouncing. Everything was upside down. The black sky was below me and if I looked down as far as I could, I saw the stars twinkling. Craig had saved me from the water. His jacket was warm but it needed to be warmer. I was freezing.

'Speak to me, Mary,' Craig said.

'Where's Johnny?' I whispered.

I couldn't get any louder than a whisper.

'Don't worry about him. He's gone. You're going to stay awake for me, aren't you, Mary?'

'I'll try. Is my granpa going to be okay?'

'Just stay awake for me. Please.'

Water was dripping from Craig on to my neck and my chin. His feet were slapping on the ground. The cold was in my bones, but I wasn't shivering.

Craig was taking me to the hospital. I knew the way. Everything was bumpy going back up the steps, then we were going past the bank. I hoped Granpa would already be there. I imagined us having beds right next to each other and wearing those silly gowns where our bums stuck out. Iain would come and visit and bring us mix-ups. I closed my eyes. I was desperate for a sleep.

I opened my eyes, then shut them tight. It was too bright. There were too many lights on. I scrunched up my eyes and opened them the smallest I could. *Squint mode.* I was being rolled along on a bed with wheels. The lights were passing above like *whoosh whoosh whoosh.* There, then gone. There, then gone. There. Gone. *Girl, eight, several minutes in the water. Possible severe hypothermia and affected brain function.* I was going too fast. I wanted to slow down or get off the ride. *She's awake. Can you hear me? Keep your eyes open for me, darling.* Darling was a special name some people called me. Granpa's name for me was *hen.*

The bed wasn't comfy. I don't think it was a bed at all. I was tucked in so much I couldn't kick my legs out. Even Granpa didn't tuck me in that much. I was feeling warmer, but I was shivering. There was something in my throat and I tried to be sick to get rid of it. It wouldn't come up. I tried to touch my mouth. *No, no, sweetheart. You have to leave that. Warm air into your lungs.* I had seen the lady in the place with the bright lights. She smiled and I knew that she would only smile if everything was okay. I wanted to ask where Granpa was, but the tube wouldn't let me speak. There was another thinner tube going into my arm. I touched it and it was clear and warm. I had only been awake for a minute, but I was the tiredest I'd ever been in my whole life.

I tried my best to stay awake. I was in a different room. It was daytime outside the window, but I didn't know which day. I was in a real bed with real pillows and normal covers. The tube had gone from my throat, but the warm tube was still in my arm. The room had cream walls and green leather chairs. I knew leather was from cows, but I didn't know how they made it green. There weren't green cows. The smiley lady was still checking on me. I had moved rooms but she had come with me and not let me get lost. She had long blonde hair and was wearing all blue. Her lipstick was red, like a Bond girl. She was definitely pretty enough to be a Bond girl. I knew Granpa was going to love her.

I wasn't as tired anymore. I could stay awake for long enough to remember things. The ball and the robbers. Johnny punched Granpa. Craig saved me. Craig was the last person I'd seen. I waited till the smiley nurse came back and asked where Granpa was.

'It's so good to hear you talk, Mary. I'm Nurse Heather. Let me go and get the doctor. He'll be pleased you're awake.'

Iain came to visit me. He had bruises on his face.

'I'm so sorry, Mary. Your granpa passed away. Heart attack. Nothing the doctors could do. You're out of the woods now, so I thought you should know.'

I hadn't been in any woods. I hadn't been in any woods, so Iain was wrong. He was wrong about the woods and wrong about Granpa. I tried to hit him, but the wires hurt in my arms and the beeps started. Iain left and Nurse Heather came in and did something to the machine next to me. The next time I opened my eyes, Iain was gone.

Every time I woke up, I remembered about Granpa. Sometimes it took me a minute and sometimes I knew straight away. I didn't want to believe it, but I knew it must've been true. If Granpa had been alive, he would've been in the chair next to my bed when I woke up. Iain wouldn't have lied to me about Granpa. Nurse Heather gave me a new dry pillowcase every time she came into my room. I used up the tissues too fast.

Grace and Mr and Mrs MacLeod came to visit me. They brought a card and put it on the table, but I didn't open it. They sat for a while and no one said anything. I couldn't think of anything to say to them. My throat was still sore from when the tube was in it. Nurse Heather told them that visiting hours were over and they left.

I slept as much as I could so Nurse Heather and the doctor would think I was still sick. If they thought I was better, they'd kick me out and I wouldn't have anywhere to go. Granpa wouldn't be there and Iain wouldn't want me in his house if Granpa wasn't there. The hospital was my new home.

Iain visited again.

'I'm sorry I tried to hit you,' I said.

'Don't be daft,' he said.

He brought a pack of cards to do magic tricks. My card was the three of spades and at first he pretended to guess it wrong, then got it right the second time. Then we played pontoon. He was the dealer and laid out my cards for me. We both got eighteen and he said I won, even though the dealer's meant to win for a draw.

'I would've taken you home by now, Mary,' he said. 'But I've found out it doesn't work like that.'

The police asked me questions. I tried to answer the best I could.

'Craig saved me,' I said. 'He saved me from drowning. His real name's Duncan.'

'Don't worry about him,' one of them said.

'Did you ever help your Granpa take money from his work?' another one asked. 'Maybe like a game? Maybe he gave you some money to sneak out in your school bag?'

'Never.'

Sometimes in films, the police were actually the bad guys and spies had to keep secrets from them. They weren't getting any of my stories about Granpa. They were mine and not for sharing.

'Do you remember a man called Mr Ferguson from the bookies in Stirling, Mary?'

'Aye, he was Granpa's boss.'

'Do you know he's no longer with us, Mary? He committed sui-...he passed away. So it's really important that you tell the truth here. Did you give Mr Ferguson a pair of shoes as a present?'

'Aye, it was his Easter present. And to make up for his old pair smelling like my pee.'

'Did you put anything inside those shoes?'

'They were already wrapped when Granpa gave them to me.'

'Okay. What about the money your Granpa brought to Portree? Do you know what he did with it? Any ideas at all?'

'He was meant to give it to the robbers.'

I was glad when Nurse Heather came in and told them to leave. I was lucky to have her on my side.

A man in a blue suit and glasses came to visit. Nurse Heather stood outside the door in case I needed her.

'Your Granpa met with me the day before he died,' the

man said. 'He wanted to change the legal guardianship part of his will. He was in a bit of a rush, I'm afraid, and he wasn't in the mood to have a conversation about it. He wanted to organise who you would live with, if anything happened to him. These things are complicated, I told him that. But he didn't want to listen. He got a bit...well, his temper got the best of him, and I'm sorry to say I told him I would sort it. I didn't want to upset him any further, Mary. I thought once he'd cooled down, I would explain how these things work. Obviously, tragically, I never got the chance. He left my office under the impression that you'd be living with a certain family, and I'm very sorry to say I can't make that happen. It's not possible.'

He talked for a long time. When he pushed his glasses up his nose, he pushed them up from the side. Granpa used to push up the middle bit that sat on his nose. It made him look clever. If I ever needed glasses someday, I would push them up from the middle.

When the man left, I tried to remember everything he'd said. He'd used too many grown-up words for me to keep up with what he was telling me. The main thing was that I couldn't go where Granpa wanted me to go. They were going to try and find my gran who lived in Canada. What if they couldn't find her? What if she didn't want me? I didn't know anything about Canada.

Nurse Heather checked on me every day. Every day that I could remember, she had been there. Iain had dropped off some of my clothes while I slept and Nurse Heather helped me change into them. She would say to me, 'How are you feeling, Mary? Better or worse than yesterday?'

Sometimes I was better, sometimes I was worse. I liked

it when she asked me because she really listened to my answer and cared what I said.

'Nurse Heather?' I said.

'Mary, I've told you before, you can just call me Heather.'

'Did my Granpa know he was going to die, Nurse Heather?'

'What makes you think that?'

'He tried to change his will. I think he wanted me to stay with the MacLeod's. But I'm not allowed.'

She stopped folding my pillowcase and sat down on the edge of my bed.

'I don't think he knew, sweetheart,' she said. 'You can't plan for things like what happened to your granpa. He was probably getting things ready for the future. He tried to make sure you'd be with people that would take care of you in the way you deserve. Just in case.'

She reached over and straightened up my get well soon cards. I had cards from people in Portree I'd never even met. I had one from Andy, too. It was my favourite.

'It's a shame you can't go where he thought was best,' Nurse Heather went on. 'But I'm sure no matter where you go, you'll be with people who will think the world of you. You granpa passing away is a tragedy, so soon after you two got here. But sometimes the worst, saddest things that happen to us can make us stronger.'

She put an empty tissue box in the bin and unwrapped a new box for me.

'I wisnae strong after I went in the water,' I told her. 'I couldnae even move or talk.'

'But you were very brave, Mary. Just think, if you can survive this, you can survive anything. Next time someone says something nasty or mean to you, do you think you'll be upset?'

'I dinnae know.'

'I don't think you will. I think you'll remember all you've been through and remember you're too tough to care about what anyone else says.'

'I could try that.'

Nurse Heather held my hand between hers.

'Please do,' she said.

'And anytime I'm sad, I can think of what Granpa used say to me.'

'And what would your granpa say to you right now?'

'Cheer up, hen.'

Nurse Heather gave me a hug. She was crying a wee bit.

'I think your Granpa would tell us both to cheer up,' she said, drying her eyes.

'Oh no, he'd like you. Granpa liked pretty ladies. They were his favourite.'

I hadn't even realised how brave I'd been until Nurse Heather told me.

'Are you worried about where you're going to stay?' she asked me. 'Or who you're going to live with, Mary?'

'No way,' I said. 'I'm stronger and braver than that.'

One day, Tom came all by himself. Because that's what friends do. He sat in one of the comfy leather chairs.

'They said it's normal to cry, Mary,' he said. 'I'd cry if Mum or Dad died. But you'll cheer up at some point.' He picked at a hole where the chair's stuffing was showing. 'I had a hamster called Hammy and when he died I was sad for three whole days. Then, when I woke up on the fourth day, I wasn't sad anymore. So it'll probably be like that.

You'll wake up one day and not be sad anymore.'

I wasn't really listening to what he was saying, but I liked him being there. I wanted him to keep talking so I could fall asleep without having to think about falling asleep.

'You want to hear something funny, Mary?' Tom said. 'When the ball was happening, someone went round to the Kerr's house and punctured Jamie's new football. He had just bought it to replace the one you threw in the water. They've no clue who did it. I was round there that night, remember, taking Nippy, but I never saw anyone else.'

♫

CHAPTER THIRTY-ONE

The next time Iain visited, I remembered something important.

'Iain,' I said. 'Why did you have Nippy on the night of the ball?'

'Oh, that's a funny one,' he said, then lowered his voice so that no one passing by the door could hear. 'I went round the Kerr's house while they were out to burst that young lad's football. No one eggs my house and gets away with it, Mary.'

He winked at me and started dealing from the deck. He had taught me a new game: *Scabby Queen*.

'While I was in the back garden,' he kept on. 'I got the fright of my life when I saw young Thomas in the house, taking that dog. I followed him and the dog round to the Lump and down the steps. He tied it up and went off without it.'

Iain finished dealing and we sorted out our cards. I quickly looked through my cards. Iain had the scabby queen.

'I went down and untied it,' Iain said. 'But then I had to hide behind a shed when I heard voices coming. It ended up being you and him and I felt like a right pleb, hiding from a couple of kids. I waited till you two left and was on my way to take the dog back. Of course, the Kerr's were outside the hall for a smoke and the rest of the story you saw. What a slap Linda gave Gary Kerr!'

Iain stayed with me while I waited on the phone to ring. My gran from Canada was supposed to be calling any minute. I was scared, but whenever Nurse Heather popped her head round the door and looked at me, I felt so strong I could throw a caber over the Lump.

'Mary,' Iain said. 'We've started dealing with your granpa's will. I'll talk you through the rest of it later, but we thought you might want to have this for the time being. I know it's a bit early but...'

He took out something from his pocket and handed it to me. It was an envelope with my name on the front. The writing on the front was Granpa's, but it had already been opened.

'I'm sorry it's been opened, that was the police,' Iain told me. 'They thought your granpa had stashed all his money inside or something, who knows. Anyway, I'll leave you to read it while I get a cuppa.'

I waited till he was out of the room and opened it. It was a birthday card. My birthday wasn't till September 11th and it was only August, but Iain had decided it was important for me to have the card early. Paul Reed from my class once tried to tell me I had a bad birthday because 9/11 was a *national tragedy*. When I told Granpa, he said the right way of saying it was 11/9 and I was a *national treasure*.

The card had a picture of Elvis on the front. It was him wearing his white leather suit. That was *classic* Elvis.

Inside it said:

Happy birthday, hen.
You've already made me prouder than you'll ever know.
Lots of love,
Granpa
x x x

I closed it right away so my tears wouldn't ruin the writing. I realised that even though I was getting used to the idea that Granpa was dead and I was stronger than I used to be, it could all come back like a flood. Part of me wanted to rip up the card so that I could never be that sad again. But I couldn't. I read it over and over.

Then I remembered about the special thing Granpa used to do with my birthday cards. The secret compartment was so well hidden. It was much harder to find than any of the other years. I had to rip open the back page of the card. A bit of paper was stuck inside. I pulled it out. It wasn't a tenner like I thought. It was a bookie slip. It said:

My grand-daughter, Mary Sutherland,
to play piano in a concert
at the Glasgow Royal Concert hall
by the time she is 30 years old, 11/9/2036
£10,000 at 100/1

I knew 100/1 meant the bet had no chance of winning, but I would try my best. For Granpa.

AUTHOR'S NOTE

Many thanks to the people of Portree, who were so hospitable during my visit. I would particularly like to thank, and recommend:

Andy Kulesza of *Stardust Boat Trips,* for a fantastic trip where no one went overboard. I hope I haven't stolen *too* much of your patter.

Michelle Rhodes of *Skye History and Heritage Day Tours,* for showing me the sights and answering my odd questions.

The staff at *Portree Independent Hostel,* which is more than a hotel for smelly people.

ACKNOWLEDGEMENTS

I am hugely appreciative to everyone who read all, or some, of *Mary's the Name* and offered feedback over the past two years.

Special thanks to:

My parents, Yvonne and Derek, and my brothers, Scott and David.

My Gran, Isabel, and my Aunt, Agnes, for making my M.Litt possible.

Mr Colin Wales, for being the English teacher every student deserves.

Liam Murray Bell, for your invaluable advice and influence.

Helen and Anne from *Cranachan*, for being so passionate about wee Mary Sutherland, and taking chances on unknown writers.

ABOUT THE AUTHOR

Ross Sayers graduated from the University of Stirling in 2014, with a BA (Hons) in English Studies (first class), and graduated again in 2015 with a M.Litt in Creative Writing (distinction).

His stories and poems have featured in magazines such as Quotidian and Octavius, and his short story, 'Dancin' is currently used on West College Scotland's Higher English course.

You can tweet him @Sayers33 or see more of his writing at rosssayers.co.uk.

Photo credit: Sally Murning

THANK YOU FOR READING

As we say at Cranachan,
'the proof of the pudding is in the reading'
and we hope that you enjoyed *Mary's the Name*.

Please tell all your friends and tweet us with your
#marysthename feedback, or better still, write an online
review to help spread the word!

We only publish books which excite and inspire us, so
if you'd like to experience other unique and
thought-provoking books, please visit our website:

cranachanpublishing.co.uk

and follow us
@cranachanbooks
for news of our forthcoming titles.

cranachan